HEART OF THE VIOLIST

Maddie Evans

Print ISBN: 978-1-942133-42-1
Library of Congress Control Number: 2020950657

Cover art by Crowe Covers
Editing by Michaela DeToma

DEDICATION

Two years ago, I covered a charity 5K for the local paper. A high school senior organized it to promote awareness of early-onset frontotemporal dementia, the illness that was taking her father from her family at far too young an age. I was impressed by her and by her family, touched by their perseverance and their resourcefulness, and by how in the midst of their struggle, they cared about making the way easier for others. Long after the 5K, their experience stuck with me.

Although the Castleton family is in no way based on the Krauss family, I'd like to dedicate the Castleton String Quartet trilogy to the memory of Mark Krauss and to all those who loved and supported him.

CHAPTER ONE

Ashlyn took a moment during Lindsey's violin solo to sneak a look at the crowd. The audience sat entranced as the melody climbed, then climbed even higher as Lindsey coaxed a song from her instrument. She bowed smoothly, her eyes half-closed. She played it so well, but she shouldn't be the one performing.

At Lindsey's side, the second violinist raised his instrument for the moment he'd provide the alto counterpoint to Lindsey's soprano. Jason kept his dark eyes focused on her for the cue, his concentration mingling with his striking features. The man should be on an album cover. He started a half-second before Lindsey cued him, and too loud. She shot him a look but kept playing.

On Ashlyn's other side, Hannah gave the quartet its bass voice with her cello. Although with her brown hair and cautious smile she tended to fade into the background, her instrument never did. She played a delighted background that emphasized Lindsey's soprano line, and once Hannah began, she had the effect of tempering Jason's strident tones.

Finally, it was Ashlyn's turn to join with the viola, the tenor voice. Always in a supporting role, the viola line could get swallowed up, but Ashlyn put her heart into the harmony. Instead of working in counterpoint like Jason's line, her notes supported the first violin. That's how it should be: Lindsey had supported Ashlyn so often in life, and now it was Ashlyn's turn—and not just in the music. Ashlyn leaned a little harder into her part so Lindsey's could soar.

The harmonies worked so well in this piece. So well. The final movement was heart-rending when they nailed the dynamics, and they should have nailed them. After as many rehearsals as they'd done, there was no reason not to score with every note, every vibrato, every transition, but to Ashlyn it felt strained. Lindsey wasn't playing well, and whenever Jason glanced at her for his cue, he looked irritated.

A violin's strings were tense, but not as tense as those two.

Lindsey shouldn't be in the first chair. Jason shouldn't be here at all. Hannah hadn't ever dreamed she would be the quartet's permanent cellist. Ashlyn was the only player in the same spot as last year, but it didn't feel the same.

The piece ended in a triumphant fanfare, all four instruments strong and proud. Lindsey closed her eyes for just a moment, her black hair shining in the stage lights, her hand tight on the neck of her violin, and her face devastated. The expression lasted barely a heartbeat before she gathered herself, but Ashlyn caught it. Lindsey had to be thinking of her father—had to be feeling like an imposter playing his role.

Poised once more, Lindsey signalled the other three, and to the backdrop of applause, the players stood. Ashlyn gazed out at the audience with her viola tucked under her arm and her bow flipped up to rest on her shoulder.

The announcer stepped onto the stage while the audience kept clapping. "A wonderful thank-you to the Castleton String Quartet for their amazing performance, their twentieth at the Latesummer Music Festival!"

Their twentieth—yet not a single player was over age thirty.

They bowed in turn as the announcer called their names. "Lindsey Castleton, Jason Woodward, Ashlyn Merritt, and Hannah Staples!" Then, with hesitation, the announcer said, "And it's with gratitude that we'd like to remember Robert Castleton, who performed at the last nineteen events and would have been here tonight if he could."

Ashlyn couldn't stop herself from pivoting toward Lindsey, who looked as if she'd been shot with an arrow.

Jason nudged Lindsey. Once more they bowed in unison, then headed offstage to their dressing room.

The announcer attempted to approach Lindsey, so Ashlyn pushed between and shook her hand, giving Lindsey room to escape. "Thank you so much. We loved playing for you." Then, with Lindsey in the clear, Ashlyn disengaged and caught up to her.

Support didn't have to be musical. Sometimes it was best to serve as tactical blocking.

In their prep room, Jason muttered, "That could have gone better."

Lindsey huffed. "Gee, I wonder why."

Silent, Hannah walked past them to set her cello back in its case. Ashlyn went for the desk where she'd left her viola case, coincidentally positioning herself between Lindsey and Jason. A blonde strand of her hair lay on the burgundy velvet compartment that form-fit around the viola, and she pulled it free so it could drift to the floor. "I wish they hadn't mentioned Bob."

Jason was locking down his violin. "That was a nasty backhanded criticism."

Hannah shook her head. "No, they were just being nice. Besides, we played fine."

Lindsey looked empty and stunned again, so Ashlyn said, "What time is Corwin on?"

Lindsey gathered herself. "Nine to nine thirty." She laid her violin into its coffin case and loosened her bow. "My baby brother's been laughing at me all week. 'Oh, you're on at six? That's when the old people will be there.'"

Hannah grinned. "Fair enough. We're playing two-hundred-year-old music."

Jason removed his tuxedo jacket and started unbuttoning the shirt. "He's not wrong. Sandwiching a classical string quartet between a punk group and an Aerosmith cover band would be a disaster."

A knock on the door. Lindsey called, "Come in!"

Corwin stepped inside. Tall and lanky, he wore ripped jeans and work boots, plus a t-shirt proclaiming, "Ask me if I care about your feelings." He high-fived Lindsey, then flashed a thumbs-up to Ashlyn across the room. "Great work, guys! A bit stiff on the transitions, but I don't think the old folks even noticed unless they had their hearing aids turned up."

Lindsey smirked at him. "You're all heart. Oh, and I got an email from DN-Amazing. You finally caved and sent your DNA?"

"What? No." Arms folded, Corwin huffed. "I told you, I'm boycotting my DNA."

Jason's eye-roll was carefully hidden by him pulling a polo shirt over his head.

Lindsey recoiled. "Excuse me? Are you telling me I didn't get an email about a sibling match?"

Corwin pointed to Ashlyn. "It's you, isn't it? After all these years, you've managed to pretzel-knot physics to become Lindsey's sister for real."

Hiding the shiver that went up her spine, Ashlyn opened her hands. "Dude, tell me how, and I'll do it."

Lindsey sighed. "I only wish. No, the email actually specified my full brother, and that's you."

Corwin grimaced. "Seriously? I'm going to have to murder someone."

Ashlyn closed her viola case. "Why would someone else submit your DNA kit? How would they even get your DNA?"

"It's a cheek swab, and I would have noticed." Corwin shook his head. "I bet it's one of those glitches, like when the Elwood College admissions office sent an acceptance letter to every single student applicant. In an hour you'll get a groveling apology email, and someone will be looking for a new job."

Lindsey shrugged. "Probably. The name attached to it was Michael something. I figured you'd used a fakie to evade your rabid fans."

Corwin straightened. "Yeah, bass players attract all the hot babes and the scam artists. But that wasn't me because I'd have chosen a pseudonym of awesomeness, not boring Michael, and I'm keeping my DNA locked up in my body until I'm back on speaking terms with it. Ashlyn, get on that sibling thing. Lindsey hasn't been annoying me enough since she turned twenty-five." He hugged Lindsey. "Well, great job! Hang around for nine tonight so you can hear the real musicians playing for the young people."

After Corwin left, Jason huffed. "He's *not on speaking terms* with his DNA?"

Ashlyn sighed. "Do you blame him?"

"It's dumb." Jason changed out of his dress shoes into something more casual. "It's not like your DNA can have a fight with you."

Lindsey glared at him. "I for one think it's awesome that you're back in Maine to dictate how my family is allowed to feel about our father's terminal illness." She picked up her violin case from the desk. "You know what? You and your attitude can just stuff down your high and mighty judgments for the few hours a week when we have to work together. Those transitions were horrible, and you're the one making them horrible."

Ashlyn stepped between them. "Guys, we're all tense."

"It doesn't have to be tense." Lindsey's gaze drilled into Jason. "He's making it tense. This is the first time in twenty years that my father hasn't played at the Latesummer Music Festival, and it's killing me, and then you dare stand in front of me saying my brother isn't allowed to feel angry at how unfair it is? No one asked your permission."

Jason opened his hands. "Oh, so it's totally not irrational to give your DNA the silent treatment?"

"The whole situation is irrational. Corwin can be as irrational as he wants in response."

Lindsey took her violin and left.

As Jason placed his dress shirt and tux jacket on a hanger, Ashlyn said, "Nice job."

"It's not a question of nice. It's a question of not being ridiculous." He zipped up the vinyl suit cover before turning to her. "You played great today. You too, Hannah."

In the corner, Hannah just looked uncomfortable. "Thanks. Are you staying for a while?"

"Until close, yeah. You know, first analyze our competition, and then hear the 'young people' music."

Then he was out the door too, and Ashlyn turned to Hannah.

Hannah shifted her weight and stared at the floor. "I hope Lindsey doesn't vent to Corwin about that. He already doesn't like Jason."

"Well, then it can't make things worse, can it?" Ashlyn glanced around to make sure they hadn't left anything behind. "Ready to go?"

"I guess." Hannah didn't move. "Bob's illness is just as hard on you, but Jason doesn't get that either."

Ashlyn shook her head. "It's not the same for me."

Not as if Bob had actually been her father. Not as if Lindsey were actually her sister or Corwin her brother. *But I wish.* If wishes could change genetics, there would be another DNA kit in the mail right now.

They exited the music hall into the chaos of tourist crowds. After fifteen years of attending the state fair just outside Bangor (and the last three performing at it) Ashlyn would have known her way back to the parking lot blindfolded. First the tent with the quilt show, then the knitting and crocheting exhibition. They passed the smelly livestock pens, out of place with their ankle-length skirts and done-up hair. They drew fewer stares among the booths with homemade crafts and glass-blowing.

Always, though, everywhere they stepped was activity. And food. And tourists. Tourists who started the day bogging down traffic, filled the day crowding all the restaurants to capacity, and then ended it by doubling the price of every hotel room. *Welcome to Vacationland!* proclaimed a sign on the highway, and Ashlyn tried not to see it whenever they drove past. She'd gotten good at not seeing things that made her cringe. Sometimes, that's how you survived.

When they arrived at Hannah's car, Lindsey wasn't there. Ashlyn texted to ask where she was, and eventually, despite the over-capacity cell phone service, Lindsey replied, "Took a walk to cool off. I'll meet you in a bit."

Jason would be locking his violin in the trunk of his own car, or possibly sitting in the audience at the music festival cuddling it against his heart while listening to the next act (a solo pianist). The other three were sending their instruments home with Hannah. Tonight and tomorrow Hannah would be on-call for her day job, but Ashlyn and Lindsey could stay until close if they wanted.

The weather had barely edged into too-hot territory, and fortunately the fairgrounds were beaten-down enough that the mosquitos and the no-see-um bugs weren't a bother. Flies, on the other hand, adored the overfull trash cans, stuffed with funnel cakes and melted ice cream.

Lindsey arrived. Hannah unlocked the trunk, saying, "I'm sorry Jason's been so lousy to you. I wish I knew what to say to him."

Lindsey handed over her violin. "Don't apologize. The only one I hold responsible for his behavior is him."

Ashlyn said, "I'm sure he knows he's abrasive."

"He prides himself on it." Lindsey unbuttoned the blouse she'd performed in, but she was wearing a sports bra beneath so she changed into a t-shirt right there in the parking lot. Then she stepped out of her floor-length black skirt to reveal shorts and sneakers. Ashlyn only doubled up the waistband of her skirt a few times to shorten it, then rolled up her sleeves. "Thanks for hauling all the instruments."

"Not a problem." Hannah hugged Lindsey. "I'm so sorry your dad couldn't be here. It's rough."

Lindsey bit her lip. "Yeah."

Ashlyn and Lindsey headed back to the fairgrounds. "I stumbled on a sheep-to-shawl competition." Lindsey sounded subdued. "They dyed the sheep all different colors. They have twenty-four hours to shear the sheep, then spin the wool into yarn, then knit the yarn into a shawl. It's been going on all day, and the judging is tomorrow morning."

Ashlyn laughed. "For real?"

"As if I could make that up." Lindsey shrugged. "We should head back to the music hall. I want to hear the quartet that's on at seven."

Lindsey didn't seem as if she'd smiled for hours, so Ashlyn teased, "Are we trying to poach their second violinist?"

Lindsey snorted. "I'd offer to trade Jason, but who'd want him?"

Her phone chimed with an incoming email, and she looked at the screen, then stopped in her tracks.

Ashlyn turned. "What?"

Lindsey's cheeks were colorless. She handed the phone to Ashlyn, and it took two re-reads before Ashlyn could understand what she was seeing.

Dear Lindsey,

My name is Michael Knolwood, and DN-Amazing informed me today that we're a sibling match. I looked you up online and was surprised to see that you'd be at the Latesummer Fair. I don't live that far away, so I went to your performance. You're a great player.

If you haven't left yet, I was wondering if we could

meet. I was adopted at birth thirty-two years ago, and I've had no contact with my birth family. But since we're a match, and we're both right here, I'm taking a chance that you might see this in enough time that we could talk.

Sincerely,
Michael

CHAPTER TWO

At the back of the music hall, Michael sat shaking, his phone face-up on his knee and his pulse so fast it left him lightheaded.

His sister—a full sister, no less—had been right here, in this building, only twenty minutes ago. Twenty minutes. On that stage, under those lights, playing for these people.

He'd managed to arrive halfway through her performance, so at first he hadn't even been sure which one was Lindsey: the brown-haired cellist with her expressive face? The long-haired blonde beauty with the bigger violin? Or the black-haired one on the end with the fierce concentration and all the highest parts?

The program was no help whatsoever. Through the entire performance, Michael had annoyed the people in the seats behind him by directing his phone to the Castleton String Quartet website, trying to figure out which was which. He couldn't help it. He needed to know, but the website was an out-of-date mess, and the lineup in the website photos didn't match the lineup onstage. Even musicians should know to do better than that. Only at the end, when the announcer gave each of their names, did Lindsey raise a hand and confirm his best guess.

Black hair, like his. Fierce concentration, not like his. Tall, smooth-walking, and with a winning smile. He couldn't analyze her features from this far back, but her website photos looked a bit like him. Those eyebrows looked like his.

Someone who looked like him. Someone who might sound like him, might think like him, might move like him...

The only contact information on the website had been an email form, so he'd used that, but she hadn't emailed back. What if the website was so nonfunctional that the email form went nowhere? What did musicians do after a performance? Was she even still in the building? She had to be. He couldn't have gotten this close only to have her put it off to another day.

A sister. He had a sister. A full sister.

When he'd sent off his DNA, he'd hoped to maybe find a relative eventually—perhaps a second cousin who could help him track down likely candidates for who his parents might have been and why they might have made an adoption plan for their son. But this? A full sister?

Was she a twin?

Oh, that would be crazy. A twin. A one-night stand that resulted in two babies who were then split up and adopted out to different homes, their records sealed, and their fates separated.

Still no reply.

Michael looked back through the program, but the Castleton String Quartet wouldn't return. Instead there were a dozen more acts appearing in half-hour sets, pivoting from classical chamber music during the dinner hour to rock later in the evening. And then he noticed the nine o'clock slot: Cor Castleton, bass player for Clear

Enigma. Another one?

Interesting. Was that Lindsey's husband? Did musicians marry other musicians? It could be coincidence, but Castleton wasn't that common a name. Michael looked up Clear Enigma's website, but service was so lousy at the state fair. The task bar stuck without giving him anything onscreen.

Michael wanted to be moving, but he also didn't want to leave. What if she was still here? But what if she'd left?

His screen lit up with an incoming email.

Michael — I got your message, and I'm not sure how to respond. I got the same DN-Amazing message you did, but there's no way we're brother and sister. This has to be a website glitch where they sent random messages to their users. I'm sorry for the disappointment. — Lindsey

No, this was unacceptable. Michael went to the back of the hall, typing as he walked. "Lindsey, thanks for replying. I don't think it's a glitch at all. I really would like to meet you and talk about things. I might be mistaken, but you might be mistaken too. I really would like to find my birth family. — Michael"

He waited. The pianist finished. Applause. An announcement. Then he got another email. *Are you still at the music hall? I'm on my way back. But like I said, it's not possible. -LC*

He went to the entrance and paced, waited, paced. Then a moment later, two women approached: the fascinating blonde from the quartet, still wearing concert clothes, and the tall black-haired violinist, now wearing a t-shirt and shorts, and with her hair gathered in a low ponytail.

She was his sister. Those features? That way of standing? He'd seen all those traits before. Seen them in his mirror.

She studied him, unnerved. "Um...Michael?"

"Lindsey?" He shook her hand, then turned to the other woman.

The blonde shook his hand. "Ashlyn."

Lindsey folded her arms and shifted her weight. "I'm so

sorry you drove through all the tourist traffic to get here because we could have cleared this up over a few more emails." She fingered the ends of her hair. "I'm my parents' oldest child, and I'm twenty-six. Before that, my father was a student in England, and my mother met him only a year before they got married. The next year, they had me. If you're thirty-two, you were born four years before they were even in the same country. The timeline doesn't work."

He studied her. "We look a lot alike."

"I don't know—genetics is a weird area, and I hear about computer glitches all the time." Inside the hall, music began, and it was another quartet. Like the piece he'd heard her play, the music started softly before adding voices. "Maybe we're related, so we should ask more questions, but my parents aren't time travelers."

Head spinning, Michael couldn't reconcile everything. The feelings, the anticipation, the disappointment.

Ashlyn nudged Lindsey. "Let's grab seats near the back. I want to hear these guys."

Lindsey said to Michael, "If I promise not to run away, can we talk more after this set? These folks are our direct competition. We lost a couple of gigs to them earlier this year, so I need to figure out what makes them so much better."

Michael followed them. "I heard you perform. They can't possibly be better than you."

"Yeah, well, a bunch of other things happened too." Lindsey hesitated, but Ashlyn led them to a table in the back with three free seats. Lindsey lowered her voice. "They're positioned more in a circle than we were. That must help with cues."

Ashlyn said, "It puts them right on top of each other. That affects the sound."

The two women didn't talk through the whole performance, but they did point at unseen issues from time to time. To Michael it was a mystery, like when Ashlyn flashed the number two to Lindsey, or Lindsey frowned and shook her head, but most especially when both of them sat up at the same moment. That time, Lindsey actually leaned forward as if to catch whatever happened next.

Between songs, the two of them conspired, but Michael just watched Lindsey.

Her denial felt wrong. Or did he want a family so desperately that he'd fall prey to a website glitch?

He wanted her mannerisms to feel familiar, but the more he was honest with himself, they didn't. Parts of her did look like him, though. The eyebrows. Her chin, maybe? The way she smiled? He couldn't be sure. It was dark back here.

The announcer closed the set, and then Lindsey said, "Thanks for watching with us, but now fair's fair. Let's talk over dinner. I need to come back for another set at nine."

Michael said, "You're not interested in the country music?"

Ashlyn quipped, "Country *and* Western," and Lindsey giggled.

Outside, the crowds remained thick. "There's a red snapper hot dog stand if we want something fast," Ashlyn said, "but you can actually smell the fried chicken, and I'm famished."

Michael said, "There are lobster rolls, too."

"Can't," Lindsey said. "Shellfish allergy."

Interesting. Michael didn't have any allergies, but that didn't rule out being brother and sister. They got in line for fried chicken, and fifteen minutes later they'd found a free table where they set up with a stack of napkins, paper cartons of greasy chicken pieces, and Moxie in paper cups.

Time to get this back on track. He wasn't actually on a date with two women, even if one of them was strikingly pretty. "So, the DNA. What if it turns out not to be a website glitch?"

Lindsey looked pained. "It's possible my father might have had a kid before he met my mother. But it's not— I mean, I know my dad. He's not the kind of guy who'd leave a pregnant gal up a creek."

Ashlyn rested her chin on her folded hands. "Something's bothering me, though. Linz, he does look kind of like you." She turned to Michael. "Your eyes, a bit. And when you laugh, you remind me of Corwin."

Lindsey glanced at Michael as if he made her skin crawl. "No. You don't look like Corwin at all."

Michael said, "The Cor Castleton I saw in the music program?"

"Yeah, and whether or not we're related, you should stay to hear his band. They've been working really hard this summer, ever since—well, since February."

Ashlyn said, "Actually, we've got something better than a DNA test. Michael, what instruments do you play?"

Lindsey laughed. It was the first time he'd seen her brighten up. Uncertain, Michael said, "Um...I play the radio?"

Ashlyn shook her head. "Then you, my dude, are by definition not a Castleton. Every one of them plays at least three instruments, and quite possibly a dozen. Musical talent is in the genes."

It certainly was beginning to seem as though music connected this family, with Lindsey on the violin and Corwin playing bass. Plus, the announcer had mentioned a different Castleton. "I don't know that it's not in the genes," Michael offered. "I never learned an instrument because I wanted to go into a profession rather than being just an artist."

Both women recoiled, insulted. Michael added an awkward, "The rent doesn't pay itself."

That didn't mollify Lindsey, who stabbed a french fry into the ketchup cup. "Maybe you're more distantly related, like my great uncle had an affair with a 'professional' insurance adjustor."

Best to take that change of subject and ride it as far as he could. Michael pulled up the email from DN-Amazing. "My email has three other matches." He handed her the phone, and she frowned as she scanned the list.

"All the names are distant relatives." Lindsey drew a sharp breath. "I don't like this at all. It's as if they attached my DNA to your profile. Tell them to re-run your test. My family's a mess right now, and—" She blinked hard. "I shouldn't even be here. My father should be first violin, and it's not right."

Ashlyn grabbed Lindsey's hand. "Hey. It's okay."

"It's not okay. If I drop a bombshell on Mom like, hey, Dad may have had an affair, it's going to kill her. It's not like he's going to be able to fix things for her."

"Mom's tough." Ashlyn slid over on the bench and hugged her. "She's a trooper, and you know it. Think about it. She and Dad gave all of us the DNA kits for Christmas, right? If Dad thought he had a secret child, he'd never have done that. But instead he was enthusiastic for you to do the kits."

Lindsey grabbed a napkin and wiped her eyes.

Ashlyn said, "Besides, when has Mom ever turned away a kid in need, even with exactly zero genetic connection?"

Shivers went up Michael's spine. "What's going on with your parents?"

Your parents. Not "our parents." Not yet at least. Possibly never.

Lindsey stared at her lap, her mouth contorting into a frown. "My father was diagnosed in February with frontotemporal dementia. FTD is...it's fatal. It's just like dementia because he's forgetting things, forgetting us, and forgetting how to live. He's losing fine motor coordination. He's losing everything. We had to move him to a nursing care facility last month."

Still looking at Michael, Ashlyn put her hand on Lindsey's. "The guy's amazing. He could play every instrument there was, but he loves violin the most. Lindsey's parents run a music school, and it kept turning out all these awesome players, people whose names you'd recognize if you heard them. But the illness—it's taking him so fast."

"He can't play anymore." Lindsey's voice broke. "If we

ask him about you—I don't know if he'd even remember a one-night stand from thirty-two years ago. It would break my mother's heart."

Michael went cold. "No, you can't do that. I figured they'd both still be alive and healthy. They'd be like fifty or sixty."

Lindsey shuddered. "FTD takes you young. It takes your language, your emotions, your ability to make decisions. He was so healthy and so alive, and then things got weird, so he went to the doctor." Her eyes welled up again. "I'm sorry. This has nothing to do with you. It's just that he's slipping away even though he's still here."

Ashlyn hadn't let go of Lindsey. "He was first violinist of the quartet, and Lindsey was second violinist. Except since February, she's the first violinist."

"I've taken over his students, too." Lindsey looked up. "All that to say, I don't want to bring you to my parents. My mother's strong, but she's hanging on by a hair. She's going to lose my dad in the next year or so. She's got us, but we're losing him too."

The greasy chicken sat like a rock in Michael's stomach.

What if Lindsey was right that they'd mixed up his DNA and hers? Could her results have been pinned to his profile, and trying to do its best, the computer decided that made them a sibling match? If Lindsey approached her mother with no way of confirming or denying with her father, this one glitch could ruin her mother's memories of the man she'd been married to for a quarter century.

That wasn't right.

Michael's shoulders dropped. "I don't know what to do."

Ashlyn said to Lindsey, "Your DNA kits all came from different companies, right?"

Lindsey nodded. "The companies give different profiles, and Mom and Dad wanted each of us to have a different pool of results. My results gave me five percent Eastern European, for example, but my sister's gave her one percent Eastern European."

Michael held up a hand. "Wait, it's you, Corwin, another

sister—and how many more?"

"Three of us. My sister is Sierra."

Sierra. Lindsey. Corwin.

Michael had arrived in the world with a different name: Dalton. His parents had always planned on naming their firstborn Michael, so when they received him, forty-eight hours old, they had it fixed.

Dalton, Corwin, Sierra, and Lindsey... It felt of a piece with the other names. Not as if the other names were Caroline, Elizabeth, and Edward.

Still.

Ashlyn sat back. "Then I have a suggestion. The company that makes Corwin's test got absorbed into DN-Amazing earlier this year—and he didn't take his test anyhow—but Sierra's test came from a different organization entirely. Michael should take the same test as Sierra, and we'll see whether that test turns up as her full sibling also."

Lindsey perked up. "There we go! Two unrelated labs aren't going to make the same mistake. You'll get your real results, and with any luck we'll find out we're third cousins once removed."

This wasn't a bad compromise. "Which company? Because I already filed tests with four different ancestry matching companies."

Ashlyn straightened. "Man! You're serious."

"I really want to find my bio family. It's bothered me for years, but this summer I finally acted on it." Michael looked again at Lindsey, with her reddened eyes but familiar features. "That's why I was so shocked when you were close enough that I could get in the car. We may have been in the same places over and over again."

Lindsey frowned. "Can't they unseal your adoption records?"

Michael shook his head. "I tried. I even got a lawyer, but everything's locked down. The DNA tests seemed like a way to make an end run around the system. I wanted to believe that if my bio parents were out there, they'd be looking for me too."

Lindsey's face softened. "Then let's wait a week and see if you get another email. You keep checking back, and I'll contact DN-Amazing to ask if there could be a mistake." She started stacking empty cartons on the tray. "You're a nice guy. It would be cool if it turns out you're a cousin."

"Even a cousin would be great." Michael stood. "It would be an entrée into finding the rest of my biological family."

CHAPTER THREE

Exhausted, Ashlyn didn't say much to Lindsey during the ride home.

Performing took a lot out of Ashlyn. She'd never gotten the impression that Lindsey found performances stressful, least of all a thirty-minute set at a music festival. For goodness' sakes, thirty minutes was what the quartet played to warm up the guests before a wedding. At a party, though, you had people going in and out, chatting, checking their phones, and drinking their coffees. While you as a musician wanted to turn out the best performance every time, you accepted that party guests weren't going to pay attention to it.

At a music festival, everyone was listening. They'd hear everything that could have been done better, and two years from now you'd wake up at midnight, cringing as you remembered that one note you missed.

Having that Michael guy turn up right after—wow. Not

something Ashlyn would ever have expected. Also "wow" because he was tall and poised and thoughtful. She'd nearly asked for his number just so she could "keep in touch" about his family hunt instead of relying on Lindsey to tell her if he ever emailed again.

Thirdly, despite being driven to find his biological relations, Michael had accepted without argument that they couldn't ask Lindsey's mother who his parents might be. Finally, although he'd wanted to meet Corwin after his set, Michael reluctantly backed down when Lindsey said it would be inappropriate to introduce them. "Corwin's not going to take this well. He already hates his DNA because Dad's condition is genetic." Lindsey had folded her arms. "Tell him you found us through the gene site, and he's going to go nuclear."

That's why Ashlyn had suggested the end-run around the family: when the first test results were sketchy, always ask for a second set of tests. Her mother's public defender had played that game for years to keep giving custody back to her. Question the cops' motives. Claim her mother was being unfairly targeted. Claim a lab error. Keep claiming it until it defied sanity to think dozens of incidents could be errors or outliers.

Ashlyn should have gotten Michael's phone number, regardless. "Just checking in," she could text. "Also, we're performing next week and maybe you could stop by and see us. Just in case."

Ha ha, no.

Ashlyn sat back in her seat and did the thing she hadn't dared to do in front of Michael: she Googled him. LinkedIn was the first place she found anything legit, and it would tell him he'd been searched up. Well, tough luck, Mr. Knolwood. He'd searched Lindsey first. If he didn't expect them to search back, then that would prove beyond reasonable doubt that he wasn't smart enough to be a Castleton.

"He works at an advertising agency."

Lindsey snorted. "Wow. So inspired. Glad he went into 'a

profession' rather than being 'just an artist'."

"Ads are a kind of creativity."

"Creatively making people unhappy in selective ways so they'll purchase your product."

"Be nice." Ashlyn fought giggles. "He insulted me too, you know. Let's see. He's worked at two places, both in Maine. He went to college in New Hampshire. Hobbies—oh, he does set building and stage direction at a community theater. And he referees for some soccer league I've never heard of."

Lindsey said, "Not quite what you'd expect from someone attempting to scam you out of your house and home."

Ashlyn said, "That worries me too. I mean, what if he was able to get Corwin's DNA? He could have submitted it as his own and then walked in pretending to be your long lost brother, waiting for the time when everyone trusts him. He could start taking stuff or doing identity theft. Whatever it is scammers do."

Lindsey shuddered. "I hate everything about this. I hate the timing. I hate the way he looks perfect on paper."

He looked pretty perfect in person, too. "He says the right things. If you were a scammer, though, that's how you'd make it sound."

Lindsey huffed. "Well, what choice does that leave? Either he looks innocent because he's innocent, or else he looks innocent because he wants us to think he's innocent."

He'd put nothing personal on his business profile. Ashlyn couldn't tell if he was married or had kids. If she really got curious, she'd need to track down his other social media, but for now Ashlyn put away the phone.

Lindsey said, "If I had to have a mystery sibling, why couldn't it have been you?" and Ashlyn laughed. "No, really." This late at night, the tourists had mostly evaporated back to their overpriced hotel rooms and rental cottages. Lindsey sounded earnest. "We're practically sisters anyhow."

"We're going to be sisters someday. I'll make you godmother to my first child, and you make me godmother to your first child, and that's as good as sisters."

"I'm still miffed that I wasn't able to set you up with Corwin."

"No, thank you." Corwin would forever be the eight-year-old brat who'd made Ashlyn's life miserable when she'd crash landed at the Castleton home at age twelve. The feeling was entirely mutual and double-sided. Corwin didn't object to having Ashlyn at the dinner table, but that was as close as it got. He had his friends, his pursuits, and his own brand of music.

"Yeah, but sisters-in-law is also close to sisters." Lindsey sighed. "I've asked myself a few times if maybe Michael could have been right, but how would that even happen? Dad was studying music at the Royal Academy of London. Mom didn't meet him until her last year of college, and a year later they got married, and a year after that they had me. There just wasn't any time."

Ashlyn said, "Where was Dad before he was in London?"

"He grew up in Lewiston. So yeah, they were in the same state, but you don't get pregnant just because you live in the same state. Plus, Michael's thirty-two. Mom would have had to be like fifteen or sixteen when she had him."

"Pregnant at fifteen..." Ashlyn murmured. "I mean, it's possible. Your mother has a heart for looking out for unwanted kids, and she welcomed me into the house at twelve. She might have been looking back at what she would have wanted someone to do for her."

"She and my grandmother have a great relationship. If she got in trouble, Grandma was right by her side." Lindsey shook her head. "Dad's a responsible guy, too. Maybe as a teenager he was flighty, but based on who he is now, he'd have taken a job digging ditches to support his child if that's what it took."

"Could your mom not have told him?" Ashlyn said.

Lindsey straightened. "That's— That would be weird. But again, Mom was part of the DNA testing gifts. She wouldn't have done that if it would reveal a secret baby she'd never told my father about for three decades."

Ashlyn said, "What if they were ashamed?"

Lindsey gestured with one hand. "If they were ashamed, why give us the kits that would reveal their shame?"

The most likely outcome really was the computer glitch. Blast it, Ashlyn should have gotten Michael's phone number.

They arrived at their apartment in the pitch dark. "It's weird not carrying instruments," Ashlyn murmured as Lindsey got the mail. In the second floor apartment, Ashlyn headed for her bedroom at the back and stripped off the concert clothes.

If Lindsey had to have a secret sibling, it should have been her.

But if Michael turned out to be her secret brother...that would be okay. Ashlyn wouldn't mind getting to know another near-Castleton, and he'd be nice enough to look at across the dining room table.

Lindsey called from the kitchen, "You don't want to look at the mail tonight."

Ashlyn groaned. At the table she found a greeting card envelope addressed in her mother's jagged handwriting. A minute later, she opened up a wall of text written around a gold "thinking of you" poem-esque script. Her mother began by saying she missed Ashlyn and wanted to see her again, followed by some weird tale of a person she'd met at a halfway house.

Ashlyn dropped the card back on the table without wading all the way through. It was certain odds the rest of the card would say her mother wanted to get together, and could Ashlyn maybe send her mother some cash? The handwritten shakedown would still be there in the morning. Ashlyn could face it then.

Lindsey stepped out of the bathroom in pajamas. "Didn't I say you didn't want to look?"

"That's what I heard too." Ashlyn turned with a forced smile. "It's always the same, so I figured I should get it over with."

Susan Castleton was Mom. Ashlyn's own mother was Rachel. Susan and Bob had never adopted Ashlyn because her mother was still alive, plus it would have messed up her college financial aid. Ashlyn was "a ward of the state." Now she was just an adult—an adult with two mothers, or with no mothers. It all depended on how you looked at it.

But, she thought as she went to brush her teeth, in the long run, didn't everything?

Chapter Four

Michael awoke Sunday morning to a message on his phone. "How did it go??? So excited for you!"

Mom. He brewed coffee while sorting through the many possible ways to answer, but finally he replied with, "Inconclusive. I'll tell you at brunch."

Mom would be at church right about now, so he took his time showering and trying to pick the right words to explain about Lindsey and Ashlyn. And Corwin. And their father.

Frontotemporal dementia. The whole thing sounded awful, but now he Googled it, and somehow it sounded even worse. FTD, as they called it, had nothing to do with flower delivery and everything to do with losing your words, losing your coordination, losing your personality—and all before age sixty. FTD hit younger people. There was no cure, no medication, no nothing.

No wonder Corwin was angry at his DNA. He could only

marvel that Lindsey wasn't furious at it as well.

The more Michael read, the more he caught himself hoping Robert Castleton wasn't actually his father after all.

The coffee maker beeped, and he poured a cup while trying to talk sense to himself. Learning his medical history was one of the reasons he'd wanted to look for his family. While it felt nice to say, "None" whenever a doctor asked about any family history whatsoever, it was wrong.

Everything about this was wrong. Michael quite possibly shouldn't exist in the first place.

On the adoptee forums, he'd read horror stories that for a decade had sidelined his own search. Many adoptees had tracked down families riddled with dysfunction. Some had uncovered secrets that left their biological parents furious and ashamed. *We wanted to forget you ever happened.* More than one had discovered their father and grandfather were one and the same. Talk about a jack-in-the-box of awfulness.

Among those, though...standing out from those nightmare stories were the good ones. The women who'd given up babies they weren't prepared to raise. The families who'd needed the space or the time or the energy or the money. There were children who'd been seized by the state and the parents who were relieved to find out their children had landed in a better life. Joyful tears. Reunions with half-siblings they'd never known and who'd never known about them.

A full sibling, though? That would be the jackpot. A full sibling who came from an intact family? One who knew all his extended relations? Not having to track down relatives for two parents? Even if they were just musicians, that was better than a lot of other things they could have been.

Michael drank his coffee staring out the window at a parking lot, and across the street another row of houses. Beyond the houses, though, stood a mountain with the trees lush, and over that was a blue sky populated with clouds. Michael had been born into a beautiful part of a beautiful world. He always figured he hadn't been taken far. There was always a chance he'd encounter the family who'd given him up.

"Don't say 'gave up'," people would scold on the forum. "You weren't thrown out like the trash. Parents who make an adoption plan are doing their best in a bad situation."

Still, Baby Dalton had been surrendered to an adoption agency, who had then presented him to Elizabeth and William Knolwood. Surrender was just a more formal way of saying "giving up."

With the coffee percolating through his system, Michael read some more about genetic matches, then noticed the time and sprang up to get dressed. He arrived five minutes early to meet his parents, but even so, they were waiting at a booth in the Main Street Diner. Mom had her mug of tea, and Dad had his cup of coffee.

Setting aside his crossword puzzle, Dad said, "Tell us! What does 'inconclusive' mean?"

Because the diner hadn't changed its lineup in the past fifty years, Michael didn't bother looking at a menu. "Inconclusive means I met the person the company identified as my full sister, but she doesn't think there's any way that's correct."

Mom frowned. "How can that be? Of course it's got to be correct."

"She's the oldest of three, and her parents met only two years before she was born." He stopped as Angie, the diner's sole waitress, came over. "Triple stack buttermilk pancakes, sausage, hash browns. Thanks," he added as she poured him a cup of coffee and refilled his father's mug. "Anyhow, Lindsey's only twenty-five, so there's no way her parents would have been able to have me."

Dad looked sad. "That does sound conclusive."

Mom shook her head. "No, honey. That's what her parents *told* her. Some people are like that and never admit to their mistakes. They must have met before, and then they released you for adoption but hid the information from everyone else."

Even though Michael had started the search under the

assumption that his existence was a mistake, it was uncomfortable to hear his mother say it that way. "I'm telling you what they told me. The father wasn't even in the country. He was studying music at the Royal Academy of London while the mother attended college here. They met after he returned from England, and then they dated a year before getting married. They had Lindsey right after."

Dad said, "An international student? He must be pretty smart."

Mom shrugged. "Do we know anything about that place's music program? Some universities have strong and weak departments, after all. And a lot of institutions are shunting money toward more useful studies."

Michael told them about the DNA kits given to each of their children. "That's how I ended up finding Lindsey. Lindsey's rationale is that if her parents were trying to keep me a secret, they wouldn't have done something that would have uncovered me."

Mom said, "Did you get a picture of her?"

He hadn't. It had seemed too invasive to ask for a photo of them together when Lindsey was so insistent that they weren't related. On the other hand, the Castleton String Quartet website did have her photo, so he showed that to his parents. "That's Lindsey, and I assume this man is her father."

It made sense now why the website was a disaster: in the tumult after her father's diagnosis, Lindsey hadn't called back their website designer to update it. Or updated it herself. Or couldn't bear to update it herself. Still, it needed to be done, and if Michael did end up being a relative, he'd offer to do it.

"That woman looks like you," Dad pronounced. "She's the one."

Mom hummed. "Is that her father? You don't look very much like the father at all."

"That's what Lindsey said. Wait, I can show you her brother, too." He searched up Corwin's band's page, and there was Corwin, his face contorted as he performed a bass guitar solo.

Mom sighed. "I should have known. Musicians are infamous for one-night stands, aren't they? Because they travel so much. We were always vigilant about making sure you grew up to have a profession instead of some kind of wild-haired save-the-world visionary thing."

"Are they all musicians?" Dad chuckled. "No wonder they gave you up. There's no money in music."

Mom nodded. "We did them a favor. You were expensive to raise, and we had two good incomes. Three more babies afterward?" She shuddered. "Your adoption was definitely the right thing."

The waitress swung by the table with Dad's omelet and Mom's Belgian waffle, along with a promise that Michael's order would be next. Mom said, "You always did like listening to music. It was only by the skin of our teeth that we convinced you to take French instead."

"That's very much grasping at straws." Michael sat back. Of course, last night he'd grasped at every single straw he could. "The father taught music for a number of years, and I guess the mother must have too. The three siblings are all musicians."

Mom said, "Oh, this isn't good. Did they ask you for money?"

Not only had they not asked for money, but they hadn't even let Michael pay for their food. "Why would they?"

"There's not a lot of money in music." Mom looked back at the quartet page. "Who is the other man?"

"I have no idea because the lineup seems to have changed. The second violinist is new, and so is the cellist. I did meet the blonde woman with the bigger violin, Ashlyn." Ashlyn's photo on the website was as stunning as she was in person. "I think she's Lindsey's partner. Lindsey is going to ask her relatives if maybe I could be a cousin, and we're both going to ask DN-Amazing to rerun our tests. Then we're going to wait in case I turn up as a match for the third sibling's test."

Mom looked momentarily baffled. "Why would they use

different companies?"

Michael sipped his coffee. "To get different results."

Mom shook her head. "Terribly wasteful. Spend the money doing one sibling and the results should be the same for everyone."

Dad said, "I've heard about this. Because there's no real regulation in place, these companies are matching DNA with what they think is true but not really. There's no reason to say a certain genetic combination comes from North Africa or from Australia, for example, so they're extrapolating by testing across wide ranges of people. The more people get tested, the more they can refine their answers. That's why every year or so, subscribers get updated results."

Mom shrugged. "Well, I'm not the scientist. It just seems like the answers wouldn't be divergent enough to pay three different testing agencies. But I wouldn't expect a family like you've described to do things the normal way, regardless."

Michael shrugged. "Well, three kids, three different companies. The brother refuses to do his test."

Corwin, boycotting his DNA. How might it feel to know you might be in line for the same thing Robert Castleton was going through—for your memories, your abilities, and a lifetime of skills to slip away in your fifties?

Michael was thirty-two. He could have fewer than twenty years before it happened to him. If Robert were his father, that was.

The pancakes arrived, and Michael forced himself to butter them and add maple syrup as though his stomach weren't tight like a triple knot. So close. So close.

Dad huffed. "I don't blame the brother for refusing. You and I discussed the problems with a corporation owning access to your DNA."

Michael sighed. "It's actually much worse."

By the time he was done explaining, Mom looked devastated. "That poor man. The whole family! They must be devastated."

Lindsey and Ashlyn had looked devastated, to be sure. Lindsey in tears, Ashlyn being strong for her. Ashlyn, so beautiful in the way she'd stood up for Lindsey and her in-laws. If Michael ever got married, he hoped it was to someone who valued his parents the same way Ashlyn valued Lindsey's. And not, for example, to someone who treated his parents the way Kristen had treated them.

But that was water over the dam, now, wasn't it? Kristen was long gone. Good riddance.

Afterward the subject meandered to other things. Mom, complaining about tourists. Dad, telling him about some project at work. Michael's search dominated his thoughts, but they still had their lives. He still had his own.

And yet.

And yet, he wanted to do nothing other than refresh the second DNA firm's website to force them to process him faster. Force them to connect him to Sierra Castleton. Finally build a bridge back to parents who'd thought it better if he were raised by someone else.

CHAPTER FIVE

At the Castleton Music School on Monday evening, Ashlyn took back her viola from Hannah. "I'll carry Lindsey's violin," she added as Hannah worked to get the cello from her back seat. "Thanks for keeping them safe."

Hannah shrugged. "Not a big deal. How did Corwin do?"

"He was terrific! Everyone was screaming."

Hannah laughed. "I wish they'd scream for us."

Ashlyn said, "Jason wishes they'd scream for him," and Hannah giggled.

In the basement practice room, Lindsey had the chairs set up in a slightly different formation. "I'm experimenting with how the other group did things. It might help if we can hear one another better."

Hannah surveyed the setup. "I don't think it will broadcast the sound as well. Remember, they were miked at the festival."

"We'll put it back if we're distorting one another's

sound." She looked up from setting new sheet music on all the stands. "Speaking of things I can't hear, I can't hear Jason anywhere."

"He'll turn up on California time." Ashlyn glanced at the new music. Beethoven? Fun. "Next on the schedule: we've got gigs on Friday, Saturday morning, and Sunday evening?"

"Believe it or not, we just picked up a Saturday evening gig too." Lindsey looked pleased as she returned to her seat. "Tourists may be a pain, but they're good for cash flow. Some guy is throwing a party on his yacht, and he thought a string quartet would be the perfect touch."

Hannah said, "I'm available."

Ashlyn nodded. "Yeah, that sounds like a good deal. I hope Jason doesn't get motion-sick. A yacht isn't very big."

Lindsey froze. "Yeah, that would make for a terrible evening. I could call one of our backups."

Ashlyn said, "Imagine the great Jason Vanderbilt Woodward, leaning over the railing to heave up his guts."

"Not something I want to imagine at all." Lindsey frowned. "Anyhow, let's tune and see when he shows up."

The Saturday morning performance was a garden wedding, and they knew that music forward and backward. Good to practice it, of course, but any one of them could do a passable job walking in cold. Wedding couples might request a different song every now and again, but seldom did they request anything so off the beaten path that the quartet had to work at it. The Sunday evening performance was a dinner party, and for that they could play pretty much anything they had prepared. The quartet would sound formal and forgettable, and the guests would chat without any expectation that they'd listen to the background music.

Jason arrived. "Sorry I'm late. Traffic on 1A was abysmal." Lindsey didn't say anything, and Jason flipped through new music she'd printed out before he even set down his violin. "Really?"

"Yes, really. Oh, and we picked up another gig for six

p.m. next Saturday night."

Ashlyn added, "Some rich guy wants us on his yacht."

Jason recoiled. "No."

"What do you mean, no?" Lindsey looked up. "Rich guy. Yacht. Lots of zeros on the check."

"Moisture and humidity. Wooden violins. Not a good combination."

"Are you kidding me?" Lindsey glared up. "How about this, pretty boy? I'll go upstairs into the instrument closet to get you a student violin, that way your precious darling can stay properly dehumidified."

He stared at her. "And a student violin will sound like hot garbage."

Ashlyn interrupted before Lindsey voiced her feelings about what actually sounded like hot garbage. "If we're on the deck of a boat, there should be enough air movement that the instruments won't have humidity issues."

Hannah said, "We won't be in a hall, though, so the acoustics will be working against us."

Jason finally set down his violin case. "That's precisely why we need the A-level instruments."

Ashlyn said, "No, no. Think about how water reflects sound. It'll carry for miles."

"Right, and for miles around, people will hear every one of us off by a semitone or when a student instrument falls flat." Jason took a seat. "This is a disaster. Tell them we can't do it."

"They paid a deposit, and I'm showing up even if I have to play five hours solo."

Ashlyn exclaimed, "Five hours?"

Jason sighed. "Well. Won't this be exciting?"

"Getting paid excites me. We'll be fine."

Yeah, assuming they didn't need to eat or use the bathroom or rest their arms. Considering their hourly rate, though, Ashlyn kept her mouth shut. Because the money really was good, and it would be nice not to have a non-music day job.

"Give me an A." Jason listened, then started tuning the

violin. "Five hours on a boat. If it's starting at six, we'll be playing until eleven."

Lindsey said, "If you plan to gripe and moan the whole time, you don't have to play it."

"Yes, pointing out two very reasonable drawbacks is the exact definition of griping and moaning for five hours." Jason plucked up and down the strings, then pulled out his bow and did a three-octave G scale. "Fine. Let's rehearse, and we'll work out the playlist later on."

Up until last January, Ashlyn had enjoyed practices. Without the tension of a performance, she relished playing together. The runs, the counterpoints, the harmonies. In the most expert quartet compositions, the composers had woven all the voices in with one another to create dynamic tension as well as resolution.

That was the beauty of a string quartet: the combinations. You could have all four voices together or any one of the voices solo. You could mix it up: just the two violins as soprano and alto, or the viola and a cello for tenor and bass, or the cello and one violin. You could combine two violins and a cello or the second violin, the viola, and the cello—then swap out the viola for the first violin. In the strongest pieces, four instruments came apart and recombined with glorious precision, each contributing to the whole.

Ashlyn missed Bob. With Bob as first violinist, Lindsey had played a relaxed and emotional second violin. The first violinist got all the virtuoso lines, whereas according to a very young Wolfgang Amadeus Mozart, "You don't need lessons to play second violin." That was, of course, untrue. Lindsey had been taking violin lessons since age five and would still have been taking lessons if only her instructor hadn't tumbled into a pit of lost memories and lost coordination.

Bob had a way of coaxing his violin to project with a warmth that left Ashlyn in awe. In her most ardent wishes she would be able to draw the same tones from her viola. The viola was the forgotten instrument, but Ashlyn preferred it that way: one fifth lower but only fifteen percent bigger, the viola was harder to hear than either the violins or the cello. The viola backed up the first violin, just as Ashlyn backed up Lindsey.

Jason Woodward, while a virtuoso soloist, made for a terrible second violinist. Too often he seemed at war with the first violin, and he didn't even realize it.

He was good. He was, quite probably, better than Bob had been—or would become better. All he needed was Bob's decades of experience, and (please) also Bob's humility. Three years ago, he'd left Maine for California where he'd have a chance to score the acclaim a violinist of his caliber deserved. To some extent he'd succeeded. But three years later, here he was back in Maine.

Jason had walked in expecting to fill the first violin chair, only that had gone to Lindsey. And Jason had gone to war.

Ashlyn set that aside as they reviewed everything they'd play this weekend. They didn't touch the new pieces Lindsey had copied out for them. Usually they'd each review their parts on their own and try combining them during rehearsal. Fine-tuning the dynamics was ten times harder than learning the pieces—and that was saying a lot when you were tackling a work by Mozart or Beethoven.

Afterward, Jason wiped down his violin before returning it to the case. "Let me look at the student violins. Maybe one of them isn't so bad."

Lindsey tossed Ashlyn two pounds of keys. "Can you?"

On the second floor, Ashlyn and Jason went through the closet. "This one's cracked," she said. "This one...the bow needs to be rehaired. That's ridiculous." She swapped bows so the cracked violin had the worn-out bow. "Okay, now we have a playable setup."

Jason looked over her shoulder. "Oh, look, there's a star carved onto the violin body. Won't that look adorable?" He plucked the strings, then played a scale. "Not terrible. Are you going to get a beater viola for yourself?"

"My instrument isn't as temperamental as yours. I think

it comes from being cheaper." Jason reportedly had a fifty thousand dollar instrument. He might be "living out of his violin case" for a while, but wow, was that beauty ever worth it. It looked gorgeous, sounded gorgeous, and probably felt gorgeous to play. Jason soloed with it every so often, and Ashlyn always closed her eyes just to listen. She also loved keeping her eyes open because Jason had the perfect style for the cover of a classical music album. He had great hair and soulful eyes, plus when he wasn't sniping at Lindsey, he carried himself with poise.

"The wood is thinner," was all Jason said. "Maybe Lindsey doesn't notice the difference, but some violins don't take well to changes in the weather, let alone a massive jolt in humidity." He pulled out another violin. "There's not much here. I may be stuck." He plucked a few strings and replaced it in the case, disgusted. "We'll just have to assume no one listening actually knows what they're listening to."

Ashlyn said, "The people on the shore are more likely to listen than the guests mingling with a champagne flute in one hand and an hors d'oeuvre plate in the other."

"True. You can't listen to music when you're flustered by the perennial problem of how to get the food into your mouth with both hands occupied." Jason picked up the violin with the star carved near the endpin. "The graffiti gives it character, don't you agree?"

Ashlyn laughed. "The star is why Lindsey loves it."

"Of course it is." He played another scale, then launched into a tune Ashlyn didn't recognize. "Do you know they did blind experiments with a Stradivarius violin, a couple of middle of the road violins, and two student violins? They had the same professionals play from behind a curtain, and they asked five experts to pick out the Strad. They couldn't do it consistently."

Ashlyn shrugged. "Knowing that, you still got yourself an amazing violin?"

Jason snickered. "I don't entirely trust experts. Plus, sometimes you encounter perfection and fall in love. When that happens, you get rid of everything else in order to have that one thing."

"It's just one performance you'll need the star violin for." Ashlyn set the rejected violins back on the shelves and returned to the practice room.

Hannah had left, but Lindsey was sorting music. "You found a stand-in?"

Jason arched his eyebrows. "Yes, and you'll be pleased to know it's got a star carved near the endpin, so our yacht-owning client will recognize our star power."

Lindsey's head came up. "Oh, did that one come back? Have fun with her. She's got nice tones."

"I will, thanks." Jason shouldered his backpack and the case for his real violin. "Also, five hours? Can you at least add up the times on the pieces you want, because—"

"I thought I'd make you happy by giving you a couple of solos so Ashlyn and Hannah can get a meal break, and later on I'll do a couple of solos so you could get one too."

"Considerate." He nodded to them both and took off.

Lindsey turned to Ashlyn. "Mom was wondering if we could stop by tonight. Things were bad when she visited Dad today."

Ashlyn nodded. "And we say nothing about Michael?"

"Not even word number one, not until we get the results from Sierra."

"Agreed. Did you talk to Sierra?"

Lindsey's eyes narrowed. "Yes, and she's... Heaven help us either way, because by the end of the conversation I thought she was going to go door-to-door collecting cheek swabs."

Ashlyn chuckled. "Well, Sierra marches to her own harp."

"She's got a good heart, but we don't even know the guy." Lindsey zipped up her backpack. "You ready?"

Susan Castleton was rattled, so Ashlyn made herself useful alongside her in the kitchen. Then Lindsey lured her mother away from the counter to allow Ashlyn to take over all the cooking.

"He was frustrated today." Never one to be still, Mom started getting glasses down from the cabinet. "He couldn't remember one particular word, and then he couldn't recognize it on the communication board. I couldn't even help him guess. He got angry at me." She blinked hard. "I used to predict the things he'd say so well that he wouldn't even have to start the sentence, and today I couldn't come up with the one word he wanted. Even now. I never came up with it."

Lindsey was leaning against the wall. "Did the nurses have suggestions?"

"Not as such. He got agitated, and their suggestion was that I leave. I tried staying longer, but he just got worse." Mom paused, one glass in front of a place setting and one still in her hand. "There are good days and bad days. I know that. This was a bad day."

Ashlyn set the timer for the spaghetti, eyes burning. Eventually the bad days would outnumber the good. Then there'd be only bad days. And a final day. Followed by worse days forever.

Michael should run. Michael should carefully file away those DNA reports and lock the drawer, then go back to his mom and dad to give them a big hug. "You know what? I have everything I want right here. You guys taught me to ride a bike and sat up with me when I had strep throat, and you listened to my recorder concert in second grade. My crayon drawings went on your refrigerator. That's what matters."

By his account he had a good relationship with them. If he stepped into this family, at this time, under these circumstances—he'd end up grieving. No one would be at their best. How can you say hello to five people while saying goodbye to a sixth?

Michael, Michael, Michael. Could her brain get any more infatuated? She'd have to hope that in a week she could contact him again on Lindsey's behalf with, "Sierra's test and yours don't show a match. I'd like to take you out for coffee to help you strategize." She didn't want him disappointed, but from the Castleton front porch, hills of disappointment lay in every direction.

Maybe not if he were a third cousin. Maybe not if he were only Mom's kid and not Dad's. But still, surrounded by grieving people, how could someone as obviously empathetic as Michael not feel it all the way to his core?

The Castleton home was one of those rambling houses that had never committed to a shape. In 1825, a stonemason had built a square two-story home with a fireplace and a root cellar. Over time, pieces started getting added, some with no records to document their appearance. A bump-out for the kitchen. A front porch. A rectangular addition off the side. Around the time of the Civil War, the chimney got replaced with a staircase, and a different chimney added between the main house and the addition. Then the addition got sealed off. It got unsealed and another addition added before World War I. After World War II, the original fireplace and chimney got restored, and a third floor showed up around the time of the moon landing.

On and on, the house had grown or shrunk to accommodate a succession of families as well as the advent of electricity, plumbing, and central heat. Twenty years ago, it got town water and sewer. "The other side of the house" had served as the music school until fifteen years ago when Bob bought the building on Granite Cross Road. Then "the other side of the house" became the kids' bedrooms, and nowadays it was a repository for books and instruments.

Mom and Dad had complained it was drafty. Lindsey had bragged it was almost big enough that you didn't have to hear Corwin. Sierra mused that it branched too much for the family to feel unified.

Ashlyn loved it. Loved how it fit the family. Loved how it had room for her as well.

Ashlyn cooked while Lindsey sat with her mother. Mom was great to Ashlyn, but Ashlyn wasn't her daughter. Lindsey was the one she needed.

Mere moments before the food hit the table, Sierra bounced into the house. "You think you've accounted for tourist traffic, and then you're still wrong." She hugged her mother. "You're heartbroken. Terrible day? I'm so sorry."

Ashlyn got to hear it again over dinner. Dad was slipping away.

Michael might be slipping inside.

This was the only family Ashlyn knew, and it wasn't even hers. It had expanded to take her in, now was contracting, might expand again.

Like breathing. Souls in, souls out.

She passed the spaghetti bowl and ached for Bob.

Chapter Six

Frustrated, Michael endured another tech support call. DN-Amazing's customer service reps had a script they followed with enforced compassion and precise wording. *Your DNA results are often surprising, but that's part of the fun in receiving your results.* If Michael recalled, they reminded him, he'd signed a waiver absolving them of all responsibility if he uncovered difficult interpersonal situations. Also, they were sure the benefits of any revealed truths were better than living with false assumptions.

That was not, Michael fired back, what he was asking about. He wanted them to re-run the tests and verify that his DNA and Lindsey's hadn't been confused. At the third level tech support, he finally heard a chuckle and a throat-clearing that meant a human being had listened.

"I've got your report in front of me. Obviously I can't look at the other client's because I don't have her permission." The guy sounded semi-distracted, as though reading and speaking at the same time. "I will say conclusively that this is not our other client's DNA because yours has a Y chromosome. But more than that, I'm an employee with magic powers, and that means I can access the premium features you didn't pay for. Don't tell my supervisor, but onscreen is your full report. You're a 52% match for the individual who turns up as your full sibling."

Michael said, "Meaning...?"

"Meaning that's not her DNA because then you'd be a one hundred percent match. Fifty-two is neatly in the full sibling range."

Michael said, "How about close cousins?"

The tech said, "Not at fifty-two percent. I'm not a geneticist, but I've seen a lot of weird situations. If a pair of identical twins had kids with a different pair of identical twins, those cousins would be genetic siblings, true. In serious cases of multigenerational incest...maybe? Otherwise, no. Cousins aren't going to be in the fifties or high forties."

Michael said, "Which puts us back at a computer glitch."

The tech sighed. "It's always possible, but all the weirdest glitches end up on my desk or one of my coworker's desks, and we're all sitting in the same room. If our company were manufacturing siblings, I'd hear about it."

Michael said, "At least one of these facts is mistaken."

"Granted, and since you have no experience with DN-Amazing, your track record suggests we're the least reliable link in the chain." The tech at least sounded friendly. "I will tell you that in my experience, nine times out of ten, when an intractable problem arrives here, by the time I've finished clearing my company's good name, the client has figured out the problem wasn't in the computer. Regardless, I've re-submitted your case. You should have updated results in five to ten business days, but most likely you'll find it only adjusts the percentages of DNA from under-represented parts of the world. Family matches seldom change."

Michael urged, "But the degree of relation—that could change?"

"That's what you're looking to change, but I don't see it happen very often. We're good with that part of the technology because it's been used for quite a while in paternity suits."

It hit Michael right then: had Lindsey's parents submitted their DNA? The moment he got off the phone with DN-Amazing, he emailed a message to Lindsey.

The quartet had a social media presence, although haphazard. Michael had stalked it but found nothing noteworthy. The second violinist had some solo work (and had ignited an online firestorm about six months ago) but not the others. The cellist existed nowhere else. Lindsey had a few pictures on the music school site, but not Ashlyn. Which was kind of a shame, because Ashlyn was beautiful. She appeared prominently in only one of their video clips, and he'd watched it a few times. She closed her eyes when she played the more emotional parts, as if every movement of the bow were a long kiss with a lover.

He'd never paid attention to how violinists and violists played their instruments, but he'd have assumed they sat straight and only moved their arms and fingers. The few times he'd attended symphony orchestras, that's what they'd seemed like. In the more intimate setting of a quartet, they seemed so fluid. Ashlyn's shoulders shifted; her spine flexed; her facial expression changed; her hips swayed; her voila pointed up or down. You couldn't call it dancing, but on the other hand, Michael wasn't sure what else you could call this movement to music.

Lindsey's reply came an hour later. "Mom and Dad didn't take any tests, so it'll just be Sierra. DN-Amazing told me the same thing about the XX and XY thing, how it would be obvious if your DNA and mine got mixed up. I didn't get my tech to dive into the paid reports. Good job getting that info."

She sounded so business-like. For him, it felt far too

personal, but he made himself withhold the emotion when he replied. "Thank you for asking them. I'll let you know when I get the new report." Just before he hit send, he added, "If you want to text me, here's my phone number."

She didn't send back hers. No, there was no reason. In the long run, they might be strangers.

Google was less help when he looked for "false positives" and DNA tests. The false positives that came up repeatedly were for detecting health conditions. But when it came to identifying relatives, which was the side of the bread the commercial testers knew was buttered, they were reliable.

His phone buzzed, and Michael glanced at the screen.

"Hey, it's Ashlyn Merritt. Lindsey gave me your number, so here's mine."

He blinked at it. That was odd. "Thanks. I promise not to blow up your phone."

She replied, "I do know how to block people when required. It'll be fine."

He laughed.

This could have gone so much worse. The family could have reacted with volatile denials, a cease and desist letter, or outright threats. Even though they were musicians, they were all employed and sounded educated. Despite the potential upheaval—despite the actual upheaval of Robert Castleton's illness—they seemed friendly.

He hoped they were his. When he'd started the search, he'd wanted to find any family. After meeting them, though, he wanted it to be theirs.

CHAPTER SEVEN

Unnerved, Ashlyn played a solo piece for the yacht dinner party so Lindsey and Jason could lock themselves in the tiny prep room and have a massive fight.

A yacht party was, as it turned out, a swanky affair. The quartet hadn't even met the host, although their bank accounts had shaken hands earlier this afternoon for the final payment. A butler had escorted the quartet to the deck of this huge boat where four chairs sat in a semi-circle, and to the side an itty-bitty room for stashing their instrument cases. Jason had gotten one look at the setup and declared, "We're doomed."

First, although they always brought their own music stands, it was breezy. They'd have sheet music fluttering in their binders and unanticipated page-turns.

Secondly, although this was what Jason had pointed out first, "We've got no light. Once the sun sets, we're playing blind."

Lindsey gave a cheerful, "Well, then, we get to work hard for every penny," and on the spot she rejiggered their playlist. Before Ashlyn had even finished reframing the problem, Lindsey had front-end loaded their playlist with the most difficult pieces, then backfilled the after-sundown slots with material that...well, material they could play with their eyes closed. As promised, she interspersed twenty-minute solos for herself and Jason, but then with extra time, she tossed a twenty-minute solo slot to Ashlyn. They'd finish with arrangements they all knew by heart.

Jason muttered, "Several dozen filthy rich clients, and their final impression will be that we're a bunch of middle schoolers who've just held our first recital."

"I'm not playing Mozart without the score in front of me," Lindsey shot back, "or we *will* sound like a bunch of middle schoolers holding their first recital."

Jason straightened his tuxedo jacket. "We could pull off Haydn's G-major string quartet without a hitch. Can we finish with that, at least?"

After Ashlyn's solo, the violinists would reappear with the Haydn question resolved. Either that or the Castleton Strings would have suddenly become a trio.

Jason returned. He nipped around behind Ashlyn and got set up again, but in the middle of a difficult run, she paid no attention because she'd learn about the revised plan in five minutes. Lindsey hadn't reappeared. Had they actually become a string trio?

With her piece ending and still no Lindsey, Ashlyn took a repeat on one of the sections. Jason wouldn't mind. Jason was the one who usually gave a smooth, "And why are we taking all the repeats? Because the composer asked us to, that's why."

Ashlyn ended, and still no Lindsey. Ashlyn had other solos she could play, but should she start?

Behind her, Hannah said, "Oh, good," and Lindsey rushed up to them. She didn't have her violin.

Instead, she had tears in her eyes. "Jason, can you solo

for about five minutes?"

Startled, he said, "What? I didn't do that."

Do what? Her tears? Lindsey said, "Not everything is about you. I need Ash."

Jason turned to Hannah. "Remember the first dance from last night's wedding? Lay down the harmony."

Lindsey hustled Ashlyn into the prep room where they had to stand nearly on top of one another. Unable to speak, she handed Ashlyn the phone.

"*Forwarded: We've found a match!*"

Ashlyn gasped. "Sierra too?"

Mouth trembling, Lindsey nodded.

Ashlyn opened the email. This output was far more detailed than the DN-Amazing report. Percentages, traits, locations—and then the likelihood of a sibling match at 98.4%.

Lindsey's voice wobbled. "Ash, there's no way. Two of them? Two separate services matching us to him? That's got to be legit. I've searched all week for what other things might make people seem like siblings. It can't happen. This is real."

Ashlyn hugged her. "Breathe. Take a deep breath and tell me, are you going to be all right to play the rest of the night? Or should we tag-team solos and duets?"

"I'll get a grip. We're doing the Haydn at the end so at least Jason will get off my case. He's right: we can do that one blindfolded...I hope. I just—" She shook her head. "Michael's going to be all over us the second this hits his inbox, and I don't know what to say. I have no idea what to do or how to handle this. Mom's going to freak."

"Tonight, no one's going to freak, and tomorrow doesn't matter. Breathe." Ashlyn put her forehead to Lindsey's and inhaled deep, and Lindsey breathed with her. They'd done this before, only it had always been Lindsey talking Ashlyn off a ledge. Breathe in. Breathe out. Focus. One thing at a time. "I will text him." Exhale. Inhale. "I will tell him you're performing tonight and tomorrow, but we'll talk on Monday." One breath out. One breath in. "We will come up with a plan." Oxygen exchange, deep and slow. "You are not in this alone."

Lindsey nodded. "Yes." Breathe. "We'll get this done." Breathe.

Ashlyn found her phone in her viola case and texted Michael. "We got Sierra's email. Let's talk on Monday morning after we've finished our weekend performances. Welcome to the family."

Ashlyn didn't know why she added that. She wasn't even a part of the family, let alone someone with authority to welcome him into it. It just didn't feel right to treat the test results as if he'd won five bucks from a scratch-off ticket.

Back outside, they took their seats while Jason and Hannah finished their piece. Ashlyn could have jumped back in with her own harmony, but that would have left Lindsey the only one not playing, so she waited it out.

Jason sat back down, pale and wide-eyed. "Is it Bob? Is he okay?"

Lindsey's voice was strained. "Nothing is okay, and it's not Dad. Let's just finish the last hour."

It was chilly on the deck, but Lindsey warmed them right back up again. They'd do one long piece, one shorter, and then end with Haydn, Opus 76, number one. That would bring them well over their contracted playing time, but Lindsey had planned a cushion in case the boat delayed getting back into the dock. The dinner party chattered on around them, guests strolling the deck while nibbling heavy hors d'ouvres, twinkle lights gleaming overhead, and the boat cruising gently.

Another Castleton brother. It was unbelievable.

Ashlyn had been playing this Haydn quartet since age seventeen, so she handled her part with no issue. Hannah struggled, but as the cello she could lower her volume and lay down notes in the correct key without attracting too much attention. The two violins made several bad transitions and had issues with the dynamics (Jason too loud, Lindsey too fast) and Ashlyn chalked that up to the night. Her own senses were better attuned while playing in the dark, so she could hear the violins' weak points every time they clashed.

The piece ended at five after eleven. They'd only just begun docking, so Lindsey started the Pachelbel Canon. That piece could wind on and on forever, and most people unconsciously knew it from every wedding and funeral they'd ever attended. The players went through the piece over and over, plus variations, until the guests exited the upper deck. Only then did the quartet start taking down.

Jason turned to Lindsey. "What were you freaking out about?"

She avoided his eyes. "I got bad news, okay? I'd never cry over something you said. You're not worth it."

He huffed. "Well, that's a relief. Now I don't have to talk to you about emotional blackmail."

Lindsey glared up. "Yes, because everything on earth is all about the pretty boy violinist prodigy Jason Vanderbilt Woodward. Except for this one thing, so please, go nurse your wounded ego elsewhere."

Smirking, Jason closed the music binder he hadn't touched since the sun went down.

The host approached. "Thank you so much! That was amazing!" He tipped each of them twenty bucks, which gave Ashlyn a thrill. "I'd love to have you back the next time we host, and I apologize again about the lighting."

Lindsey thanked him, followed by a demure, "We managed without it."

He shook all their hands. "I have to say, I was worried when I heard that Bob was stepping down, but there's just something about the Castleton genes that gives your music its sparkle."

Lindsey flinched, and Ashlyn put a hand on her arm. "Thank you, sir. It's wonderful of you to say so."

Chapter Eight

By the time Michael arrived at the specified chain restaurant on Monday evening, he hadn't slept for two nights straight, and he wasn't sure anything he said would be coherent.

Ashlyn rushed to him in the lobby, and she hugged him. Even distressed, she looked gorgeous. "This is going to be tricky. Lindsey picked this place because it's public, but there's also a second exit to the parking lot, plus we requested a table way in the back. And unlike the Mexican restaurant right in Hartwell, the owners won't recognize us on sight."

Michael steeled himself. "I'm as ready as I'll ever be."

"Then you're the only one." Ashlyn led him through the different dining areas to a room at the back. The only occupied table had Lindsey between two others, a guy and a gal.

Lindsey stood, unnaturally formal. "Michael. Thanks for

coming. This is my sister, Sierra, and my brother, Corwin."

My sister. My brother.

Corwin didn't even hide his appraising look, as if Michael were a two-story colonial he was assessing for curb appeal. Opposite him, bedecked in a gauzy blouse and ankle-length skirt, Sierra stood with her arms wide open. "Michael! It's so good to finally meet you!"

Corwin snorted. "All the self-restraint of a tsunami."

Lindsey murmured, "Behave. We need to do a lot of planning tonight, and that means you need to check your emotions at the door."

"Not me." Sierra arched her eyebrows at Lindsey. "I'm just amazed. How could you ever have thought he wasn't one of us? Look at him. Isn't it obvious?"

Corwin rolled his eyes with enough panache that a decent amplifier could have turned it into a guitar lick. He wore a black t-shirt printed with "You laugh because I'm different. I laugh because you're all the same."

Ashlyn grabbed the chair next to Corwin, so Michael took the last remaining one, between Ashlyn and Sierra.

A waitress brought two baskets of chips and bowls of salsa. "Are we ready to order?"

Sierra threw her arms around Michael. "We just met him, and he's our long-lost brother! Isn't that amazing?"

Lindsey said, "She means no, we're not ready to order. The poor guy hasn't even opened a menu."

Michael laughed. "Actually, I'm familiar with the menu, if you guys know what you want."

The waitress must have wished she'd gotten the night off, but she wrote everything down, and all the while Sierra kept gazing doe-eyed at Michael.

Corwin drummed his fingers on the table. "I still don't understand how this guy exists. Mom and Dad didn't meet until he was five years old."

"No, that's only what they told us." Sierra rested her chin on her folded hands, eyes low-lidded. "They must have conducted a forbidden romance across the miles."

Lindsey said, "When Mom was fifteen? Because that's

how old she'd have had to be."

Sierra sighed. "That is so romantic. Love at first sight."

Ashlyn said, "Romantic and possibly illegal...?"

Michael hesitated. "Oh, that would be awful."

Lindsey shook her ahead. "No, I worked it out. Nine months before your birthday, Dad would have been seventeen. Both minors. Not good, but not illegal."

Sierra closed her eyes. "Followed by a four-year long-distance courtship, him dreaming of her during his studies."

Corwin huffed. "Get your head out of the clouds. The first thing we do is drag this dude in front of Mom and ask if it's possible." He turned to Michael. "I still don't know if you're a fraud or what, but if you nabbed my DNA in order to pose as one of us, I will have you murdered. I have friends who will dispose of your body in the most unreachable gorge in Baxter State Park, and no one will ever know what became of you. And that I swear on my father's actual living soul."

Michael stiffened, but Ashlyn rolled her eyes. "Get over yourself. Just because you play bass doesn't make you a gangster."

Lindsey snapped, "Submit your stupid DNA to the service. If it comes back that you've already submitted your DNA, then you have your answer."

Corwin folded his arms. "I told you, I'm boycotting."

"Then shut up about murdering people because I'm boycotting violence." Lindsey took one of the chips. "The bigger question is what we do about Mom. I'm terrified for her."

Sierra frowned. "She was so upset last week. I cannot imagine what this is going to do to her, particularly if Michael is Dad's kid but not hers."

Lindsey said, "The agency says there's no way we're half siblings."

Sierra said, "The agencies admit they don't really know what they're doing in fringe cases. Anything is possible."

Ashlyn shook her head. "I've been trying to think of a

way to bring it up casually, like as a hypothetical question. I'd be the best one to do it since I'm not a blood relative, but I'm coming up blank."

Corwin leaned back in his chair, fingers woven behind his neck. "So hey, Mrs. Momma Castleton? I was wondering? If, hypothetically, someone had their *nullius filius* show up after thirty-plus years—how would they feel?"

What an edgelord. Michael folded his arms. "You could go right ahead and say it in English."

Corwin mocked a distressed face. "And bruise Sierra's delicate ears?"

Michael huffed. "It's no secret I was born on the wrong side of the bed," and that drew Corwin up short (finally) but got a laugh from Lindsey.

Round-eyed, Ashlyn still sounded distressed. "You laugh, but I'm not coming up with much better. I could ask what she'd think if my mother had adopted out a baby before I was born."

Sierra leaned around Michael to put a hand on Ashlyn's. "You wouldn't get the real answer. Mom cares too much about you to speak badly of your mother. What might she feel about herself, though? Shame? Guilt? Grief? That's what worries me most."

Lindsey reached for another chip. "She could feel anything, and right now, with Dad...?"

"Yeah, this one's tough." Ashlyn shivered, and Michael longed to do what Sierra had and settle her with a touch.

Sierra looked at the tabletop. "It's too bad this is happening this year. A year ago, you could have met our father. He's a gentleman and a wonder, so smart and strong, always a rock for all of us."

Michael shuddered. "Lindsey told me. It sounds horrible."

Corwin raised his water glass. "Here's to nonfluent variant primary progressive aphasia, the bane of our lives, and may it rot in the deepest trench of the Pacific."

Lindsey raised hers. "Hear, hear. A toast to all the

researchers who will someday find a cure: may they succeed sooner rather than later."

Sierra sighed. "Not soon enough. But at least they've found some meds that help him stay centered."

Ashlyn said, "A toast to SSRI medications, which keep Dad less agitated and help me tread water."

The waitress brought their buffalo wings, and they ate in silence. Finally Michael said, "Would it be possible for me to meet your father?"

Not *his* father—not with Corwin on so short a fuse.

Lindsey frowned. "Maybe...? Dad wouldn't expect to recognize you."

Sierra said, "Does Dad know Michael exists? What if Mom never told him?"

Silence descended around the table. In that moment, Michael refitted all the puzzle pieces. Their father, giving them DNA kits. Their mother, frozen with the fear that her husband would discover a son she'd never revealed.

Ashlyn shook her head. "That would make everything a whole lot worse. Except for Michael meeting Dad. There'd be zero chance he would suspect who Michael is."

Corwin huffed. "I don't know why this guy would even want to go. Dad's about fifty-fifty with recognizing me."

Sierra said, "Normally he does recognize me, but I also bring the lap harp. He recognizes the instrument."

Corwin turned to Michael. "Speaking of harps, which instruments do you play?"

Michael shook his head. "None."

Corwin's nose wrinkled. "Poser."

Ashlyn said, "That might have been an opportunity thing, not a talent thing."

Corwin raised his eyebrows. "According to Mom, Lindsey was stretching rubber bands over dresser drawers at age two in order to pluck different tones. Opportunity is what you make of it."

"Michael should at least meet Dad." Sierra rested a hand on his arm. "Don't say who you are, and don't sign the guest book. Just visit, and go home."

Lindsey recoiled. "Is that wise? If Dad does remember Michael between visits, he'll have to unlearn everything afterward. Plus, won't it look suspicious if we all show up with Michael in tow?"

Ashlyn raised a hand. "Let me bring him. The nursing staff will assume he's my boyfriend, and Dad enjoys visitors. If it's a good day, we can talk. If it's not, we can leave, but at least they'll have met before Dad slips too much further."

Puzzled by the boyfriend comment, Michael looked at Ashlyn. "If you don't mind."

"I don't. I wish you could have met him years ago." Her lip trembled. So beautiful. So sad. "But this is how it happened, and time is the enemy."

Time, indeed. Time was the enemy.

Time might have been the culprit that kept a fifteen- or sixteen-year-old girl from raising her baby.

Tonight, time separated Michael from Corwin again. Midway through the meal, when Sierra barraged Michael with a thousand questions about his history, Corwin handed Lindsey a twenty. "I'm done. Sorry." He shoved his chair into the table. "If this guy's legit, I'll just have to cozy up to him later."

Lindsey said, "Stay classy, Cor," and he snapped back, "I always do."

They picked through their meals after he left. Michael tried not to feel defeated. If Corwin took time to adjust, it made sense. Sierra was one hundred percent employed in romanticizing Michael's existence, but that too felt like a coping mechanism. Lindsey, her initial denial undermined, was just deflated.

Ashlyn said, "Stop me if I'm wrong, but don't the nurses

complain that Dad stays awake nights? How about I take Michael right after dinner? This late in the day, there's no chance we'll run into any other visitors. The nurses will even appreciate it because we'll be keeping Dad occupied."

Lindsey frowned as she thought. "Well...it does make some sense."

Michael said to Ashlyn, "Are you okay with that? I don't want to drag your night out to all hours."

"We don't normally visit for long unless he's lucid." Ashlyn looked to Lindsey. "That gives you a break, and you can maybe talk sense to Corwin."

Lindsey shook her head. "He'll cool down if we wait. Right now, it's better I give him breathing room."

Sierra sighed. "Mom, though."

Lindsey nodded. "Mom. Indeed."

Michael tried to pay for everyone's meal, but none of them would hear of it. In the parking lot, Ashlyn followed Michael to his car, and Lindsey drove home alone.

His father. His *father.* This was awkward and wonderful and horrible, all at the same time.

Still, it was too quiet in the car. In an attempt to make some kind of conversation, Michael said, "How long have you and Lindsey been together?"

She looked up. "Huh? Oh, I met her in third grade. We weren't in the same class in fourth, but we started interacting a bit more in fifth when the school started the orchestra program."

He nodded. "That's neat. You're childhood sweethearts?"

Ashlyn laughed. "No, not like that. I'm single. So is she."

He turned to her. "You're not a couple? But you call her parents Mom and Dad."

"It's so much more complicated than that, you have no idea." Ashlyn crossed her long legs and leaned back in the front seat. "We're roommates and practically sisters, but we're not romantic partners."

Huh. "Then why the mom-and-dad thing?"

She fell silent. Then, "You're not going to like it."

"Why wouldn't I like it?"

"See... No, you're really not going to like it. It's a long story, and you're going to hate me afterward."

She didn't follow up with an explanation, and now Michael burned with curiosity. Had she been married to Corwin? Was she herself the child of an affair partner?

Ashlyn said, "Take a left at the next light." He'd have to wait for an explanation. She wasn't going to pony it up on her own, but if it was that complicated, surely it would get mentioned at some point.

They parked in a mostly-empty lot, then went to the front desk. "Hey!" said the security guard. "Late night?"

Ashlyn signed in. "Yeah, I didn't get a chance to see Bob this weekend because we had three gigs one after the other. I wanted to stop by."

They were way outside the posted visiting hours, but the guard buzzed them through. Ashlyn brought Michael upstairs and through one of the corridors.

Oh gosh. Oh gosh. This was insane. His father. He was going to see his father.

The place smelled. It didn't smell *terrible* but smelled... well, artificial. Artificial air, artificial lighting, artificial temperature. It smelled artificially clean, as though covering over the normal odors of too many bodies in too small a space.

At the nurse's station, Ashlyn exclaimed, "Hi, Lucy! Hey, Theodosia! Oh, look at the gorgeous flowers! Who from?"

One of the nurses beamed. "My husband sent them for my birthday."

"I love yellow flowers. They make everything happy." Ashlyn was either stretching out Michael's nerves to the breaking point with the skill of a master torturer, or else she was trying to keep the nurses' attention off him. "Is Bob still awake?"

Theodosia said, "He just gave me a keyboard lesson, so yes, he's quite awake."

Ashlyn grinned. "You can take the teacher out of the school, but not the school out of the teacher. Happy birthday!"

Ashlyn escorted Michael all the way to a corner room with the lights on and music symbols covering the door. Two steps ahead of him, she entered with a cheerful, "Hi, Dad! It's Ashlyn, and I brought my friend Michael."

Okay, okay, okay—go.

Bob sat in a wheelchair in front of a bedside table. Before him were the remnants of a late-night snack, a small keyboard, and a jigsaw puzzle partly assembled.

His father.

His biological father.

Michael was in the same room as his biological father.

Bob beamed at Ashlyn. "Ash, it's so good you're here." Then looked at Michael. "Good to see you, too."

Michael's brain whirled. His father. "My pleasure, sir."

Ashlyn sat in a chair opposite Bob. "I didn't visit this weekend because we played three different gigs, but I missed you. I was hoping you'd still be awake."

Bob waved over Michael with perhaps a bit of confusion. Corwin said he was fifty-fifty, but tonight he'd recognized Ashlyn. "Pull up a chair! Sit!"

"Yes, sir!" There was a second chair in the corner, and Michael carried it over, fighting wonder.

Bob. He was tall. He had bright eyes. Black hair, like Michael's. Long fingers, again like Michael's. His voice sounded a bit like Michael's. He— He just was. He was here.

Here. His father. His dad.

Ashlyn picked up a wood and metal contraption from alongside the keyboard, then started pushing the metal bits to make sounds. Was that a finger-piano? Did it matter? For the first time, Michael was in the same room as his biological father.

Absentmindedly creating a tune, Ashlyn regaled Bob with a story about reporting to a yacht to play for an all-night dinner party, only to find no lighting and the wind blowing papers off the music stands. She was making noise and distraction, but Michael had no idea what he'd have said anyhow, or whether he could have borne up under silence.

Ashlyn said, "We could play only what we'd memorized, so we ended up having to play a few solos and some duets to fill out the list."

Bob shook his head. "What did you play?"

Ashlyn gave a few different titles that were just names with numbers. Michael didn't recognize them, but he resolved now that he would. Usually he listened to rock, sometimes to jazz. He was always careful when selecting background music for a commercial, so he did know the names of a few pieces. He could switch his roster to classical and learn about this world his relatives inhabited, a world where numbers and parts factored into the titles with perfect ease.

Bob reached for the finger-piano, and Ashlyn handed it over. He twanged some notes, saying, "Did you bring your harp?"

"Sierra has the harp," Ashlyn said without any self-consciousness. "I'm Ashlyn. I play the viola, and I didn't bring it tonight."

Bob flinched. "I'm sorry. You know."

"I know." She looked up with a smile, and her eyes were beautiful. So gentle. "I love when Sierra plays the harp. Her fingers breathe over the strings, and it's like heaven."

Bob fumbled with the finger-piano, but he kept going. "Just like heaven. Tell me about your viola."

Ashlyn sounded wistful. How many times had she told Bob this story? "I needed a better instrument because I'd been playing the same viola since I was thirteen. One day you drove us to the string shop, I thought just for fun, and Lindsey disappeared into a practice room with a 19th century French violin. You walked me through the viola section, and then you surprised me. You said I needed a better instrument because I was playing professionally, but you knew I couldn't afford one."

Bob nodded and smiled, but Michael wasn't at all sure he remembered any of this. Maybe he was re-experiencing it for the first time.

Ashlyn sounded dreamy. "There were dozens of violas hanging from pegs on the wall, and I was reading the descriptions. You walked right over to one I thought was terrible and told them I wanted to try it. It had blonde wood and no flame on the back, but you insisted. You promised I wasn't playing the color. I trusted you, but I did a few scales to show you how terrible it would sound, only it didn't sound terrible at all. I played it for half an hour, and then I brought it home to try for a month. Now it's my baby."

A baby. Musicians called instruments their babies? What did that make an actual given-away baby?

Transported, Bob was gazing past her. "You fell in love."

"I fell in love." Ashlyn's voice was soft. "You knew right from the start."

Bob looked at Michael. "Have you fallen in love?"

Michael glanced at Ashlyn. "Not at the moment."

Ashlyn chuckled. "I don't think he plays anything."

Stern, Bob waved a finger at him. "A man should play an instrument. Music frees...."

He stopped and struggled.

Ashlyn finished, "Music frees your soul."

Bob nodded. "Your soul."

Michael leaned back in his chair. "What instrument should I play?"

Bob studied him, and a sudden frustration came to his face.

Ashlyn reached for Bob's hand, but still he kept trying to get the words out. Michael thought Bob could see the instrument in his mind but couldn't come up with the name. Or maybe he wanted to ask a question about what kind of music Michael liked to listen to, but he couldn't fabricate the words for that either.

Ashlyn squeezed Bob's hand and let go. "It's okay. Michael's stubborn and probably won't learn anyway."

Michael nodded. "I should do what you did. I could go to a music store and see if any of the instruments want to come home with me."

Ashlyn brightened. "Sometimes the instrument does pick the person."

From behind them, a voice said, "Oh, what a surprise!"

Panic flashed over Ashlyn's face. "Mom?"

CHAPTER NINE

Michael jumped out of his chair, but Susan Castleton said, "Oh, please, don't worry. I'll grab another from the hallway." She glanced from him to Ashlyn. "I don't believe we've met...?"

Oh, but they had. They'd met and bonded and then been parted, and now Michael could only manage, "I'm Michael Knolwood. I, um—"

Ashlyn interrupted, "We met at the Latesummer Fair, and we've been talking ever since."

Mrs. Castleton smiled broadly. "Oh, well, it's nice to meet you, Michael." She shook his hand, and electricity jolted up his arm. "I'll be right back."

When she left, Michael turned to Ashlyn. She was pale like a ghost. "Should I leave?"

Ashlyn shook her head. "No, but—awkward."

At the very least, Susan's presence had distracted Bob from his frustration over the instrument names. When

Susan returned, they all shifted to make room. She kissed Bob, then settled back in her seat.

Ashlyn couldn't quite keep the nerves from her voice. "Usually you visit at lunchtime."

"I did. But you know how it is. All of you were busy tonight, and the house was too quiet." She turned to Bob. "Theodosia said *you* were still up and giving her a keyboard lesson." When Bob chuckled, Susan addressed Michael. "Where do you live?"

"Haverstock, just outside Bangor." He wasn't prepared for this. Lindsey wanted a fully-scripted revelation, and whatever Michael said or didn't say now would send her plans up in flames. Even without giving the real reason for "talking ever since," the half-truths would dig the pit deeper. Now, when they did reveal who he was, Susan would know their first encounter had been a deception. "I heard the quartet's performance at the festival, and we listened to some other acts afterward."

Ashlyn interjected. "Before you ask, he doesn't play an instrument."

Bob seemed frustrated again, and Michael said, "Bob was telling us about Sierra's harp."

Ashlyn said to Michael, "She brings the lap harp, but the viola can't work in here."

That was odd. "Why not?"

"Too loud. The neighbors complain." Ashlyn turned to Bob. "You hate muting a viola."

He nodded. Susan said, "And you're absolutely right. Mutes deaden the viola's natural voice. Also, a mute throws off the musician's intonation."

Someday Michael might sit with these people at his desk while he talked them through the process of designing an ad with Photoshop, and he trusted that it would sound exactly the same.

Michael said to Ashlyn, "I'd like to hear your viola. Solo."

Ashlyn said, "The viola is a supporting role in the quartet. It's harder to hear than the violins."

Susan smiled. "But you can't have a string quartet

without one."

Bob laughed. "What's the difference between... between..."

Once more the frustration swirled over his face.

Susan said, "What's the difference between a washing machine and a viola?"

Ashlyn quipped, "In a pinch, you can use a washing machine in a string quartet. What's the difference between a viola and a chainsaw?"

Susan replied, "You can tune a chainsaw."

Bob laughed again. Okay, this was interesting.

Ashlyn said, "What's the difference between a violin and a viola?"

Michael had actually looked this up: the viola played one fifth lower than a violin and was fifteen percent larger.

Susan said, "The viola burns longer?"

Ashlyn beamed. "Probably because it's still in the case."

Susan added, "And no one cares if you spill beer on a viola."

Bob said, "What's a string quartet?" which frightened Michael until he realized it was the lead-in to another joke.

Ashlyn answered, "A good violinist, an okay violinist, a failed violinist, and someone who hates violinists."

Susan added, "All getting together to gripe about how much they loathe composers," and Bob laughed again.

Michael pushed back his chair in amazement as an entire world opened before him. In-jokes for musicians about musicians—that wasn't a thing that had occurred to him. There were probably online support groups for musicians, memes, stories, legends, and a whole vocabulary he'd never touched. A world he'd never even grazed, but which he could have grown up surrounded by.

"Which instruments do you play?" Ashlyn had asked, and later on, so had Corwin.

Michael turned to Susan, "Which instruments do you play?"

Bob said, "Which instruments *don't* you play?"

Susan winked at Michael. "I play piano and pipe organ,

but also trumpet, trombone, and some guitar."

Ashlyn said, "Sometimes you play French horn."

About to ask Bob what he played, Michael hesitated, but Bob anticipated the question. "Violin. Saxophone. Flute."

"Oboe," Ashlyn added.

Susan said to Michael, "Don't be too impressed. Flute and saxophone and oboe are all very similar to one another, so it's just a matter of accustoming your fingers to the different positions. Also, flute is played transverse."

Ashlyn leaned over with her hand on Michael's shoulder. "Psst—be very impressed."

Michael was on fire right now, in the presence of both his biological parents and now with this gorgeous woman's hand on his shoulder. Gorgeous and single. He felt alight with the vibrancy of all three of them and the comfort they had in one another. Bob looked relaxed with Susan at his side, and Susan had warmed up with her husband near. They were wonderful together.

They'd given him up, though. He could have been theirs.

Mom and Dad were awesome, and Michael loved them. They'd done well by him and made sacrifices for him. He was blessed and lucky, and he knew it.

Here in this room, though, he saw a different road for his life's journey, one that would have led him down music clefs and up scales and into concert halls.

After ten minutes, Ashlyn said, "We need to be going now." She kissed Bob on the cheek, then turned to Susan and kissed her too. Michael hung back, uncertain, until Susan shook his hand. He shook Bob's as well.

Bob said, "Thank you for being here," and Michael wondered if Bob even remembered who he was. Michael might just as well have walked in saying, "Do you remember a baby boy named Dalton? That was me."

Susan said to Ashlyn, "I'll email you later, honey," and to Michael, "It was nice meeting you." Then Ashlyn herded him out the door.

All the way across the parking lot, Ashlyn was whispering to herself, "Oh my goodness. Oh my goodness." Michael couldn't even speak.

Both his parents. In the same place at the same time, with no preparation, no nothing.

He started the engine but didn't take it out of park, just struggled to quell the tension.

Ashlyn had her arms wrapped around her waist. "That wasn't supposed to happen."

"No kidding." Michael put the car in gear. "I need to take you home."

"We need to talk to Lindsey because that just blew everything right out of the water." Ashlyn slackened into the seat and looked at the roof. "Yeah, um...make a left out of the parking lot."

Michael treated the drive back as what he'd call "blizzard conditions," taking everything slowly, making sure to keep three car lengths between him and anyone he followed, and doing his best to focus rather than careen back into his own thoughts.

Because— Because he'd just found his parents. Because —

No, he wasn't supposed to be thinking now. Think about it after he got Ashlyn home, that way he didn't meet his biological mother again in an emergency room trying to explain how he'd crashed with her pseudo-daughter in the passenger seat.

Five minutes of nerve-wracked driving later, they pulled into a dirt parking lot behind a three-story Victorian. Ashlyn looked up with, "Good, she's awake. You'd better come in," then led Michael through the back porch, a dooryard, and up a set of narrow steps that listed to the left. Violin music filled the stairwell. On the second floor, she unlocked "2" and simultaneously increased the volume.

The apartment smelled of an apple-spice candle burning in a jar on the stovetop. Lindsey was on her feet in the adjoining living room, a music stand before her, and she raised her eyes from the sheet music as Ashlyn and Michael entered.

Ashlyn gave no preamble. "Your mother showed up."

Lindsey's hand dropped, but the violin stayed under her chin. "Oh, for crying out loud."

"Yeah. I made it sound like Michael was trying to hook up with me, but I have no idea how much she figured out. She asked Michael all these questions, and I was sweating like a snowman in a sauna." Ashlyn walked halfway up the kitchen and then turned back. "She has to have noticed how freaked out I was. Mom can pick up a lie at fifty feet."

Michael raised his hands. "I didn't lie."

Putting away her violin, Lindsey snorted. "It doesn't have to be a technical lie. She knows everything that's going through everyone's head, and she senses half-truths the same way a smoke alarm would have detected the Chicago fire. She probably couldn't read you clearly, but she can read Ashlyn." Lindsey looked over her shoulder. "Also, Ash, you're not exactly subtle. Did you knock over your chair trying to escape?"

Michael flinched. "Does it count if I knocked it backward?"

Ashlyn gave a mini eye-roll. "I didn't climb out the window, either. She had us dead to rights, so I told her I'd met Michael after our performance at the Latesummer Festival and that we'd been talking ever since."

Michael added, "Which is true."

Lindsey closed the violin case. "Which only means now she's concerned that you'd bring a guy to see Dad when you're embarrassed to be moving so fast with him."

Ashlyn said, "Not to mention Michael could do way better than me, so she's really going to wonder."

Michael snorted. "You're stunningly beautiful. If anything, she's confused why you're wasting your time with me."

Lindsey flicked her hand at them. "You two can get a room later. Right now, let's do damage control."

Ashlyn's cheeks reddened. Maybe as a diversion, she pulled out her phone...and then groaned. "Linz...yeah, um..." and she handed it over.

Lindsey's eyes widened, and she handed the phone to Michael. It was an email from Susan.

> *Ashlyn, honey, it was so sweet that you were there tonight to see Dad. I saw how surprised you were when I walked in. Michael is very nice, but I'm worried that a man you only just started talking to wanted to meet Dad so soon, and what else you might have told him. I trust you, but please be careful. I love you. Mom*

Michael made his way to the couch and read the email again. Susan thought him a predator. Nice.

What did she mean by, "What else you might have told him"? Was that related to why Ashlyn called them Mom and Dad?

Lindsey paced the living room. "Okay. We're going to have to move a bit faster. But Ashlyn, you won us an opening. Tomorrow before quartet practice, go to Mom's for dinner and have a cozy chat. Ask about the dangers of a guy moving too fast. Ask about being naive and young while a dashing, smart guy sweeps you off your feet. Ask what can go wrong."

Michael's ears rang. "That's your plan?"

Ashlyn paled. "I hate this. If I do that, I'm really lying to her."

Lindsey shook her head. "You're not lying. You're asking for advice based on her experience. You're asking why she's concerned. The fact that you're also digging for one very specific bit of information is incidental."

Ashlyn bit her lip. "She's never going to admit she had another baby."

"You only want her to admit she met Dad long before she told us she met him." Lindsey turned to Michael. "I hope you'll forgive me, but I want independent confirmation from Mom. Then, and only then, do we go ahead and disclose."

CHAPTER TEN

Reluctant to let Michael go, Ashlyn walked him down to his car. "That could have gone better."

Michael's voice was thin. "It could have gone worse, too. I'm in shock."

He reached his car, but instead of getting inside, he leaned against the quarter panel. If he didn't want to leave, Ashlyn certainly wasn't going to press him. Not after all those emotions. It felt better having him here, having him rehash the fright, the longing, the surprise.

In a bid to keep him close, Ashlyn said, "What did you think of everyone?"

Michael obliged by not getting in the car. "It's overwhelming, but they're not what I expected from being musicians."

Ashlyn tilted her head. "Meaning?"

"Drugs, drinking, rebellion, that kind of thing." Her skin crawled, but he went on. "Instead everyone was articulate and enthusiastic, more professional."

Ashlyn fought annoyance. "Well, they're mostly into classical and jazz, Corwin aside. What about Bob and Susan?"

That stunned look returned to his eyes as he smiled. He probably didn't realize how attractive he was while actively detangling a problem. "I liked them both. Susan is smart and friendly. I mean, even warning you away from me, she was tactful about it."

Ashlyn smiled up at him. "Yeah, she's always had that way. You can tell she's not happy with something, but then she'll express it in the most charitable way possible."

He was handsome. If Susan noticed his looks at all, she'd have felt familiar with him. Didn't women tend to choose men who resembled their fathers, if only because they associated those men with how a man ought to look? Never having met her own progenitor, Ashlyn wouldn't experience that. Or if she did develop that tendency, maybe it would be toward men who resembled Bob.

Susan would be detecting flashes of her children in Michael. She'd feel comfortable with facial features composed of half her and half her husband. Someone as intuitive as she might know without knowing. Sierra, by far the most intuitive of the Castleton kids, had said it was obvious.

Maybe Ashlyn was keying on that too because every time she looked at Michael, she noticed more and more his strong jaw, his soft eyes, his black hair.

She inched closer, heart racing. "You didn't have to say that about me, you know. Mom would see that you *are* a catch. She's more worried that you're a Casanova who's using your looks to take advantage of someone who's hopelessly naive."

"You don't strike me as hopelessly naive." He felt magnetizing.

This wasn't real. Her attraction was only a response to the heightened emotion because of everything they'd uncovered. If Mom was telling Ashlyn not to let Michael move too fast, it meant Mom had sensed that in some ways Ashlyn did want to move faster. Michael was a man in the teeth of uncertainty, and Ashlyn wanted to give him solidity.

Anchor him, or he'd drift away like a boat on the ocean. He'd find what he wanted, then withdraw to Haverstock and reduce his contact to the annual Christmas card. Michael had grown up already. He did have a family. He was searching for his roots, and once he'd uncovered them —once he'd answered all his questions—then he'd be settled with no need of further contact.

Ashlyn looked at the ground. "Mom's going to tell me not to let a handsome guy get my head all turned around."

Michael leaned against the car. "She'll probably tell you not to date a non-musician because if a guy doesn't love music, all his tastes are questionable."

Laughing, she crinkled her eyes. "Really?"

Michael nodded. "I've heard people say that about guys who don't love cats and guys who don't like *Lord of the Rings.*"

Ashlyn grinned. "She never told me to prowl for musicians. She may even have said to avoid them. What did your mother say about dating musicians?"

"Not to do it." Michael was so matter-of-fact that Ashlyn cringed. "Remember, musicians and artists are universally into drugs and drinking and rebellion, and that doesn't work so well with the nine-to-five and the suburban three-bedroom home."

Prickly, Ashlyn said, "Maybe if someone doesn't love musicians, *their* taste is questionable."

"Fortunately for everyone, it's been about fifteen years since I asked for my mother's approval on who I should date." Michael stepped away from the side of the car. "I'll try not to crawl out of my skin tonight and tomorrow. I do want to hear what happens when you talk to Susan." He turned back. "Would you mind updating me yourself? Lindsey is strained to the breaking point."

Ashlyn straightened. "Consider it done."

"Thanks." His voice was worn. "This is like an earthquake centered in your living room, especially with the timing."

"Maybe it's better this way. Another year and Bob might not be here." Ashlyn's voice broke. "At least you're getting a chance to see him. Maybe he'll even give you a keyboard lesson."

Michael got into the driver's seat, and Ashlyn stepped back toward the house.

Goodbye. He did wave at her as he pivoted the car and brought it back out to the street. She thought she could hear the GPS voice through his windows, but then he pulled away and left her alone.

When she arrived at Mom's after work, Ashlyn went straight into the bathroom and stripped off her khaki shorts and the "We Scream for Ice Cream!" uniform shirt. Mom knew better than to talk to Ashlyn for the first few minutes after she got off shift. The ice cream stand had been mobbed all afternoon.

In the bathroom, Ashlyn scrubbed drips of chocolate off both forearms, then washed her face and neck. She changed into her spare t-shirt and a more comfortable pair of cargo shorts.

Mom called through the door, "You can start the washing machine if you want."

Would she be here long enough to run a load? Did she even want to be? "I'll do it at home, thanks." About half the time she'd hand-wash her uniform clothes and drip-dry them in the bathroom rather than use the machines in the apartment's basement.

Mom put her to work preparing a salad. After a whole day making frappes and scooping out cones and slicing bananas for sundaes, Ashlyn would have preferred if Mom had magicked down a pizza from the sky, but that never happened. Some families did takeout on a regular basis, but Ashlyn hadn't experienced that since...well, not since her own mother. Not that her mother had brought home food that often, but when she did, it was takeout and Ashlyn got some of it.

Lindsey had learned to cook at her mother's side, starting at age three when they'd stood her on a chair next to the countertop. Ashlyn remembered Corwin kneeling on that same chair back when she'd first started visiting the Castletons.

Visiting. Crash landing, more like.

The Castletons always got dinner on the table. Either Bob or Susan would come home from the music school and prep so everyone could eat the minute the other one walked in. Then they'd both be out the door to teach more students until nine o'clock at night, leaving Lindsey and Sierra (and later Ashlyn, and still later Corwin) to clean the kitchen by themselves. When the kids got older, they took over the cooking too so their parents could fit in more evening lessons and make the drive together.

Ashlyn liked that routine. Lindsey taught her how to be useful, and in that way, Ashlyn was paying for her own upkeep. At least, that's what she told herself before it became obvious she was costing them more than they'd ever have benefitted.

Susan breaded and fried a pair of chicken cutlets, and she'd made biscuits to go with them. Ashlyn set the table. It wasn't equitable. It never had been.

Two minutes into the meal, Mom said, "Tell me about Michael."

That was the worst possible opening. "He was at the music festival, and we met while listening to a different string quartet. He and I and Lindsey ate at the fairgrounds, and then we went back in to listen until Corwin's gig at nine. He was nice enough that I kept texting him."

Mom nodded. "Why did he want to see Bob?"

"That wasn't his intention." Ashlyn felt more secure here. "We went to the Mexican place for dinner, and when we were about to leave, I said I was going to see Dad. On the spur of the moment, Michael offered to go with me. I didn't think it would be a problem. Dad doesn't mind visitors."

Ashlyn felt like the plastic sheeting you affix to a window so it looks like stained glass but people could still see you were home; it just wasn't obvious what you were doing on the other side.

Mom shook her head. "I'm worried that he's pushing you too fast."

"He's a nice guy once you get to know him. He works at an ad agency as a designer, and he volunteers at the community theater. He builds sets and does stage direction."

Mom nodded. "All that's good, but are you sure he is who he says he is?"

Ouch. What was that Lindsey had said about Mom sensing everything you were thinking? She'd picked up the exact question, just not what Ashlyn was thinking it about.

Ashlyn chose her phrasing carefully. "Everything he's said so far seems legit. I looked at the community theater website, and I searched his LinkedIn profile." She paused. "I'm naive, but not stupid."

"I didn't say you were either, but I do want you to be careful. Him coming to see Bob so soon—I wasn't sure why you'd even bring him that quickly."

Ashlyn looked down.

There was no way she could answer that question. "Because I wanted him to meet Dad before he slipped away even further" would be the most hurtful thing in the world for Mom to hear. It would almost be better to say, "Because Dad is important to me, and I'm losing him too. But I'm the one who's always on the sidelines."

Mom's heart was the one that would break worst. The others—they'd lose their father, but they were adults whose destinies were to leave their parents and operate in the world. Dad himself said fatherhood was a self-defeating job, that if you did it correctly, the kids set sail and fended for themselves.

Mom and Dad had been together twenty-eight years, though. Or if Michael was to be believed, thirty-two.

Which, she realized, she did. Lindsey was holding back, but Ashlyn wasn't.

Ashlyn groped for a path forward. "It was spontaneous. Lindsey and I hadn't talked to Dad all weekend, and I figured I ought to go. I didn't see any harm if Michael came with me."

Distress crossed over Mom's face. "Does it bother you that much, seeing Dad this way?"

Blast. That was a worse interpretation. Usually Ashlyn and Lindsey went together because it was convenient. It also gave them one another to lean on afterward.

"It's hard. Like when he forgets the name of an instrument." Or the name of a child. Or when he got frustrated because his hands shook too much to fit the puzzle pieces together so he had to point, one to the next, to get them to fit the pieces for him.

Dad's memory was like that too, except one at a time, the pieces were falling to the floor, and no one was able to retrieve them.

Mom's eyebrows were an inverted V. "I could go with you if it's that hard."

Since it was already this bad, Ashlyn decided to make things worse. "You sounded really worried about me, though, like I was going to get swept off my feet by a shyster."

Mom laughed. "Michael didn't look like a shyster to me."

"Well, to be fair, a good con man wouldn't look like a con man."

Mom paused. "Do you get that vibe off him?"

"No, or I wouldn't have let him within a thousand miles of Dad. But do you think it's a possibility?" Now to push the boundaries harder. "I mean, he's smart and good-looking, and he's a little older than me. That's a sweet combination."

Mom nodded. "I can see why you'd be attracted to him. He was also soft-spoken and polite, although I think we startled him with the music terminology."

Ashlyn laughed. "You should have heard him with me and Lindsey." She cut herself off before adding, "and Corwin and Sierra." Yeah, that wouldn't completely tip their hand. *Wait, why did everyone else in the family meet Michael only ten days after you met him the first time?* Oh, no reason, Mom. Please pass the salad dressing?

Ashlyn did reach for the salad dressing. "Anyone ever do that to you? Sweep you off your feet?"

Mom's eyes crinkled. "Well, Bob certainly did."

"But he wasn't a con man." Ashlyn stated that as fact because it was. "What was he like when you first met?"

Mom sat back, wistful. "I told you about meeting him right after he got hired as music director for the church on Main Street, this prodigy from the Royal Academy of London who could play any instrument that ever existed as long as you left him alone with it for half an hour. If an alien civilization sent us one of their instruments, he'd have messed around with for a while, then tuned it and experimented with a medley of the Moody Blues."

"And was he gorgeous?" Ashlyn thought of Michael. "Did he have dreamy eyes?"

Michael did have dreamy eyes, didn't he?

Mom nodded. "It was his smile I loved most. He saw me and just... He smiled at me, and I knew."

Ashlyn had heard this story before. She needed the rest of it, the prequel. "That was it? One smile?"

"It was a jolt like nothing I'd ever felt." Mom looked away. "I look back at photos of that time... We were so young."

Push the thin red line. Push it. "You were nearly done with college. That's not young."

Mom's gaze dropped. "Even at that age, what did we know?"

Ashlyn said, "You knew you loved each other. You can

know that at twenty—or younger."

Mom gave a rueful smile. "We did, and we didn't. You never know what love is going to demand of you. It's easy to say 'forever' and resolve to live through the hard times, but that doesn't make the hard times not come."

Ashlyn said, "Were there really hard times?"

Mom fell totally silent.

"Now is a really hard time," Ashlyn added. "I know that."

"This is worse than a hard time. It's—" Mom stopped eating. "We went through ordeals together, but we knew it would be okay as long as we stayed the course. 'We'll muddle through,' he'd promise me. But this—it's a slow parting. It's an unbecoming rather than the marriage adapting. We're being disassembled."

Ashlyn stared at her own half-eaten plate.

Mom blinked hard. "I'd have done it anyway. But I was so young and so confident we could handle everything together. The next step was always obvious, but the one after the next wasn't. He'd make music, and I'd harmonize to him. We'd make it to the top of the mountain, and that's where we'd plant our flag. I believed in him. He would do right by me. I'd give him everything for love. But sometimes—" She looked at Ashlyn, haunted. "We created a lot of good together. But yes, we were far too young for what we were doing. We had no idea."

Ashlyn's mouth trembled. "Were you really that young?"

"Young enough to be stupid. Old enough to be stupid in just the right way." She swallowed hard. "I'm sorry. I'm ruining dinner for you."

"I asked." Ashlyn ventured further into forbidden territory. "Was Dad the first person you fell in love with?"

Mom swallowed hard. "I didn't date much in college. I went out a few times with some guys. Nothing serious."

Ashlyn said, "Not even when you were really young? No crushes? No prom date in his first tuxedo?"

If the previous territory was forbidden, this was an active minefield.

Ashlyn pushed. "I love the fairy tale aspect of love at

first sight, but now that I'm older, it sounds like magic that the very first time you saw Dad, you fell that hard and that fast. If you hadn't dated much, how would you know?"

Mom studied Ashlyn a moment, and when she answered, her voice was a little deeper, a little softer. "You asked if I thought you were naive. There are different ways of being naive. Not suspecting danger exists at all—that's one kind of naiveté. But there's another naiveté that's not ignorance. It's more like...purity. That's the special kind, where you can recognize the danger for what it is, and at the same time, you embrace it because you love all the hidden sides."

Ice ran down Ashlyn's spine. "I don't understand."

"In the second kind, you know you're young, but you've found something so valuable that even if it destroys you, you have to have it. Life without it won't matter, so death with it becomes a trifling thing."

Ashlyn imagined Mom at age fifteen, gazing into the eyes of seventeen-year-old Robert Castleton, embracing danger like a dagger into her soul.

Mom glanced out at the back yard. "In some ways, the second kind is worse. You're not getting hoodwinked by a con man. You're hoodwinking yourself."

With her hands folded in her lap, Ashlyn said, "Isn't that just...you know, youth? Invincibility?"

Mom sighed. "Idealism, maybe. It's more than being naive and less than being stupid. You don't realize when you volunteer to get hurt...you could hurt others too."

Ashlyn looked up. "No one got hurt. You and Dad dated and got married."

Mom nodded. "I've never regretted marrying him, even knowing how it's going to end."

Ashlyn prompted, "You're talking like you were still a little girl, though."

"I guess I am. I'm feeling old. I'm losing him too soon." She gestured to Ashlyn's plate. "Go on and eat. It's just that I've been thinking a lot lately about our lives and how it's all worked out. Bob and I... I would do it all over again."

With that, the door was closed. Ashlyn gave it one last try. "No changes?"

"Maybe some." Mom bit her lip. "I don't think a couple could be together as long as we have and not have at least one regret."

CHAPTER ELEVEN

Ashlyn called instead of texting, which sent Michael's heart rate into the stratosphere. "Hey, Ashlyn."

"Hi." She sounded subdued. "Do you have a minute?"

This was all formality. With the way she sounded and the fact that she'd phoned, Michael couldn't imagine this was good news. She could have texted, "Confirmed!"

"I have a lot more than a minute." Michael turned off the TV and paced his apartment. "Did you talk to Susan tonight?"

"I did. It's... She was thoughtful. First off, she does like you. We agree that if you're a con man, you're doing a great job."

Michael laughed. "Is that a good thing?"

"Either you're honest, or else you're trying to appear honest."

Michael had ended up in his bedroom and therefore was out of places to walk. He turned and moved back through the living room and toward the kitchen. This was the smallest apartment he'd ever lived in, but he didn't need much space. After breaking up with Kristen, he'd wanted everything simple, compact, and ready to hand.

Michael said, "Well, I liked Susan too. I told you that."

"She was concerned about you visiting Dad so soon. I told her we'd had dinner together, and you offered to visit him with me. She thought that meant I didn't want to see Dad alone, but that gave me an opening to ask about the other things."

The other things meant Michael's entire existence. So frustrating, to be this close and not have answers. Indisputable answers.

Ashlyn said, "We were talking about being young and stupid. That seemed like a good entry point."

Michael said, "Was she telling you not to be stupid about me?"

"Absolutely, but she was very diplomatic. You have to admit that you going to see Dad—Bob—would make no sense without knowing why you wanted to see him."

Michael said, "Therefore she immediately assumed you needed backup."

"It's very hard seeing him that way. Usually I go with Lindsey. Once she said it, I realized I hadn't ever gone alone." Ashlyn wasn't taking the conversation in a straight line. Was that nerves, or did she never tell stories in a linear fashion? "If it's just him and me—what if there's a lag in the conversation? What if he never recognizes me?"

"Has that happened?"

Ashlyn didn't respond.

The rest of the story: Michael wanted it. "So, you were talking about being young and stupid. Did she tell you about herself being young and stupid?"

"You have to know the way she talks, but to me it sounded like she was referencing something specific." Ashlyn lowered her voice. "She was warning me, but she was talking to her younger self too. She never said what about. She said there were hard things about being married, and decisions you made knowing you'd get hurt, but preferring being hurt to living without the thing that hurt you."

Okay...? "And that makes exactly no sense."

"I don't know that she intended to make sense. She's a musician through and through, and as far as I know, she thinks in music. She understands her marriage as harmony, not as a pair of interlocking solos. Whatever she was cautioning me about, she wasn't warning me away as much as letting me know she understood why someone would willingly throw themselves into the fire."

Michael was back in the kitchen and stopped, wide-eyed. "Do you think she thought she was playing with fire when she was with Bob the first time?"

"Not playing with fire. More like, stepping right into the heart of a furnace."

Michael wasn't sure whether to sit or pace the length of the apartment again. Instead he remained in place, reeling.

If Susan released him for adoption, she had looked right down the highway of her own sacrifice. Or maybe she was referring to something far earlier, the decision to commit to one man for a lifetime when she herself was barely out of girlhood.

"Susan's in such a bad spot now. She's watching the disassembly of her marriage, memory by memory. It's awful, Michael. They promised a lifetime, but he can't keep that promise."

Michael recoiled. "Of course he kept it. He can't help what's happening now."

"But to her—to her it feels as if he's crumbling like dry concrete. Whenever she touches him, parts slip away like sand down the side of a cliff, and he's... All the things he was, they aren't still there. Or they won't be forever."

Now Michael did sit.

"So...I never got a real answer. But I might have gotten something like an answer because of the things she didn't answer, like whether that was the first time she saw Dad, or whether she'd ever dated anyone else before him."

Michael said, "When you say 'that,' you mean what they've told you about the first time they met?"

Ashlyn sounded broken. "I don't know that it really was the first time anymore. It's a story, nothing more."

"Tell me." Michael closed his eyes, and he found himself smiling. "Tell me the story they always tell you about the first time they met."

July. Tourist season.

Susan's best friend's car had no air conditioning, so Susan and Amanda drove up to Hartwell with the windows down. Susan had the map on her lap and kept checking their progress. They had a cooler full of snacks and a back seat full of camera equipment.

They pulled up in front of a stone church on Main Street. Susan craned her neck and shielded her eyes to study the bell tower, then the tremendous wooden doors. Read and re-read the sign. It was definitely the right church.

Amanda hefted their camera bags out of the back seat. "Well, here goes nothing."

Susan mustered a smile. Amanda took photos of the bell tower, but Susan was afraid she'd drop her camera. She photographed the wrought iron fence instead. The steps. The statue in front. A bronze plaque greened up by weather and time.

People passed on the sidewalk, curious at the pair of college students photographing an unremarkable church. "It's for a class," Amanda explained. "Art in the everyday."

Susan kept finding other things to photograph. A tiny white flower with roots in a sidewalk crack. A deep groove in the granite steps, worn by a hundred fifty years of churchgoing feet.

Amanda finally hissed at Susan, "Are we ever going

inside?" It was hot as blazes.

Amanda made Susan go first. Afternoon on a weekday: no one should be in the dark interior. The door weighed a ton but opened soundlessly, and Susan slipped through with Amanda at her back.

Someone was singing. A man.

Susan froze. Amanda nudged her forward, and with both hands clutching her camera, Susan crept through the narthex into the body of the church.

Fifteen feet up, where the wall met the beginning of the roof, a dark-haired tenor sang on a ladder while adjusting the speakers.

In her blush the rose was born,
'Twas music when she spake.
In her eyes the light of morn
Sparking seemed to break.

Susan couldn't move, her camera forgotten, her heart burning. He was tall and strong, his head near the rafters, singing with a precision that left her dizzy.

Aura Lee, Aura Lee, maid of raven hair.
Sunshine came along with thee
And swallows in the air.

He jammed his screwdriver in his back pocket and started down the ladder. Only then did he see the two women.

He met Susan's eyes mid-descent. His jaw dropped. His foot slipped, and he plummeted to the floor.

Susan and Amanda rushed for him, and there were multiple apologies. Susan kept trying to say she was so sorry, and he kept apologizing for scaring them.

He promised he wasn't hurt. He was the church's newly-hired music coordinator, choir director, and organist. He offered to show them the whole building. They could get photos for their class, and he'd tell them about what they were looking at.

They got photos. They got dinner.

Susan got Bob's phone number.

A year later, Susan and Bob got married.

After hanging up with Ashlyn, Michael spent the rest of the evening on YouTube finding clips of the Castleton String Quartet.

He'd assumed musicians would have no marketing smarts, and these didn't disappoint. They didn't have their own channel (which he'd have to suggest they do immediately, if not sooner), but they did have clients who uploaded videos and occasionally credited them. Again, he'd have to make Lindsey link to those videos on their website, but that was for later. Tonight, he wanted to listen.

The long-ago videos featured a different lineup, Bob in the first chair, Lindsey in the second. When Bob disappeared, there came the new guy, the dark-haired one with the expression-filled face and the dusky eyes. In really old videos, both Bob and the dark-haired guy appeared together, but not Lindsey. The cellist in the videos previous to this year was always the same man, older than Bob, but the recent ones had the brunette woman.

Ashlyn seemed a constant. Once she started showing up, there she remained. Michael watched her in every video. He didn't mean to. He meant to watch Bob, meant to watch Lindsey. Instead it was Ashlyn who drew his eye whenever the camera passed over her. The blonde hair, the sweet expression, the fluid motion of her with that instrument.

The viola didn't stay put. Now that he'd gotten used to her movements, he began watching the instrument too. It tilted and pivoted, shifting in the air while that bow did its magic across the strings. Did Ashlyn know how amazing she looked when she performed? Did she realize how she drew the eye and never let it go?

No, likely not. She sat toward the back and only ever glanced to the others for cues. They never stood for applause in these videos because applause wasn't the point of their performance. The playing always seemed incidental to whatever else was going on. The wedding. The funeral. The special occasion. The dinner party.

Ironically, the one time he'd seen them perform was the far outlier in their repertoire. That was the only time people had shown up for them, rather than for something else where they happened to be present.

One video, and only one video, had the camera set up at an angle that really caught Ashlyn at her best, and Michael kept replaying it.

She was beautiful. She was kind. She had an empathic sense of what her not-quite-a-mom was thinking. She was protective of Lindsey. She respected Bob, and she respected Susan.

Half an hour ago, she'd gotten off the phone with Michael, and since then Michael hadn't stopped thinking of her. Ashlyn had ached about Susan's assertion that dying with the pain of love was better than living without it.

Ashlyn had known pain. What kind of pain, he didn't know, but pain had visited that heart. Pain she thought he'd hate hearing about.

Yes. He would hate that. He'd hate whatever caused her to suffer. In some way, though, she thought he'd hate however the Castleton family had stepped in to resolve it.

He had his phone in his hands before he was thinking clearly enough to stop himself. But it was late. He kept dwelling on his biological parents. On his siblings. On Ashlyn.

"Do you want to get together again?" he texted Ashlyn. "Maybe dinner?"

It was too soon, too rushed, too emotional. Everything was in upheaval.

"That would be good. When?"

Right now would have been fine. "Tomorrow? Thursday?"

"Hang on."

Hang on for what? Was she checking her social calendar? Actually, they'd mentioned the quartet practiced on Thursday nights. But they performed Fridays. They performed Saturdays and Sundays, too. Scheduling was starting to get tricky.

She texted again: "Lindsey is coordinating with Sierra and Corwin."

Michael hesitated. Not just him and Ashlyn? He should have more clearly defined his "we."

"Lindsey has a plan. Wait a minute."

Michael sat back and stared at the phone. *Really, Ashlyn?* "Wait a minute" and "Hang on" like he was tapping his foot with impatience?

He played the quartet video again. He was starting to feel familiar with this song, whatever it was. The family that posted the video hadn't given the title. What kind of ad would play in front of this music?

"Lindsey has a plan. Can you come to Hartwell tomorrow night?"

"Sure," he texted.

"Lindsey and Sierra will talk to their mother together. Corwin wants nothing to do with this. He won't sabotage us, but he won't help. I'll go to dinner with you nearby. If Mom wants to meet you, we'll see her. If not, at least you didn't waste your time."

Was Ashlyn not feeling the same pull toward him that he felt toward her? She'd made it so...practical. Or was that Lindsey's doing? Lindsey, who saw a rudderless boat and set her hand on the tiller because somebody had to.

At least it got Michael to dinner with Ashlyn. "I'm paying. Pick the place and the time."

"Thanks."

Michael would be putting hundreds of miles on his car because of this. You know what? That's what cars were for. Cars were for leaping into when you got an email saying a DNA search had turned up a full sibling, and a Google search said she'd be performing two hours away in approximately an hour and forty-five minutes. Cars were for shooting northward when your other two siblings wanted to meet you for the first time. If he burned more gas this month than he'd burned the entire year previous, it was worth every drop.

Ashlyn told him a restaurant and a time, and he acknowledged. Google maps indicated he'd need to leave work early. Fine: that's what personal time was for, the complement to the existence of his car.

She said, "I hope you don't mind."

Maybe he needed to be pushier. "I did ask if you wanted to go to dinner. Why would I mind?"

A long pause. Then, "I don't know."

He said, "We can talk more tomorrow."

She wrote, "Yeah, either the night will be really long or really complicated."

He replied, "Don't rule out that it could be both."

She didn't reply until the YouTube clip had reached the end of the song, and then he looked down to find it had appeared. "I'm not sure what I'm hoping for. Only that there's a peaceful resolution."

CHAPTER TWELVE

In the lobby of Paolo Lui's, Ashlyn found Michael pacing between the fish tank and the welcome stand. The moment she entered, he turned and smiled broadly.

Her heart skipped. *Well.*

He *had* wanted to meet her, hadn't he? On Tuesday night she'd played it off as though he'd been using "you plural" when he asked about dinner. Would it be okay if I met you for dinner? Sure, *we all* would love to have dinner with you.

"We all" was a shield. It was easier to clear it up if he wanted to meet alone than if he was only interested in the family.

After all, why would anyone be interested in Ashlyn? Even her mother wasn't interested in her. Michael could just be using her for access, and that would hurt even worse than assuming he was interested and finding out he wasn't.

Ashlyn squeezed his hand. "Are you nervous? Because I've been dying all day."

Wordless, Michael nodded. A greeter appeared, and seeing Ashlyn with him, she offered to seat them.

On a Wednesday night there weren't many diners, so they took a table by the window. Ashlyn said, "When you're nervous, do you find you can't eat? Because I could eat the left side of the refrigerator."

"Savage. Pick out an appetizer and save room for dessert."

"I manage an ice cream stand, so I'll just order an entire pan of lasagna." She laughed. "Rockway's owner says we can eat all we want during our breaks, but let me tell you, after the first week, that loses its luster. I bring home ice cream for Lindsey, but most days I just want a hamburger."

Michael smiled. "I didn't realize you worked at an ice cream stand."

"May to October for the last four years. This is Vacationland, after all, and the quartet alone doesn't pay the bills. We all have 'real' jobs for now. Hannah's a vet tech. Lindsey teaches music. Corwin does welding. After Rockway's closes, I do seasonal work with a catalog company until January. I don't actually know what Jason does, but I'm sure he's important at it." She rolled her eyes. "You haven't met Jason, but his ego casts a shadow."

"Good to know. I'll wear my sunglasses."

Ashlyn settled back in her chair. Although nervous, Michael looked pleased to see her. The more they joked around, the more he relaxed.

They gave their orders, and then Ashlyn slumped forward. "Corwin was emphatic that he didn't want to go tonight. Lindsey thought he ought to be there, but he went to go sit with Dad over at the rehab hospital."

Michael said, "Why rehab?"

"Okay, technically it's a 'skilled nursing center for sub-acute rehabilitation and long term care.'" Ashlyn shuddered. "He doesn't belong in a major medical center.

Hospice isn't appropriate. Not yet. Neither is a nursing home. Most of what this place does is rehab, but they do have a memory care unit, and they're close. Insurance will keep paying, so he's there for the duration. It's..." She choked momentarily. *For the duration* was such a nice way of saying that was the room he'd die in. "Why did this thing have to take his memories? Parkinsons would be bad. Cancer would be bad. But at least it would have left *him*."

Michael's voice softened. "He's still the person you knew."

Ashlyn wanted to throw something. "He's not the same person! He's losing who he is, and I hate every minute of it. If it had to happen to me, I'd rather get hit by a meteor."

She shouldn't have said that. The genetic lottery was still Michael's to lose, same as Corwin, Sierra, and Lindsey. Instead she shoved the subject sideways. "Since Corwin's being a jerk, Lindsey's going to tell Mom without him. Sierra thinks it'll go over like a dream, that Mom will breeze over here to give you a hug and a kiss, and then she'll produce some long-hidden souvenir of your birth that will match you to her like the fulfillment of a prophecy. You'll join at the heart and feel mystically completed."

Michael laughed. "And when that doesn't happen...?"

"Then we test out Corwin's theory, which is that Mom will be outraged that we could believe she lied to us all these years, and she'll spend the evening convinced Dad hid a fling thirty-plus years ago and then abandoned his by-blow on the side of Route 1. After which I guess you'll twirl your mustache, bilk us out of millions, and disappear to pull the same scheme on someone else."

Michael frowned. "Corwin's attributing a lot of talents to me that I'm afraid I lack."

Ashlyn forced a smile. "For one thing, I notice the absence of a long mustache to twirl."

"Nor do I laugh like an evil villain. If you want, we could practice before I meet her."

"That would be for the best, otherwise we'll have to go with Lindsey's prediction."

Ashlyn's stomach clenched as she remembered Lindsey staring into the mirror this morning, her eyes sad. Just so sad.

Michael prompted, "Which is...?"

"That you're legit. That Mom will be shocked, then excited, then want to know why we didn't tell her right away, then upset that she actually met you and I didn't say a word. Hurt that I kept the secret from her too."

The waitress brought their sodas. Michael said, "There isn't a script for this, so we're all stumbling through the best we can. I'm actually mad at myself because I didn't think to bring her flowers."

Ashlyn felt queasy. If she'd have walked in to find Michael holding flowers, she'd have assumed they were for her, and she'd have made an idiot of herself. "Why?"

"A gift. I don't know. Aren't you supposed to do something like that?" He shrugged. "You said you love yellow flowers, so I'd probably have gotten yellow in hopes that she liked them too."

Ashlyn stirred the straw around her glass, releasing a cascade of bubbles. "See above. There isn't a script for this. Besides, if you brought flowers, it might make things worse. She'd think of Dad."

Michael flinched. "Point taken." Then he looked up with focus. "Can you tell me now? Why do you call them Mom and Dad?"

All the hair stood on Ashlyn's arms. "You're not going to like it."

"You said that before, but I can't come up with what could possibly be that bad. Unless they kidnapped you...?"

"They kind of did. But a good type of kidnapping." Ashlyn twisted her napkin and then laid it back on the table. "This is all a mess. They've been really, really good to me."

Waiting, Michael didn't appear enlightened. Ashlyn blew off a long breath. "Okay, so... My mother isn't well. My mom—Rachel—got sent to prison when I was three, and my grandmother in Lincoln took over. I think my mom was picked up on theft or drug charges or something—it changes any time I ask, so I've stopped asking. It doesn't matter. It could have been anything."

Michael said, "I take it there was no father in the picture?"

That was such a blameless way to say it, as though Ashlyn's mother had simply *gotten herself pregnant* the way you get a cold. "Not in the picture" meant no man had ever been involved, neither in using a mentally ill woman for sexual gratification, nor in absconding from all responsibility afterward.

Ashlyn looked down. "You're going to think I'm horrible for saying this, but I figure my mom was turning tricks in order to score drugs. I'm most likely a nasty souvenir after one of those trades. My grandmother gave me back to Rachel when she got out of prison, but she's not...she's not stable?"

Ashlyn looked up. Michael had a flat expression, working hard not to appear horrified.

Well, now Ashlyn knew for the future: if he ever again asked if "you" would like to grab dinner, he meant "you and a large group of random people so there's no chance this looks like a date."

The damage was done. That meant it couldn't get worse. "Rachel's diagnosis changes based on who's diagnosing her. It could be paranoid schizophrenia, and it could be bipolar disorder—but who knows? I'm diagnosed with anxiety, by the way, and I take sertraline. It helps. Rachel on the other hand self-medicates with anything she can find, and that makes it hard to do things like hold down a job. Or raise your kid. Like, Lindsey and I were classmates, but I'm a year older than her because when I should have started first grade, my mother was too strung out to enroll me. No one noticed until the next year, when Rachel was back in prison for a few months."

Michael frowned. "And this wasn't a red flag to anyone?"

Ashlyn waved a hand. "Yeah, but really? Social services just kept bouncing me between Rachel and my grandmother. Around the time I was ten, after my mother's third or fourth stint in prison, my grandmother refused to take me anymore. She wanted to stop enabling my mother with tough love or whatever, but that left me fending for both of us. Now the cops *couldn't* take her or else I'd be all alone. I had to be the one to keep my mother solvent and make excuses for her."

Michael's eyes went wide. "No way."

"I'd already started orchestra, so I knew Mr. Castleton, and I was classmates with Lindsey. I'd been in and out of their house for sleepovers and because they always had snacks after school."

Ashlyn stopped while the waitress brought their salads and a basket of garlic knots. She let the heat of the garlic sting her tongue and crawl through her head.

She liked this place. She was glad to share it with Michael, even if it would be the only time. Where she came from had never been her own choice, but too often it forced other people's choices.

Michael grimaced as he poked at his salad. "You're right. I don't like this at all. Your family treated you terribly. Didn't anyone step in to help?"

"Mr. and Mrs. Castleton—see, this is the actual part you're not going to like." Ashlyn looked up. "I'd almost rather skip this? Just jump ahead to when I was twelve. Rachel had no food in the house, and they'd turned off the lights. I packed all my school supplies and my viola and went over to Lindsey's. Lindsey let me stay in her bedroom. We figured I could live there."

Michael laughed. "You thought no one would notice?"

"Oh, for sure, Bob and Susan noticed. They fed me dinner every night, and in the morning, I'd go to school to get the free breakfast and the free lunch. They were teaching nights, though. As long as I stayed in Lindsey's room after they came home, they didn't notice I hadn't gone home. Before the bus came, I'd sneak outside. After a week, some cops showed up at the school, and I got called into the guidance counselor's office."

Michael had stopped eating. Ashlyn picked up her fork and started on her salad. "You don't need to be horrified. I promise you, I'm still alive and sitting across the table."

"Why were the cops there? Your mother died?"

Ashlyn snorted. "She's also still alive and sends me letters every so often asking for money—which I do give her sometimes. I dread the day she figures out I work at Rockway's because free ice cream? We'll never get rid of her." She speared one of the wrinkled black olives. "The cops had come to the school asking about my last known whereabouts because Rachel had reported me missing. How long was I gone? She wasn't sure. Maybe a week? Imagine their surprise when the school secretary paged me to the front office, and I appeared in two minutes, clean and healthy, my perfect attendance record unsullied. Child protective services got involved before the end of the school day, and that's where it gets complicated."

There really was no way to keep telling this story without upsetting Michael, was there?

Michael looked to be forcing down bites of his salad, one at a time. "It's already complicated. I don't know a single person whose history is this complicated."

"Yeah. Um..." Ashlyn stared out into the parking lot. "Lindsey had suggested I live in her room because her parents were licensed foster care providers for the state. She didn't know all the rules, but she knew they'd get kids who'd stay a few days because of problems at home, and I'd already been in the foster care system, so we figured I could crash there indefinitely." Ashlyn laughed nervously. "What did we know at eleven and twelve? Only then Bob and Susan got in trouble because I shouldn't have been staying."

Michael had gone quiet. She hadn't buried the lede well enough.

Finally, "They were taking in foster kids?"

They'd made an adoption plan for their baby. Then

they'd raised other people's kids instead.

While not a mind-reader like Susan, Ashlyn could see those thoughts in his head. His biological parents hadn't wanted him. They'd taken in other kids. They hadn't given him love. They'd given love to others.

"I said it was complicated."

Michael took a garlic knot without saying anything.

"I also said you wouldn't like it."

He grimaced. "You did say exactly that."

In the parking lot, a family of five was climbing out of a minivan. Ashlyn looked back at her food. "I begged the social worker to let me stay with Lindsey. Susan told them it would be less disruptive since I could keep going to the same school and keep the same activities. Rachel either wandered away or got taken away because she hadn't been paying rent anyhow, and I'm not sure where she went after. They can't incarcerate you for being insane, and she's not enough of a danger to incarcerate her for that."

Michael set his fork on the table with a click. "She was endangering you. A lot of people were."

"And a lot of people weren't. The state kept putting me in someone else's care, and then when everything calmed down, they'd put me back in hers. For years at that point I'd been on the social services' radar. Then the Castletons took me as a permanent foster kid, and twelve months later, with my mother nowhere to be found, I was officially a ward of the state."

Michael said, flatly, "So the Castletons adopted you?"

Ashlyn took another bite of salad rather than answer.

His voice was grim. "That's why they're Mom and Dad?"

"I hung out at their house so often they were already Mom and Dad." She pushed a cherry tomato to the far side of her salad bowl. "They didn't adopt me. It would have messed up my financial aid for college. If you're a ward of the court, you get free in-state tuition." Ashlyn tried to meet Michael's eyes, but he looked away. "I'm sorry. I didn't know at the time that you even existed. I didn't mean to take your place."

His head jerked toward her. "What? I'm not thinking of you like some kind of usurper."

With a startled laugh, Ashlyn said, "Usurper?"

"Dethroning me from my rightful heirdom at my father's right hand...or something." Michael's fist clenched on the table. "It's just— It's not that they didn't want kids. They very clearly did want kids. They didn't want *me*."

"The timing," Ashlyn said. "If they were that young—"

"Please stop. There are a thousand good reasons why they did what they did." He sounded upset. "Just let me be angry for a few minutes. I'll talk myself out of it. A lot of things in life that are the right thing to do still aren't fair."

Ashlyn finished off her salad and was being tempted by another garlic knot when their entrees arrived. Michael had a five-cheese ravioli dish, and she had chicken parm. *Be careful! These plates are hot.*

Everything was too hot to handle. Michael's situation. Her past. Her here-and-gone-again mother.

The place made good food. It was a shame Michael would always find it as bitter as his disappointment.

Still glowering, he said, "Are you paying them back now? Did they railroad you?"

Puzzled, she looked up. "What do you mean?"

"Into being just a musician?"

She caught herself, about to ask if he was content being just an advertising designer. He wasn't really sniping at her. Yes, he looked down on jobs he didn't think of as *professional*. No, he wasn't trying to hurt her. He was too unsettled to filter his words, that was all. "I love the viola. I wouldn't choose anything else, even if I'm scooping ice cream for six months and then working phones at a catalog company from November through January."

He let that settle. Then, "What was it like to grow up with them?"

Ashlyn always had a ready answer for that one. "Noisy."

Smiling, he chuckled. "Really?"

"Yeah, really. Corwin had endless attempts at bands. Eventually Bob and Susan just let him refinish the basement so he could have his own studio. His first band recorded their first album down there when he was sixteen."

Michael grinned. "And Sierra had a harp going all the time?"

"Don't sell her short. She also plays trumpet and trombone, like her mother. Corwin's more into the woodwinds. Corwin's first album featured Corwin on bass guitar, but also Corwin on lead guitar and Corwin on saxophone."

Michael's eyes widened.

"Lindsey was forever on her violin. That's when I really got into the viola. When I first started crashing there, if they asked why I was at dinner again, I would say we were practicing. Well, if I said that, then I had to practice. For years, Mr. Castleton would listen to us playing and then give me an impromptu lesson. We were always getting those. He'd walk past Lindsey's room to grab an apple from the kitchen, stop in and correct her fingering or her stance, then go back to his room having forgotten the apple. Two minutes later he'd be back because he'd just remembered he was hungry, and then there'd be more advice about intonation."

With Michael looking less fragmented, Ashlyn sorted through her head for other things to share. "You've got relatives around the state, too, and we got to see them a lot. We'd pile into the car and drive to Brighthead for a day at the beach with Lindsey's cousins, or we'd end up way in the north hiking a mountain. Sometimes Dad would leave us to fool around in a state park while he played a wedding. We saw everything. Corwin started bringing his guitar and busking near tourist traps for extra cash, and then Lindsey started doing it too. If you were wondering, the state police and the park rangers don't want you doing that, so if you get caught, the trick is to look super young and super stupid. *You need a license? To play guitar? Really?*"

As they ate, Michael kept settling down. He was right:

he'd just needed time to talk himself out of his own anger. Now he wanted to know everything: did the Castleton kids play sports? Travel teams? Were they ever into theater? Did the parents come to all their performances? Where had Bob Castleton's quartet played?

She realized after a while: Michael was asking about so many locations because he wanted to believe they'd met. What if there had been contact at one of their performances? At a contest? At a science fair? At anything?

With empty plates and glasses before them, they were talking at top speed when the waitress encouraged them to leave by asking about dessert. Michael said, "Do you want something?" and Ashlyn was about to answer when her phone buzzed.

A text. Lindsey.

"No." Ashlyn's eyes stung. "We have to leave now."

CHAPTER THIRTEEN

Michael's heart hammered as Ashlyn asked for six cannoli in a to-go box, plus the check. From across the table, he caught the alert just before it disappeared. "*New Message, Lindsey Castleton:* Mom wants to see him."

He looked up. "It's on?"

"It's on." Ashlyn took back her phone and messaged. "*We can be there in fifteen minutes.* I guess this is good."

Michael fought a nausea born of tension. "Too late to back out now."

Ashlyn fidgeted with her napkin again. She met his eyes, then looked away. "Are you going to be okay? Actually, leave your car here, and I'll drive us. Your head isn't in the game."

His brows contracted. "And yours is?"

"I'm less nervous. Plus, I know the roads. I'll drive you back to your car afterward."

When the waitress returned with the box and the check,

Michael didn't feel like doing math. It said a little under fifty bucks for dinner. He left three twenties and a ten on the table, then carried the box. Ashlyn led him to an older model Honda Civic.

As he buckled in, he heard himself saying, "How does this handle in the snow?" As if it mattered.

"Like a cross between a toboggan and a balloon with the end untied." She backed out of the spot, then lowered all four windows. "Also, note our state-of-the-art air conditioning."

His mind had already flown away from the conversation. Ashlyn was right: he shouldn't be driving, but he wasn't sure about her either. He lost track of the roads as they navigated from the town into the empty space where it petered out into nothing, and then they emerged from the woods into a smattering of houses here and there, and finally many houses.

He could have grown up here. These streets could have been as familiar to him as to Ashlyn.

At a traffic light she made a left, then a right, then she pulled up in front of a white farmhouse with black shutters, an addition that stuck off the side, two chimneys, and lights in all the downstairs windows. In the driveway stood Lindsey, Sierra, and Susan.

Susan ran right for the car, dove through the window, and hugged him.

He embraced her, eyes closed, heart racing. She felt soft and sad and sweet and amazing. In Bob's hospital room, he'd shaken her hand and felt lightning, but here came the thunder. Here were the storm fronts melding, the world changing around the force of the two of them.

The engine went off. Michael just held Susan, breathing and being close.

Susan stepped back, tears on her cheeks. Michael got out, and she hugged him again. Then Sierra wrapped her arms around them both.

"You're here." When Susan—his mother—finally choked out words, that's all she said. "You're here."

Susan's living room was full of books and couches, a battered coffee table, and landscapes on every square inch of wall space. Michael sat on one couch with her (with his mother—with his *mother!*) while Sierra curled up on the edge of another, and Ashlyn sat on the floor. Lindsey was in the kitchen making tea, but with the wide entry between kitchen and living room, she could both see and hear them.

Susan had already apologized for not recognizing Michael when they'd met at Bob's bedside, and Ashlyn had fallen over herself apologizing for not saying who he was. Sierra just listened with tears streaming down her face. Michael didn't know where to look first.

While Lindsey put the cannoli on a serving plate, Susan wrung her hands. "It's all so complicated."

Sierra said, "There's time to explain later. Right now, just get to know Michael. You've waited for him for so long."

"You ought to know." Sitting with a box of tissues on her lap, Susan turned to Michael. "I wanted to find you. When I signed the papers, they told me the adoption would be open. I could send you letters, and I could find out where you went. When I tried to write to you later, they said that wasn't true, that it was a sealed adoption."

Sierra exclaimed, "They lied to you?"

Susan closed her eyes. "The agency said whatever they had to so I'd sign the papers. I don't know who said it. Maybe the social worker, maybe my family. That was my condition for making an adoption plan, and they agreed to it, but the paperwork was different from the verbal agreement, and they pushed me to sign in a hurry. I trusted them, and I shouldn't have."

Michael's eyes stung. "That's awful."

Susan shuddered. "It's more than awful. Last year, Bob— your biological father—made a plan for finding you. If we got our DNA out there with a bunch of different services, you could find us if you went looking. But at the same time, we didn't want to tell the kids because if you didn't want to be found, we didn't want to break their hearts knowing the way we did that you were out there somewhere but with no way to contact you."

Sierra tucked up her knees. "Why didn't you submit your DNA?"

Susan tried to steady herself. "Your father thought it best if you guys submitted the kits, that way it looked fun and less redundant. I disliked that the first contact would come through one of you, but your father had read up on adoption searches. He decided a sibling would be more approachable than a parent."

Michael sat back. If that first email had indicated a parent, would he have been so quick to reach out? A sister did feel more like a peer. The parents were the ones who'd rejected him. Would caution have ruled the day? Or would he have been equally quick to get into a car for two hours on the off-chance that he might catch a glimpse of a parent? Once he'd gotten that glimpse, would he have dared send that email?

Susan looked down. "We were holding our breath all of January waiting to see if a match was already in the database, but nothing happened. Then with Bob's illness, I set it aside. When Ashlyn brought a guy she'd just met to see Bob, I didn't make the connection because I'd already decided it wasn't going to happen. I had no idea what to think. Were you a predator digging for information? An abuser trying to move too fast? I'm sorry."

Sierra breathed, "We had no idea you'd be there Monday night."

Susan sounded chastened. "It wasn't something I'd planned. The house was too quiet."

"Because all of us were out meeting Michael together.

Excellent planning on my part." Lindsey shook her head as she came into the living room with the cannoli. She bent so Ashlyn could take one, then brought the plate to Susan and Michael, and then to Sierra. They all ate where they sat, so Michael bit into his too and tried not to stress about crumbs. Mom and Dad still had a "no eating in the living room" policy. They also had a living room with a cream-colored carpet and matching furniture.

One kid versus three kids—or four kids if you counted Ashlyn. Two executive jobs versus two musicians. It all made sense, but the differences kept startling him.

Ashlyn said, "I'm sorry I asked all those prying questions."

Lindsey returned to the kitchen. "Mom knows I put you up to it."

Mom said, "We did want you to know, but the potential heartbreak if you never found him...or if something terrible had happened and he'd died...? It was too much to put on you."

Lindsey returned with a tray filled with mugs and a ceramic tea pot. "Okay, now that we're all in one place, I need to know—how does Michael exist? You always said you met Dad after he returned from London."

Mom winced. "We did meet after he returned from London. We hadn't seen one another for four years, although we'd been writing and sometimes calling. We'd agreed to wait until he came back, and we'd see if the magic was still there. Everyone told me he wouldn't wait and I was better to forget all about him, but when I snuck up to Hartwell and saw him, it all came back." She wrapped her hands around one another. "We first met at a music camp. He was seventeen and a junior violin teacher. It would be his last summer in the States before attending the classical music program at the Royal Academy of London. I was one of the advanced piano students."

Sierra gasped. "That is *so* romantic."

Lindsey, on the other hand, looked unnerved.

Susan traced a design on the tissue box. "He wasn't one

of my instructors, but of course with only a hundred students, we were meeting one another all the time, practicing and performing, trading sheet music, trading instruments... He was the most captivating boy I'd ever met. Any instrument you handed him, within five minutes he'd be playing scales. We'd stay up late talking about music theory, or he'd take me on a hike under the stars to tell me stories about Mozart's life. I know that doesn't sound exciting to you, but he knew everything, and he was so well-practiced at everything. I fell head over heels."

Ashlyn said, tentative, "That's what you meant about recognizing the danger and walking straight into it?"

Susan looked defeated. "I was so young. But I knew if I didn't live with this man—well, in retrospect he was still a boy—then I didn't want to live at all. When I came home, I was pregnant. He promised to marry me, but our parents stopped us."

Lindsey said, "You were fifteen?"

"I turned sixteen at camp. My parents wouldn't hear of it. They wanted me to go to college, and he was going to go to London. Both our families said I shouldn't ruin his life by keeping the baby." Susan's eyes glistened. "The Academy was one of the top five music schools in the world, if not the top. He had a world-class opportunity and he'd graduate at the pinnacle of his profession. He shouldn't give it up for a girl. Not for me."

Susan pulled out a wad of tissues and buried her face. Michael's hands clenched in his lap.

Lindsey poured tea and sat on the carpet. "So they separated you?"

"If your father... He's a good man. He was always a good man, and even then, he always fulfilled his obligations." Susan shook her head. "If I'd said I was keeping the baby, he'd have refused to get on that plane and taken any job he could to support us. I couldn't have that. Music was part of the person I loved, and if I was the reason the world stripped that off him... The baby couldn't stay. The baby needed to be raised by stable parents who were older and married and had a good income and a good education."

Michael's throat tightened.

"I told Bob to go to the Academy. I had the baby alone and made an adoption plan. They let me keep you for two hours, and then they took you away." She pulled out another wad of tissues. "I wrote Bob after you were gone, and then I couldn't bear to write him again for another year. But he kept sending letters, and he waited for me just like he promised. Four years. He got offers from around the world, but instead he returned to Maine, and he wrote me that he'd accepted a job as a church musician. But I didn't know— I didn't even know how I still felt about him. My best friend told me we should sneak up to Hartwell one day, just look around at the town. We wouldn't meet him. We'd see where he was working, and I thought, if I can see he's settled, maybe that will be enough."

Sierra whispered, "You weren't sure?"

"It had been so long. I'd been so hurt. I was scared. Amanda and I used our summer photography class as an excuse to drive up here." Susan blinked hard. "That story is entirely true. I met him in the church. He was up on a ladder singing 'Aura Lee' and fixing a loudspeaker. When he saw me, he fell off the ladder. All the feelings came back, and before we went home, I knew. He promised me we'd make a family for real this time." She turned to Michael. "But you were already gone. They wouldn't tell us where. The records were sealed. Our baby was gone."

Susan was weeping freely now. Lindsey set a cup of tea on the side table and knelt before her, hugging her. "I'm so sorry, Mom. That's terrible."

"It was like my baby was dead, but he wasn't dead. They said I had no right to be sad. They said it was for the best. It was my decision. I had to cheer up and forget all about it." Susan's shoulders jerked. "I'd made a stupid decision, but it was over. I had my whole life to look forward to. I should be happy."

Michael closed his eyes and pulled into the corner of the

couch. Then, a moment later, he felt a hand on his.

Ashlyn's. She had tears in her own eyes.

Sierra whispered, "Whoever said all that to you—I want to kill them."

Lindsey jerked back. "Sierra!"

Sierra's eyes were huge, her mouth set, her whole body trembling. "Whoever devalued you like that—whoever silenced your voice—you tell me their names. They are nothing to me. If they're my relatives, if they're friends of the family—whoever they are, they are *nothing*."

Susan just cried into Lindsey's arms, and then Ashlyn climbed up on the couch between her and Michael to hug her too.

Sierra stood, fists clenched. "You had every right to feel what you felt. You were grieving. Even with Michael still alive, your baby was made dead to you by liars, and you were separated from your lover by people who cared more about his future than your present. They should be mauled by bears and their corpses devoured by coyotes."

Ashlyn murmured, "It does no good. The damage is done."

Sierra hissed, "They haven't even seen damage."

Michael offered, "I've had a good life. The couple you gave me to—they're good people. They want me to thank you for making what had to be an impossible decision."

Still encircled in Lindsey's arms, Susan said, "But we could have kept you. If my family had been willing to help me raise you, then when Bob returned, we still could have married. You'd have grown up with the others. We'd have been your family."

Ashlyn said, "That's in hindsight. You did the best you could."

Lindsey said, "If Dad had come back and married you... married you while you were raising his four-year-old son... think about it. Would you believe he'd married you because he loved you? Or would you believe he'd married you to take care of an obligation?"

Michael went cold all over.

Lindsey said, "Dad loves you so much. You're his everything. He loves music, but he loves you more. You know that now, but you'd never have been sure."

Ashlyn said, "You told me you were impossibly young. You believed the people who should have looked out for you, and you made the only decision you could."

Sierra said, "And would you really want your baby raised by people who scolded you for being heartbroken when liars and thieves stole a piece of your soul?"

Susan just kept crying, and Michael deflated.

"I'm sorry." He bit his lip. "I'm sorry I caused you so much pain."

Susan reached for him. "It's not you. We walled it up because we had to. There wasn't a grave to visit or a way to acknowledge you."

Lindsey tucked up her knees. "But you did acknowledge him. You used to have mini-celebrations in the middle of May. I never knew why. You'd say you felt like baking a cake because it was springtime. You'd say it was someone's birthday somewhere, and we'd have a party and pretend we were giving someone ridiculous gifts."

Sierra exclaimed, "Oh! A zebra! And one year I gave the anonymous birthday boy Mount Denali."

Susan smiled at Michael through her tears. "We couldn't talk about you except with each other. Maybe Bob sensed that he was running out of time this year, and he convinced me to search for you. Within weeks, he was diagnosed. But now you're here."

She reached for him, and Ashlyn slid off the couch so Michael could hug her. Susan held him so tight he could feel her heartbeat against his chest.

He'd grown beneath that heartbeat. He'd been outside it for two hours, and then he'd never felt it again for thirty-two years.

Chapter Fourteen

They stayed at Mom's house far later than Ashlyn was used to. Talking. Listening. Crying. Sierra declared she wouldn't go home tonight. Mom was worn to the bone, and Lindsey didn't know what to do next. She kept moving about: making more tea, washing the dishes, asking if anyone wanted something to eat, shutting windows, turning off lights in rooms they weren't using.

It was past eleven o'clock. Mom was pale, and Ashlyn felt so tired she was nauseated. Sierra had moved next to Mom on the couch and dozed with her head on Mom's shoulder. Ashlyn was sitting again on the floor.

Lindsey said, "Michael, how far a drive is it for you? I don't want you getting home after one o'clock."

Mom looked at the clock. "Oh! You need to get back. I'm so sorry."

Michael looked as drained as everyone else, but the nerves were gone. Sitting in the restaurant, he'd been about to jump out of his skin, his eyes quick and his hands unable to keep still. The worst was over. He'd met them and been acknowledged. He'd asked questions. He'd gotten answers.

Lindsey said, "Michael, I'll drive you back to your car."

"Let me take him." Ashlyn pulled out her keys. "You have to be at the school earlier than I have to be at the ice cream stand."

Mom hugged Michael in the doorway as if she didn't want to let him go. By now, they all had one another's phone numbers, but she was crying just as hard as if a social worker were taking him again.

"I hope she'll get some sleep tonight," Ashlyn said as she started the engine.

"Me too."

Ashlyn said, "You too, but get all the way home first."

"No, I mean I hope she gets—whatever." Michael gave a low chuckle. "I can't even think anymore. This was..."

"Unexpected?"

"A lot better than I thought. Not that I thought it would be anything." Michael stretched. He was too big for the Civic, his legs too long for the front seat, his head up by the ceiling. "I didn't dare fantasize about what meeting my bio parents would be like. I wanted to find them, but everyone told me not to build up any hopes. They said for all I knew, I was the product of a whole lot of dysfunction and maybe abandoned behind a dumpster."

Ashlyn said, "You mean, like me."

Michael drew a sharp breath. "I'm sorry."

Ashlyn didn't reply.

He was right, of course. No adoptee hoped to uncover a story like, "My mom got pregnant trading sex for drugs." The fantasy story should sound like, "My parents were happily married and died in a car crash, their last thoughts their undying love for one another." Schizophrenia and drug addiction didn't place on the list of fairy tale endings.

It wasn't fair. But you didn't get to choose your parents, nor did you deserve the parents you got, nor did parents get babies because they deserved a baby. Rachel hadn't wanted or "deserved" Ashlyn, but here Ashlyn was. Michael's parents hadn't been able to have a baby, but arguably they'd deserved a baby (and proven it by being good parents).

Ashlyn blinked hard. Everyone had cried too much tonight. If she started thinking about Rachel, she'd be worthless to drive the rest of the way home.

Michael said again, "I'm really sorry. I didn't mean it that way."

"I get it." Michael was thinking about himself because that's who he should be thinking about right now. If any part of his brain wasn't tangled up in himself, it was thinking about Susan, about Lindsey, about Sierra. About Bob. Ashlyn had never been more than a sidecar to the family in the first place.

Michael said, "I want to see you again."

Ashlyn kept her tone neutral. "I'm sure you will. Mom's going to wait four hours tomorrow morning and then text to ask if she can meet your parents, and she'll likely invite everyone to an upcoming performance so they can listen."

"I mean, I want to see you."

She couldn't imagine why. She was *just a musician* and a product of dysfunction, the equivalent of crumpled fast-food wrappers tossed behind a dumpster. Also, given her exhaustion and bewilderment, she was just a bit oversensitive.

The restaurant came into view, lights still on but few cars in the lot. Ashlyn got the space next to Michael's and set it in park.

"Can I meet with you again? Maybe go somewhere, see something?" He reached for her hand, and she took his. "I know it's soon, but I want to know you more. I want to spend time together."

Heart racing, Ashlyn said, "I'd like that."

Her voice came out soft, surprised, sensitive.

He put his hand on her shoulder, and she leaned toward him. He ran his hand up her neck and brought her closer, and then he kissed her.

Slow and sweet, his kiss flooded her body with warmth. She raised her hands to his shoulders, and he kissed her again, this time with urgency. With her eyes closed, she inhaled the scent of him until Michael filled her mind, filled her senses, filled her whole world.

He brought his hands forward to cradle her chin, and when she opened her eyes, he was gazing deep into her, his breath punctuated.

She fingered the ends of his hair. "And I really liked that, too."

He was breathing fast. "I wasn't— I was taking a risk there." In the parking lot's dim light, his delighted smile drew an answering smile from her. "Maybe this weekend?"

"Performance Friday night, two weddings on Saturday, some other function on Sunday afternoon. Maybe Sunday night?" She ran her hand down his arm until she could weave her fingers into his. "We'll find a time. You're going to be in town a lot now, aren't you?"

He squeezed her hand before getting out of the car. "Yes. For more than one reason."

Michael was amazing.

Dazzled as she drove home, Ashlyn forced herself to turn on the radio, desperate to focus on the road rather than the lingering warmth of his kiss.

So unexpected. So amazing. So distracting.

He was handsome. She'd admit that to herself now, handsome and with that humor in his eyes as well as an abiding concern for everyone around him. He'd listened to Mom while she cried off and on all night, never blaming her for the decisions she made at sixteen years old. Instead he'd been gentle in his patience and tender in his questions.

Then, instead of justifiably thinking of himself, he'd reached out to Ashlyn and let her know he'd begun to care for her too. He wanted to be with her and get to know her. It didn't matter to him that Ashlyn was the door prize from a drug den.

Guilt flared through her: Mom hated when Ashlyn referred to herself that way. Whether Ashlyn described herself as a door prize or an unwanted side effect, Mom would scold her. "Don't disparage yourself. Your mother needed help, but she never found it. Rachel was doing her best, and no matter how you arrived, the world is better for having you. You are loved, and you deserve your self-respect."

Maybe Michael would feel the same way.

Maybe someday, Ashlyn could too.

A low light shone in the kitchen window, and Ashlyn bubbled over with warmth again. Lindsey knew Ashlyn didn't like coming home to a dark apartment, so she'd lit the little lamp on the kitchen counter. Everyone cared about her tonight.

Upstairs, though, Lindsey was still at the table, drinking hot chocolate.

"I figured you'd be unconscious." Ashlyn left her bag on the chair. "Are you okay?"

"No, and I don't know how I could be. Corwin's blowing up my phone. He's outraged. He's mad at Michael for pushing on this, mad at me for going along with it, mad at Mom and Dad for keeping this a secret. He's not mad at you, but all I have to do is mention your name and he'll find a reason you're evil too." She gave a wry chuckle as her phone sounded again. "He asked if Sierra was just as deluded as before, so I'll ignore that and let him get mad at the next thing. She doesn't need his anger."

Ashlyn said, "But... Since it's legit, why would he be mad?"

"Hello, have you met Corwin? He's shocked and sad and protective, and with his trademark tenderness, he demonstrates it by being a jerk." Lindsey wove her fingers behind her neck and flexed her spine. "I nearly jumped out of my skin when Sierra went off tonight. I never expected that."

"She's protective of your mom, too." Ashlyn leaned against the fridge. "I never saw your mom fall apart like that. She always knows exactly what to do and then does it."

Like Lindsey, actually. Lindsey's "let's-solve-the-problem" insights came directly from her mother.

"That's the real reason I'm taking Corwin's hate right now. I don't want him messaging Mom, and I couldn't sleep even if I wanted to." Lindsey screwed her eyes shut. "Mom was so hurt. I never realized she'd been traumatized by anything, but that was trauma. She never let on, and now I feel awful."

Ashlyn shuddered. "She's been my rock."

Lindsey pressed her eyes into the heels of her palms. "No one's ever been a rock for her. Not even Dad—not really. Dad's great, but when it comes to strength or planning or dealing with tragedy, he passed the football to her. Now she's dealing with Michael on her own."

Ashlyn shivered. "Are you okay with Michael? Do you think he's safe?"

"We know nothing about him. He could be Mom and Dad's kid *and* a scammer. There's no way of knowing except going forward. He doesn't seem like he wants things, but like we keep saying, if he was playing a con game, he'd ease in nice and slow." Lindsey looked up. "Why are you asking me? You've spent more time with him than I have."

Ashlyn braced herself. "He kissed me."

Lindsey straightened in her chair. "And what did you do?"

Ashlyn bit her lip. "I kissed him back...?"

"Oh, look, I've found the thing that will make Corwin mad at you." Lindsey's brow contracted. "Is that smart? Everyone's riding an emotion wave right now. Plug us into the grid and you'd power Maine for a month. Exactly no one is thinking clearly. Why would you let him do that?"

Ashlyn tried to smile. "I like him?"

Lindsey made a face. "I thought things were weird before. This just went to a different level of weird."

Ashlyn took a seat at the table. "Weren't you trying to set me up with Corwin?"

"In a thousand years you and Corwin wouldn't so much as eat lunch together, let alone hold hands." Lindsey angled her head as she studied Ash. "How does this work? If you're kind of my sister, and he's kind of my brother, isn't that kind of creepy?"

"I'm not really his sister, and he didn't grow up with you."

"It's not illegal or immoral. It's just...tangled up." Lindsey shook her head. "Don't let him pull you in for the wrong reasons. If he wants to get in tight with our family, and you look like a way to lock us down, he might find that attractive."

Ashlyn said, "And there's no other reason?"

Lindsey snorted. "You're gorgeous, and you know it. If the quartet is ever on the cover of a magazine, they're putting you and Jason front and center, facing each other, with me and Hannah blurred out in the back."

Ashlyn rolled her eyes.

Lindsey rubbed her temples. "I'm sorry. It's really late and my head's all turned around. If you two get together, I'm happy for you. He seems like a great guy, and with any luck, he's going to be around for a while." She looked up. "Plus, I'd get my wish. You'd finally be my sister."

CHAPTER FIFTEEN

"Hey, honey." Michael's mother's voice on the phone was both cheerful and tentative. "Are you free to talk now?"

"Sure." Michael logged off the computer and stepped away from his desk. "I was about to get lunch."

"How did it go? You texted that you met them all, but you didn't sound...I don't know."

"There's a lot." Michael headed down the stairs rather than take the elevator two floors to ground level. "It did go well, but I'm still processing."

Processing Susan's story. Processing the siblings' reactions. Processing Ashlyn. Ashlyn's story, her feelings, his feelings, and where this was going to go. He didn't have a plan. Everything had shot off the rails.

He gave his mother an outline of the night, how he'd met Ashlyn first for dinner so they'd be waiting nearby. Mom kept making encouraging sounds as he told the story en route to a local sandwich shop, and she murmured,

"That poor woman," when he told her how Susan had hugged him through the car window.

"We talked until eleven o'clock. I didn't get home until way after midnight." Coffee this morning had been a lifeline. Given the caffeine he'd consumed to compensate, Michael might not sleep well for another month. "There were so many things to catch up on."

"Thirty-two years," Mom mused. "Your entire life. Those girls' entire lives. I'm so sorry to hear the agency lied to her."

That part still bothered Michael, how someone took advantage of a sixteen-year-old, quite possibly a dozen someones. "You'd have sent her letters and photos if you'd known."

Mom said, "No, I wouldn't have. I wouldn't have adopted you under those circumstances. When we first applied for an adoption, I told the agency exactly that. No hippy strung-out teenager was going to show up on my doorstep trying to claim her child."

Michael froze.

Mom said, "We waited too long for you. I wasn't going to risk losing you if the baby-daddy came back and sweet-talked the mother into changing her mind. It was better for the baby to have a clean break. You waited until you were an adult to find them, and that's how I wanted it."

Michael's head reeled. "Well, Susan feels guilty that they went on to have more children, as if they could have raised me too. But she was sixteen. She hadn't even finished high school."

He remembered Sierra's eyes like fire as she defended her mother.

He remembered Ashlyn fighting tears. Ashlyn, the only blonde in the room, the only one not related to everyone else. Ashlyn, the only one sitting on the floor.

He wondered if the agency had changed the terms of the adoption because his mother would have refused to adopt him under the original terms.

Before those thoughts finished stampeding through his

head, he realized also that his mother's unflattering fears about Susan were all applicable to Ashlyn's mother—and not in a good way.

Mom said, "Did you take photos with them?"

"I have a few." It hurt to look at them this morning. Susan's eyes were red, her face blotchy, her smile forced. They'd need to take pictures again.

He'd need a picture with Bob.

He'd need to give his heart a break because this was so much, so fast. He'd heard warnings about that: if you search, prepare to feel anything. Anything at all. Hopelessness. Joy. Anger. Grief. Delight. Prepare to revisit every feeling you've ever had about your adoption, but triple it and then add forty percent.

Mom said, "Can you send the pictures?"

He snapped, "Why are you all over me about this?"

Mom didn't answer, and Michael flinched. "I'm sorry. I shouldn't have said that."

"I'm not trying to be pushy." Mom sounded subdued. "This matters so much to you."

"I know. I know. I'm sorry. You're not pushing me."

"I'll back off. I'm just so glad for you that I want to share your joy. Don't get angry."

Michael stopped outside the sandwich shop. Joy? Was that what he felt? The universe whirled in his head. "I don't even know half the things I'm thinking right now. The full siblings, the dementia, the foster kids, the music. Like, my brother hates me even though he hasn't exchanged ten words with me, and everything is like that. It's too high intensity."

He leaned against a brick wall between two shop windows. Mom asked, "What foster kids?"

"The Castletons were taking in foster kids for fifteen years. They got cleared to provide emergency foster care with the state. They—"

His throat closed up.

Bob and Susan were taking strangers' kids into their home and standing in place of their parents, while across the state someone else had taken in their kid and stood in place of Bob and Susan, and that wasn't fair at all. It wasn't fair to Michael that they were happy raising other people's children but not their own.

Mom said, "Did they do that hoping they'd find you?"

Michael didn't answer.

Mom said, "Or were they doing that because they knew how important it was for a family in a terrible position to have a stable home for their child?"

Michael said, "Susan was only sixteen."

"Oh, that poor woman. That poor girl."

"She married him five years later, and they had Lindsey the year after. It was the right thing. I keep telling myself it was the right thing."

He'd arrived at the wrong time. That was the only way it made sense. He'd just been too early. If he'd waited five years—

—But if he'd waited five years, would Bob and Susan have waited for one another? Or would Bob have found a British wife and remained in England, performing in concert halls instead of outdoor weddings and an old stone church? Was Baby Dalton the glue that kept them bonded to one another through those years of separation?

Mom said again, "That poor girl. It must have been so hard for her."

Yes, but it was hard for Michael too.

He'd had a good life. His parents had told him from the start that while most families just had a baby, any baby, he'd been a chosen baby. They'd wanted him, prepared for him, passed tests for him, and in some way selected him. He'd grown up thinking himself some name-brand top shelf product in a highly selective market. Not an accident of chance, but cultivated and chosen.

Heaven help him, he'd said that out loud to his friends. Other kids got to have one birthday, but he had two: the day he was born, and the day he was adopted. Other kids were delivered in a hospital, but he'd been delivered in a sedan. "My parents wanted me and worked hard for me."

He'd been eight, nine, ten years old. May the universe and all that was holy forgive him for that. What do you know at age eight? Because all those things he'd said he wasn't—he was. He was both of them. He'd been an inconvenience and a blessing. He'd been unwanted and wanted. He'd been a source of grief and a source of joy—and all of that, without any intention or action on his part. To lay claim to that—to lay claim to any of that—was to be the cause of Susan's heartbroken sobs.

Mom said, "Well, I'll let you have lunch."

"It's okay. I'll tell you more."

"No, you're right. You need time to process. You just eat, and I'll see you on Sunday. I love you, Michael."

"I love you, too." The response was automatic. Then she was off the phone.

Inside the sandwich shop, Michael stared at the wall and wanted nothing. He ordered one of his standards, thinking instead about one of the more bizarre combination subs that had always intrigued him but which he'd never braved himself to order. He picked up a bottled soda from the cooler and mindlessly grabbed an apple from the bin. They totaled him out and handed him a boring sandwich wrapped in white paper in a brown bag.

It was too much. It was too little. It was too fast. It had come far too late.

With his head not in the game and an hour left to work, Michael texted Ashlyn. "Can I see you tonight?"

She replied, "Impatient, aren't you? I actually have practice tonight with the quartet."

He sighed. "Sorry. I forgot about that."

"Not a problem. You're not supposed to know my whole schedule." Then, "Wait, I have an idea."

Not even thirty seconds later, his phone sounded with an incoming video chat. He opened it, and there on the screen was Ashlyn.

"Hi!" The phone was looking up at her from beneath. "You said you wanted to see me, so voila! Now you see me."

Michael laughed. "You do realize I'm still at work."

"Well, I'm not." The screen gave a dizzying series of angles all at once. "Given our schedules, I'm going to assume that's as close as we come to meeting again until next week. Practice tonight and performances all weekend."

Michael said, "Is it always like that?"

"Summers, yeah." She positioned the phone in one place, and now he recognized her kitchen. "I'm making dinner for me and Lindsey whenever she gets home, and then after we'll go to the music school and practice."

Michael said, "Don't you play every day?"

"Oh, sure. But we don't all play together except twice a week, and any performances. Tuesdays and Thursdays, usually." She looked far more energetic than he felt. "Anyhow, now you get to watch me making potatoes."

He grinned. "I would watch you peel potatoes."

"There you go. Potatoes, hamburgers, some kind of vegetable. We live an exciting life here in Hartwell." She turned on the kitchen tap and started scrubbing. "Talk to me. Now that you've found everyone, what made you start looking?"

Michael said, "It was the right time."

Ashlyn huffed. "That's such a non-answer. I've been reading a bit about adoption, and they talk about *the search* as though it's a universal, but a lot of people do it younger than you did. Plus, you're happy with your family-of-origin. So what made it be time now?"

She kept working on the potatoes, and Michael sat back in his chair. "Last January, I broke up with my girlfriend of five years, and that's what got me thinking."

Ashlyn turned off the water. "What kind of parting shot

did she give you that made you think, 'Hey, I should track down my relatives'?"

"She didn't actually say anything. Kristen—she was an insurance agent—she and I had been growing apart for a while."

Ashlyn got down a cutting board and then dug in a drawer for a knife. "Yeah?"

"Things blew up right after Christmas. I moved into my current apartment, and I started trying to figure out who I was again now that I was on my own."

Ashlyn started cutting. "Oh, I see. And when you were putting the pieces together as to your future, you started wondering about your past. That makes sense."

Ashlyn was fully focused on the knife, not on the camera. Michael said, "It felt like assembling a giant puzzle with tens of thousands of pieces. Why I'd gotten involved with Kristen, why things fell apart, what was wrong with me, what I could have done differently."

Ashlyn said, "Why did things fall apart with her? Five years is a while."

"I had a chance at a high-powered client, but I knew they were a nightmare to deal with, so I let another designer take them. She was furious. She wanted me in a better job, a better apartment, a better neighborhood, a better car. I wanted to keep my sanity. I wanted not to have to work nights and weekends as if I were on-call all the time. She hated that. She wanted me to take this client, make a lot more money, then poach them and open my own ad agency. When I refused, she went all-out with the ridicule." Michael hesitated. "Then one night, I had an epiphany."

Ashlyn glanced at the camera. "A voice from the past?"

"Something like that. It hit me while I was driving home, dreading the passive-aggressive attacks that would be waiting for me. Suddenly I thought: *know your own value.*"

Ashlyn's brows shot up. "That's an awesome epiphany."

"Right? I went straight from not knowing how to keep her happy, to thinking, I don't *need* to keep her happy. My value as a person didn't depend on giving other people what they want, but she only valued what I was giving her. I decided she didn't have the right to judge me."

Ashlyn whistled. "There you go. That's your ticket right out the front door. It's just a shame it took you five years to remember that."

Michael glanced at his office door, but no one was around. He really should be working, but since he wouldn't be meeting Ashlyn tonight, he could stay later to make up the time. It wasn't as if he'd been doing anything productive prior to now. "Things had started out good, but after a while it was always criticism. Anything I did, anything my parents did—it wasn't good enough. It gets tiresome."

Ashlyn said, "Especially when you're not even doing it wrong, just different?"

"Right. I drive too slowly, and the car is too old, and my parents do holidays the wrong way, and we watch TV the wrong way, and we like the wrong movies, and on and on and on."

Ashlyn switched to a singsong voice. "*Why are you cutting the potatoes in cubes? Don't you know they should be cut lengthwise?*"

Michael snickered. "Oh, then you've met Kristen."

"I've met a lot of Kristens." Ashlyn sighed. "After a while, criticism becomes scorn, and scorn destroys everything. When someone doesn't respect you, you stop respecting them, but you also stop respecting yourself."

Michael nodded. "Well, I got out of there with no sense anymore of what was right, and everything I did, I was second-guessing myself. Then I thought, *know your own value,* and I realized I was worth more than that. But I still wasn't sure what I actually was worth."

Ashlyn dumped the potato cubes into a mixing bowl, then doused them in oil. "I can see that. After a head trip like that, you'd need time to figure yourself out again. The criticism echoes on and on and on even after the person's not there."

Michael hesitated. "Did you date someone like that too?"

"My good sir, I was *raised* by someone like that." Ashlyn opened a cabinet and stared inside. "A therapist told me people who criticize everything are deeply unhappy, but they see themselves as victims. To do that, they have to externalize their focus and badger everyone around them."

That sounded like a lot of expensive jargon. "I never had a therapist."

"Therapy might have helped. It depends if the therapist is even remotely competent, which I'm going out on a limb and assuring you they aren't all." Ashlyn huffed. "Don't even get me started on some of the 'professionals' the court ordered me to talk to when I was a kid. One of the useful ones told me about something called 'locus of control.' People who are healthy have what they call an internal locus of control, where they see themselves as in command of most situations in their lives. When something terrible happens, they see themselves as having power to change it, or at least adjust to it. Some people have an external locus of control, which means they see themselves as victims at the whim of fate."

Michael hummed. "Sometimes the force making things go to pieces really is outside yourself."

"Like with Bob's illness, sure. But Susan sees herself as in control of her own decisions in response to his illness. If Kristen was constantly on you for everything, then she was assuming you were in control of her feelings, and therefore she was badgering you whenever she felt bad."

Michael said, "Which I couldn't live with. I had to get out of there."

"Obviously, but after five years of being undermined, naturally you weren't sure who you were anymore." Ashlyn dumped the bowl of potatoes into a roasting pan, then covered them in a blizzard of salt.

Michael said, "That's when I started searching. I tried to get my records opened, but that dead-ended. I interviewed lawyers, but it didn't seem like they would help. I was thinking of hiring a private detective, but when I added up the cost, I thought I should try the DNA services first. And that brings us to August."

"Which brings up another question, which is whether finding the Castletons gave you the answers you wanted."

Brows raised, Michael sat back.

Ashlyn looked at the camera. "I'm not making fun of you. I get what you're saying: you're looking for who you ought to be. I did that too, only I was lots younger. Someone at school called my mother a crack whore, and I spent the night crying because I didn't know if it was true."

The words stung, and Michael didn't know what to say.

"What did that make me? Was my very existence a sexually transmitted infection?" Ashlyn's eyes narrowed. "Mom shuts me down when I say things like that, by the way, but that doesn't mean I didn't think them first. I did find my answers in the Castleton home. I found exactly the kind of value you're talking about—because they valued me even though I gave them nothing. You might find your answers there too. The question is, what if you don't?"

Michael said, "They've already given a lot of answers."

"Aren't the answers raising more questions? You've been mining us for every tidbit you can think of, but are those details telling you who you are? Or who you aren't?"

Michael's boss knocked on the door, and he held up two fingers. His boss nodded and walked away.

Ashlyn said, "Oh, right, you have a job."

"Yeah, they frown on paying me to hang out ruminating on the past." Michael shook his head. "But you are giving me information, and that's a good thing."

"Is it?" Ashlyn looked momentarily haunted. "I grew up there, but I'm not one of them. You're one of them but didn't grow up there. You can't crawl into me and re-live what you lost. That's not fair to you or to me."

He frowned. "I don't get it."

"All I'm saying is, I'm not merely a byproduct of where I grew up." She slid the pan of potatoes into the oven. "And neither are you."

CHAPTER SIXTEEN

Ashlyn's phone vibrated in her pocket during practice, and she caught herself smiling.

Michael had begun texting her during the daytime, not about anything in particular. Just stuff he wanted to share, photos of places he'd seen and silly things he'd found on the internet and a flyer for an event he thought she might like to go to. Scattered throughout the day like sprinkles on an ice cream cone, the texts meant he was thinking about her all the time.

She played through the whole piece, not checking her message until the end of the movement when she could count on Jason and Lindsey to argue about intonation or dynamics.

Jason said, "This was interesting, but hadn't we better do the piece *as written*?"

Lindsey sat taller, but Hannah blurted out, "Do we know who the vocalists are for the weddings on Saturday?"

Lindsey gave Hannah a slow smile. "Why, indeed, we do." Then nothing more.

Grinning about Hannah's open secret, Ashlyn said, "How interesting, Lindsey! Is either of them Enrique?"

Soloist Enrique Almendarez crossed paths with their group on a regular basis. For one thing, Lindsey always recommended him. *"Have you hired someone yet to sing for your wedding? You hadn't considered a vocalist? We know a tenor who would do justice to the songs you've selected. He's even got some clips online."*

Lindsey gave a sly smile. "Maybe?"

Hannah shifted uncomfortably. "I was just wondering if I should offer him a ride."

Lindsey said, "A ride would be very convenient for him if he were singing with us."

Jason glared up. "Guys? What's the big deal? Enrique: yes or no."

Lindsey huffed. "Yes. The morning one."

Hannah brightened. "Okay. Then I'll ask if he needs a ride."

Ashlyn glanced at Lindsey. "Odds are he does."

Jason sounded puzzled. "Pretty sure Enrique has his own car."

Ashlyn only shrugged. "One fewer car on the road can't hurt."

This Saturday they'd be playing a garden wedding at ten o'clock in the morning, followed by a church ceremony starting at six in the evening. Lindsey would happily book three weddings in the same day if the clients all turned in their deposits. *Do we have to be in two places at once? No? Then I'm booking them.* Days like that meant careful pre-planning in terms of coffee ingestion, getting to bed on time the night before, and packing food you could eat at red lights while traveling between gigs. But take note: money. Money was good.

Lindsey had worked out the travel time and determined these two weddings didn't violate the "two places at once" rule, and therefore both deposit checks had gone straight to the bank. As a bonus, Hannah would spend time near Enrique.

Jason looked up from making notes on his score. "Why does the soloist matter?"

Hannah shifted and looked at her music. "I like to know."

It was obvious to anyone in the world, including random houseflies that passed through a performance, that Hannah was carrying a torch for Enrique. Obvious to anyone in the world except Jason, who only shrugged and went back to noting things on his music. Probably things like, "Remember to annoy Lindsey" and "Grandstand a bit here so people never doubt my importance."

Lindsey said, "Let's do that piece over from measure one-twenty-five," and with that Ashlyn lost the chance to check her phone. "Oh, and Hannah, if you could play just a tad louder, the effect would be magnificent."

By the next break, two more messages had come in. That was over the top for Michael, so Ashlyn pulled out her phone, and her heart sank. Unknown number, but the first message was, "Ashlyn? It's Mom."

Ashlyn usually blocked her mother's number, but given Rachel's general stability, her number was something of a moving target.

Second message: "Ashlyn, are you okay? It's Mom. Just wondering what you're up to."

Third one: "I love you, sweetie, so let me know if you're okay or else I'll call the cops and have them check on you."

Speaking of over the top, Ashlyn would have to find a ladder and assume the previous "top" was merely another floor on the skyscraper of her mother's unpredictability. Ashlyn turned off notifications and put the phone back into her pocket.

It made no sense, and it never would make sense, but mental illness made no sense in the first place. By definition. From time to time, Rachel would remember Ashlyn and feel some kind of maternal stirring. She loved her daughter and wanted to be a mom, so she'd send her daughter a card or hunger to hear her voice. The impulses never lasted long enough for Rachel to travel across the state to see Ashlyn, but until the impulse faded, Rachel would try doing whatever it was she thought mothers did. Up to and including calling the cops for a wellness check.

The police loved that. Two years ago, a cop had shown up at Ashlyn's apartment, laid eyes on her, and said, "You're how old? Not our responsibility. Your mother wants you to call her."

Ashlyn had said, "Call her yourself and tell her I'm fine."

Who knew how often Rachel had tried it since then? The Hartwell police didn't have a lot to do, so on a boring night, they might actually drive by her place to have something to fill in on the report.

Lindsey had the quartet play the next movement, but Ashlyn's heart wasn't in it. You could play viola by rote mechanics if necessary. First-year students could run the bow over the strings and use the correct fingering to achieve the right notes. Emoting, though? That took emotional effort, and three stupid texts had tapped her out.

When Lindsey stopped to examine one of the weirder sound combinations, Jason said, "Ashlyn? Are you alive? I've heard music boxes with more feeling."

"Thanks for noticing." Ashlyn checked the tuning of her A string, which sounded a bit off. "I had my heart removed so I could play more like you."

Lindsey laughed in surprise before she smothered it. Jason said, "While I understand your admiration, that's not the way to master the instrument."

"Then I'll work harder on my gentle supportive nature." Ashlyn narrowed her eyes. "Shall we try again?"

Jason drummed his fingers on his knee. "What's actually going on? First Lindsey turned on the waterworks this weekend, and tonight you're acting like your puppy died."

Hannah glanced at Ashlyn. "I think she's playing fine."

Jason's face darkened. "And I'm not an idiot. Is it Bob? Is he okay?"

Lindsey sighed. "My family had a huge upheaval this week. You both ought to know, so let's call practice done for tonight." She laid her violin across her lap and loosened the bow, and then piece by piece she laid out the story about Michael.

Jason interrupted. "No way. There is no way that guy is legit."

Lindsey recoiled. "Except that he's totally legit."

Jason shook his head. "The guy's scamming you. He's scamming the whole family!"

"How? Are you suggesting he found out about a secret pregnancy that no one else knew about, then stole Corwin's DNA and submitted it to exactly the two services Sierra and I submitted ours to, and at the same time managed to commission a plastic surgeon to make him look just enough like the rest of us to fool our mother?" Lindsey's brows raised. "At this point, it's easier to believe he's the real deal."

Jason's eyes widened. "What now? Are you going to turn us into a quintet and invite him and whatever instruments he plays so he can be our new headliner?"

Ashlyn sighed. "Your position is secure. He doesn't play an instrument."

Hannah recoiled. "But he's a Castleton."

"Don't do this." Jason stood. "He's bad news, and he's going to take you for everything."

"Are you losing your mind?" Lindsey looked up at him. "My father isn't dead, and this guy isn't a scammer. The first rule of scamming is to scam people who have money, and we have nothing."

"You have a music school and a whole lot of intellectual property." Jason stalked over to his violin case. "And don't forget the instrument room. Do not give that guy any of Bob's violins."

Lindsey said, "He doesn't *play* anything."

"Yes, but he can *sell* anything, and then they'll be gone. Don't give him a thing." Jason set down the violin and turned to her. "So help me, Lindsey, before you sell any of the violins, talk to me first."

"Because you're a violin appraiser? Because I'm an idiot? Because I'm going to throw away a bunch of instruments that aren't even my property to dispose of? What's gotten into you?"

Jason snapped the case and grabbed his music off the stand. "What's gotten into me is *sanity,* and I don't think it's occurred to you how much danger you're in. How can this guy even exist? Bob told me the story of how he met your mother. Does your mother have a time machine?"

Ashlyn said, "They don't have a time machine, but they did have a secret."

Jason whirled toward her. "You too? You believe him? After everything?"

Ashlyn met Jason's eyes. "Yes. After everything, I do believe him."

The cops weren't idling in front of the apartment when Ashlyn and Lindsey got home, nor was there a note on the door. Ashlyn didn't bother sorting through the mail, just in case her mother had sent another card gilt with guilt.

Lindsey said, "Help me out here. Why would Jason think I'm going to give my father's violins to a guy who has never shown an interest in them?"

"Maybe for the same reason Corwin thinks the family is about to collapse in on itself under the weight of one more member?" Ashlyn turned away. "Did Corwin freak like that when I first showed up?"

Lindsey stood over the recycling bin, dropping in junk mail while she sorted it midair. "You don't remember? Yes, he lost his marbles when he realized you weren't going home. 'Like we need one more girl in the house!'"

Ashlyn chuckled. "I don't remember that. He was like

eight."

"He slammed doors for months. That's also the month he took up drums. You probably didn't realize it because you'd never lived with him before, but he acted like twice the toad he normally did. He's lucky Mom and Dad didn't keep you and jettison him."

Ashlyn relaxed when Lindsey didn't hand her any of the envelopes. "I'm lucky they kept me. Your parents turned everything around."

"Yeah, and Corwin wouldn't get rid of you now. Maybe he's jealous by nature." Lindsey brought her violin to her room, but she just kept speaking. "What's going on with Michael? You hear from him today?"

"We're texting and talking. He wants to come to the performance tomorrow night."

Maine being "Vacationland" meant a lot of towns got creative about drawing in the tourist dollars. "Live music on the town green" was a staple in most of the coastal towns, and Lindsey wanted the quartet at every one they could get to. Did a local farmstand have an end-of-the-school-year concert? She'd ask to play it. Town spirit day? Are you having a concert at the bandstand? How long is the slot? How much will you pay? Lindsey always put in an application to perform at every town. Since the Castleton family knew every musician in the area, most places approved the quartet the minute the application hit their inbox, and even the ones "by invitation only" usually found it in themselves to issue an invite.

With rentals turning over on Fridays, many of the towns held festivals on Thursday evenings. On a good week, the quartet could have events from Thursday through Sunday evening. It mattered. It mattered because not only were they "out there," but also, they needed the money to make it through the winter when the tourists went home and no one in their right mind would attend an outdoor concert—including the musicians. Ski lodges were nice, but this part of Maine didn't have a lot of skiing, and most ski lodges didn't hire live musicians anyhow. Then there was the holiday season work and music at Christmas parties. From January until April, Ashlyn had to survive on her bank balance.

Ashlyn said, "If Michael comes to the performance, Mom might come as well, just to see him again."

Lindsey stepped back into the hallway. "I'm still drained."

"No kidding." Ashlyn leaned against the wall. "Michael had time to prepare for all that. We didn't really. Mom had even less. And how do we tell Dad?"

Lindsey blinked hard. "Yeah. I hate to say it, but what if Dad doesn't understand?"

Ashlyn's throat closed up.

"I don't even know anymore. It was awful when I told him about my cousin Aileen's wedding and showed him the photos. He was so happy every single time he saw them, like it was a great surprise. 'Well, good for her! She's beautiful!' Then five minutes later, I could show him the same photos, and he'd be just as happy and just as surprised and say exactly the same thing."

Ashlyn trembled. "I hate this."

Lindsey nodded. "I hate it too."

Later, in her pajamas, Ashlyn propped herself on her pillow and texted Michael. He was running a rehearsal for a performance in two weeks, and every so often he'd send her a picture. Ashlyn watched a YouTube video about giraffes, pausing in between his messages.

He showed a picture of an empty cubby. "If they don't put back the prop umbrellas, I'm going to lose my mind."

She texted back, "Who'd steal a prop umbrella?"

He replied, "They put things down anywhere, and then it's my fault when they need the same prop in the next scene and can't find it."

She laughed. He added, "These are grown adults," and she laughed harder.

Michael sent her photos of the stage. She texted him, "Are you wearing a headset to talk to the director?"

"Of course I am. How else could I enjoy her continuous

sarcastic quips about the actors?"

"I demand a headset selfie."

A headset selfie appeared within the minute, Michael looking moderately tolerant before a partially-assembled wooden balcony.

Ashlyn replied, "You look like a general about to order an air strike."

"The director just called a meeting and sounds like she's about to order an air strike. Later."

Ashlyn looked again at Michael's selfie before saving it to her photos. From this angle, she could see Sierra in his cheekbones, and definitely Corwin in the tolerant smirk. Those were Lindsey's eyebrows, half-raised in an unspoken question that looked an awful lot like, "Are you satisfied?"

She texted Michael, "Bronze leader, standing by."

It unnerved her when he didn't reply to that. She hadn't figured out his cultural likes and dislikes, or whether he'd get the same references she got. In the musical world, no. When it came to some of the major blockbuster movies of the past decades, Ashlyn was more likely to own the soundtrack than the DVD, more likely to name the composer than the lead actors. One of the gals at the ice cream stand had gushed over the climax of a recent movie, and Ashlyn's response had been, "But they didn't take enough chances with the score." The background music needs not just to support the storyline, but also to add to it. A good score matched the scene, but a great score raised questions and added meaning in the way it contrasted.

Kind of like how the first and second violins could play together or play against one another. Sometimes the viola opposed the melody line in order to render the melody even stronger. Trying to explain this had left both Ashlyn and the employee in confusion, so she'd abandoned the conversation.

If Ashlyn married Michael, she'd be a Castleton for real. Except no, she'd end up with Knolwood. He'd gone looking for his biological family, but he wasn't going to abandon the family who'd raised him. To him, Mom was "Susan." Dad was "Bob." If he married Ashlyn, would he call them Mom and Dad too? Would he ever?

Of course, a second date was a far cry from marriage, especially considering they hadn't technically had a first date. He'd asked her to dinner, and she'd turned it into a project.

Michael texted, "Guess who's going to be building props all weekend?"

Ashlyn replied, "Friday night too?"

"Oh, blast. Yes, Friday night too."

Ashlyn replied, "It's okay. Lindsey told the other quartet members about you, and there's a little tension about whether you are who you say you are. Maybe we should let them settle before you meet them."

He replied, "Hm." Then, "I don't suppose you'd want to come build sets on Sunday?"

Ashlyn snickered. "I'm not sure which end of the hammer goes where, but sure."

Not entirely true. She could do minor instrument repairs.

Michael replied, "Can you get here by ten?"

Considering the drive, ten would be wicked early after an evening wedding. "I can do that."

"Awesome! I'll let Emma know we've got help coming."

Ashlyn said, "Looking forward to it. Try not to laugh too hard when I hammer my hand."

He replied, "Don't hammer your hand. You need it to keep playing music as beautiful as you are."

Ashlyn's heart froze.

"I'm heading home now," he texted. "Have a good night."

"You too," she replied, but kept re-reading the previous line. *Music as beautiful as you are.*

CHAPTER SEVENTEEN

Michael met Ashlyn in the parking lot behind the theater. She wore jeans and a t-shirt, plus work boots, and she'd pulled her hair into a thick ponytail. She stepped up to him, and he gave a quick kiss. When she didn't object, he let the excitement build: this was the real thing. She wasn't just humoring him, and their mutual infatuation wasn't just one overwrought night. She'd driven a far distance to hammer things together with him, and she was glad to see him besides.

Plus, she hadn't brought any of the Castletons. Today, she was all his.

He introduced Ashlyn to Emma Hall, the director. Of the others assembling sets today, three were actors, one was a high schooler getting service hours, and two were the lighting crew. In another part of the theater, the sound guy was testing the equipment, plus one of the lighting guys would be turning lights on and off the entire time.

Michael and Ashlyn would be building a fireplace and a mantlepiece. After they got that set up, they'd need to find or make trinkets to set on the mantle. Ashlyn pulled a pair of work gloves from her bag (good thinking!) and they started gathering what they needed. One of the actors set up a table saw in the alley behind the theater.

Emma said, "Someone needs to retrieve the green sofa from the basement."

Michael turned to Ashlyn. "You up for hauling furniture?"

"With you? Sure." She followed him down a set of winding stairs to a sub-basement full of props from performances past. "Haven't you needed a living room before today? It looks like you guys saved everything."

Michael flipped on the lights. "We re-use anything we can, but sometimes the previous props aren't right. A fireplace in Victorian England won't look the same as a fireplace in the dark ages."

Ashlyn walked through the props. A sleigh. A bed. "You could maybe use that," she said, pointing to a grandfather clock. "Oh, and a wardrobe! That looks amazing."

He laughed. "You're acting like it's Christmas."

"It is exactly like Christmas. There's even a tree!" She turned her phone into a flashlight and scanned the corners. "Is that a tent? Oh, and that looks like the bow of a ship! I love it."

After pulling dust cloths from several pieces, he located the correct sofa and shifted a desk to one side so they'd be able to free it from the other props. "We'll just get this on the lift," Michael said. "Once it's there, we can raise the thing up to stage level."

"Thanks, I was wondering." Ashlyn tugged one of the desk drawers, but it didn't open. "These look so real. They'd definitely fool you if you didn't know."

When the sofa was in the right place, Michael texted the director. "I'm asking if there's anything else Emma wants brought up. Like maybe the grandfather clock."

It was the perfect time for Ashlyn to sidle up next to

him and continue the kiss from the parking lot—from both parking lots, actually. Instead she climbed through more of the props. "I just found ancient Egypt. Were you doing *Joseph and the Amazing Technicolor Dreamcoat?*"

"Those were from a murder mystery, for a scene set in a museum." He swung his own flashlight around. "It was the first play I stage directed."

"Oh, exciting!" She raised a drop cloth, then froze. A moment after, she had withdrawn the coffin case of a violin. Kneeling before it, she unsnapped it without asking, then shone her light on the instrument strapped inside.

After she was silent two minutes, he felt as if he ought to say something.

Emma texted, "I'd forgotten about the grandfather clock. Bring it up."

Michael said, "You're sad? It's just a broken violin."

"It looks fixable. Some kids don't have instruments, and this one is just fading away." She stroked the wooden body. "If you don't play them, they lose their voices."

"Bring it upstairs and check it out, but it's probably here because something's wrong with it." He shrugged. "Emma agrees with you about the grandfather clock."

Ashlyn glanced at all the things between the clock and the elevator. "It's hollow," Michael added. "We can portage it like a canoe."

While he was right about the weight, he wasn't right about the maneuverability. It took twenty minutes to get the clock into a position where they had any hope of extracting it from all the other pieces, and then they had to carry it. "Remind me never to hide a body with you," he said.

"I'll remind you myself because I don't do murder." She was gasping as they got the thing clear of a merry-go-round pony. "There's also the matter of staining my eternal soul."

"Details." Michael gave the clock a bit more height, and then they had it nearly to the elevator. "Set it upright again. I'll walk it from here," and then he nudged it forward, corner by corner, until the prop stood on the elevator floor. Ashlyn rejoined him holding the prop violin, and he pulled the chain for the bulb.

Her hand found his as they walked up the stairs. This time he did stop and kiss her in the stairwell. She snaked one arm around his waist, the other on the violin handle.

He wanted to stay right there, but the crew had hours of work to do, so with reluctance, he gave one last soft kiss before they returned to the stage floor. Michael pressed the buttons to raise the elevator, and the floor vibrated.

Ashlyn's eyes shifted around. "Is that thing safe?"

"Probably?"

Saying, "Better part of valor," she carried the violin to the first row of seats.

While Michael and one of the guys hefted the sofa to the center stage (much easier here on a clear surface), Ashlyn sat with the violin on her lap. First she examined the whole thing with her flashlight, even though the seating area itself was well-lit. Then she peered inside the curvy holes on the violin body, studying what Michael had assumed was empty space. Next she worked the pegs in the top part, giving gentle twists until one popped loose, and then the next.

With so much work to do, he should ask her to take care of that later, but realistically, she didn't even have to be here. Emma Hall was chatting up the lighting guy, so Michael went to Ashlyn. "Diagnosis?"

"It's not in terrible shape, but the neck might be warped." She pulled a flimsy wooden piece from the case. "The bridge collapsed, but that may have saved it by lowering the tension on the neck for however long it's been in storage. The bow is a disaster, but it's fifty bucks to rehair a bow. I'll put peg compound on the tuning pegs. They're too swollen to turn easily. All the strings need replacing." She swiveled the violin in her hands and peered again into those curvy slits. "There's something written on the bass bar, but I can't read it. At least the soundpost is still upright."

Michael sat a couple seats away from her. "I'm going to interpret all that as a positive?"

"It needs a little help, but it shouldn't have been abandoned. Whoever gave this to you should have asked for it back."

"Maybe they found it in an attic and didn't realize what they had."

"Most people don't." Ashlyn looked up. "Since you don't need this right now, I'll take it to Lindsey. If it's just a matter of sprucing it up, we can do that, and you could maybe do something with the violin. Auction it off to raise money, or maybe if you ever have live music here."

Emma approached. "What's this?"

"She's a violist, and she found this in the prop room."

Ashlyn looked up. "It shouldn't be there. It's going to lose its voice."

Emma shrugged. "We don't do musicals, so it's not an issue."

Ashlyn said, "I'd like to check it out, if you don't mind."

She nodded. "Whatever. It's not as if we're using it." She clapped to get the attention of the men on stage. "If I could get you guys to bring the wood in from outside?"

Ashlyn was about to close the case when she paused and pulled a fabric bag from the second bow slot. She loosened it, and out slid a smaller instrument. "A tin whistle."

Michael shook his head. "I wonder what performance this came from."

Ashlyn said, "*The Music Man*? I know nothing about theater, in case you were unsure." She sighted along the whistle, then raised it to her lips and blew.

A sweet, haunting note filled the theater. At the door, Emma turned.

Ashlyn repositioned her hands, then closed her eyes and blew again, echoing the sound through the theater. Her fingers changed position, and the note went up, then further. She started again on a low note and did a full scale, then back down.

Emma was walking back to them, and Michael battled the urge to stop Ashlyn. This wasn't the time for idle musings about giving voices to mute instruments. They needed to hammer and paint and push and adjust. Ashlyn, on the other hand, kept her eyes closed and started a tune that made all his hair stand on end.

He didn't know it, and he did. It haunted him, sad and beautiful and uplifting all at once. He'd never heard it before, only somehow he'd always known it.

She messed up a note, then backed up and took it again, but after the second mistake, she lowered the instrument. "Sorry. I haven't played one of these for a long time."

Emma clapped. "Bravo! How did you happen to find two instruments you play in the prop room?"

"This was just a hitch-hiker." Ashlyn looked up. "I can play a few, actually."

"You're very good."

"Humans have been playing these for fifty thousand years." She stood with a shy smile. "With all that history, it's an honor to be one among them."

Pizza arrived at one o'clock, and the stage crew broke for lunch. Michael had taken pictures of everyone working, but he'd made sure to get a few especially nice photos of Ashlyn hammering together that mantlepiece. He'd post his photos on the community theater website as well as their social media in a drive to create some publicity ahead of the show.

Attracting tourists was tricky. Only the locals truly cared about the local culture. Some of the visitors had homes up here for the whole summer, and those folks could be induced to purchase season tickets, but that never would keep the theater filled. The majority of tourists were weekenders only interested in having a good time during their numbered hours, and you had such a narrow window to capture their attention. If they arrived on Friday and the performances were Saturday and Sunday, you had to hit the publicity hard and bring them in quickly.

Ashlyn settled next to Michael with her pizza and a bottle of water. One of the guys said, "What were you playing before?"

"'Nearer My God to Thee'. We play it sometimes at funerals, but it's hard to transpose from the viola to the penny whistle. Also I only know the harmony." She shrugged. "Sorry."

The guy said, "Well, I don't play anything, and it sounded great to me."

Michael said, "My parents gave up on me after my school's recorder concert where we made a total hash of 'Hot Cross Buns'."

Ashlyn winked at him. "You realize the recorder is just a version of the penny whistle, right? They give kids plastic instruments and next to no instruction, so it sounds like trash. A real recorder sounds rather nice."

Emma looked startled. "Really? Why do they start on the bad ones?"

"Plastic is cheap. With a recorder, you don't need to position your mouth specially to make notes. You just need to puff into it, as opposed to a trumpet where you need to buzz." Ashlyn was rattling this off without needing to think about it. "A recorder's got diatonic tuning, and the notes are a perfect scale. Finally, the soprano recorder is the right size for a child's fingers. As opposed to, say, a sousaphone." She shrugged. "There are hundreds of complicated pieces you can play on recorders because they're deceptively simple, but they've got depth."

Michael said, "Play it again."

Ashlyn retrieved the penny whistle and warmed up with a scale. He'd never realized before that even the simplest breathing techniques of a professional musician were so much more...well, professional. Powerful. She didn't appear to be blowing with force, but her notes vibrated through the whole auditorium. She thought a moment. "I'm not sure what to play... There's an upper and lower limit to what this will produce." She brightened. "Oh, okay."

She didn't play "Hot Cross Buns". Instead she began a sweet folkish-sounding tune that Michael almost recognized—and then he did. It was "Arkansas Traveler", and she was playing it right there on the whistle as though it had been written for that instrument in the first place.

She got through one verse before meeting his eyes and laughing.

"See, now if we'd done that in kindergarten, we'd all be playing today." The other guy shook his head. "You make it sound easy."

Michael said, "It took twenty years of experience to make it sound easy."

She smiled. "Easy to play, difficult to master. That's the idea. As opposed to the violin, which is difficult to play and then difficult to master."

As if that had reminded her, she set down her pizza and brought back the violin case. This time when she opened it up, she removed things from the compartment beneath the violin's neck. "Rosin. You're supposed to use this to make the bow slippery, but it's long since turned to rock." She pulled up a tiny metal hinge with a long screw. "That's a fine-tuner. Some people have these on the tailpiece to make the tuning adjustments easier." A U-shaped fork. She banged it into the metal leg of a seat, and it resonated. "This poor baby was in nearly play-ready condition when she got buried. I wish we knew who left her behind."

Uncomfortable, Michael glanced at Emma. "Could we find the old owner?"

Emma shrugged. "I can't even imagine what performance it came from. For all we know, it might have been salvaged at random from an antique store."

Ashlyn worked the light wooden bridge under the strings until it was upright, then started tightening the pegs at the top. "I'm going to tune it a fifth down," she said, almost as if asking for permission except that she wasn't. "I don't want to take a chance that it isn't ready to withstand that kind of tension. It'll have to sound like a small viola for a while." With the instrument on her lap, she plucked strings and adjusted pegs, starting in the center and then working outward, finally testing the center ones again.

She'd hit that tuning fork before and sent an A all around the theater, but right now, she was doing it from memory. What would it be like to hear all those notes in your head and know what they were?

Given his genes, shouldn't Michael be able to do that?

Standing in her lap, facing her, the violin began answering when she asked for sounds. Instead of relaxing, though, her focus intensified as the notes sounded truer and truer, and she started plucking parts of the strings to make them sound the same as the open ones. Finally, she tightened the bow. "Here goes nothing."

She tucked the violin under her chin and drew out a long, sweet sound, then laughed. "You know the joke that a violinist's fingers are like lightning because they never strike twice in the same place?" No, Michael had never heard that joke. "I'm going to be even worse because I'm used to an instrument that's a lot bigger."

Michael offered, "Only fifteen percent."

"Wait until my fingers are all crowded together in the higher positions." She worked slowly through a scale, stopping every so often to re-take the notes. "I wish Lindsey were here. She'd make it sound awesome."

Ashlyn was making it sound awesome all by herself, and Michael had no such desire for Lindsey to be here. He wanted Ashlyn to perform for him. For them all, but really for him. He wanted to see her work with a valueless combination of wood and horse hair and metal to produce sounds that mimicked a human voice and filled the space between the walls. Ashlyn was giving her heart to this abandoned creature and breathing life into it, giving it a voice and a history, as well as possibly a future.

Once she was more comfortable with the fingering, she started a piece he recognized, the "Ave Maria". This she played all the way through, bringing the song up through the lowest register of the violin-turned-viola and right up to the highest notes. Her eyes closed, and then she got to her feet as if she needed movement to bring this one to fruition. Again her body shifted with the playing, her hips and her spine and her shoulders all in motion while that instrument responded to her touch.

Michael was responding too, his heart rising and falling with the song while he grew ensorcelled by how she merged with the tune, until there was no more distinction between the player and the sound being played.

You can do that? The thought kept rifling through him. *You really can do that?*

Before this moment, even knowing his family were all musicians, it had never occurred to Michael where music came from. Music came from the radio. Or it came from concert halls. Songs involved words. But here was one person, one "found" instrument that was jury-rigged to work at all, creating a melody extracted into its purest form.

Her soul. She was voicing her soul. No wonder she'd been offended by a violin losing its voice. The violin in her hands was beautiful.

She was beautiful.

She drew out a few final long notes, her finger pulsing on the string to make the notes vibrate while the whole instrument resonated. Then she lowered the violin and opened her eyes. The muse had disappeared. Ashlyn had returned.

She offered Michael a nervous smile. "I'm sorry. It's playable, but that wasn't very good."

His heart thudded.

Emma said, "After what you just did, bring it home. Make it play for real."

"It was more than very good." Michael made room so

Ashlyn could sit beside him. "It was like hearing another world."

CHAPTER EIGHTEEN

Everything ached by the time Ashlyn got home, although it shouldn't have. Playing the viola demanded she be in good shape, since for the duration of her playing she had both arms higher than her heart. That meant a lot of core strength and arm strength, not to mention awesome posture. She and Lindsey did Pilates videos on a semi-regular basis, but even playing their instruments a couple hours a day kept them in reasonable condition.

"Reasonable condition" had not been sufficient for shifting furniture and portaging a faux grandfather clock. Ashlyn's arms hurt, and during the drive home, her back and legs had gotten stiff. She'd have a great time working the ice cream stand tomorrow, wouldn't she?

In the kitchen, she found Corwin with Lindsey, splitting a platter of nachos. Lindsey brightened. "Pull up a chair. Is that a violin?"

"It's a violin." Ashlyn set the case on her seat. "The

theater people had shoved it into the basement to rot, and I convinced them that's a crime against all that's holy."

Corwin reached for the case. "Idiots. Even if they didn't care about playing it, they could have sold the thing."

Ashlyn threw her jacket over the chair back. "Typically clueless. How many people know what a decent instrument costs?"

Corwin opened it. "No one, the same way nobody knows what a decent musician costs."

Lindsey raised the pitch of her voice. "*Oh, but you'll do it for the exposure!*"

"If I want to expose myself, I'm going to get arrested." Corwin pulled out the violin and examined it in the light. "Not too bad. Dad had students playing on worse."

Ashlyn said, "It has a nice tone, but I—"

"—tuned it like a viola," Corwin muttered as he plucked the strings.

"—wasn't sure it would be able to handle the higher tension if I tuned it correctly."

"Yeah, snapping the neck off the body would run into money." Corwin tried to turn the pegs. "It needs a liberal dose of peg dope, too. And better strings. Oh, and the bow is a nightmare. You played this thing?"

Lindsey said, "To be fair, how much worse could it sound than an actual viola?" and Ashlyn giggled.

Corwin spent the next few minutes lubricating the pegs (and muttering imprecations about people who left sweet violins to die) while Lindsey explained Corwin's presence. "He still isn't sure about Michael. We want to rule out any chance that Michael somehow used Corwin's DNA to pretend at being the long-lost baby Dalton."

Ashlyn said to Corwin, "So you're going to submit it?"

He huffed. "Don't say 'submit'. I'm not in submission to a set of genetic codes I never chose and which doubtless have it in for me." Corwin plucked the E string that was now playing an E rather than an A. "What I am doing is sacrificing myself in order to protect our mother."

Ashlyn said, "While I acknowledge your generous

sacrifice, how would anyone even know to steal your DNA?"

Corwin tested the A string, then the D, then the G. He adjusted the D. "You don't get it: that information was out there. Some of her relatives knew she had a baby. There were doctors and nurses who knew, plus the adoption facilitators who established for a fact they were liars and thieves. Liars and thieves only move on to other methods of lying and thieving. Steal a baby, then thirty years later, you can send back an adult to steal everything else."

As conspiracy theories went, it wasn't a bad one.

Lindsey added, "Mom likely tells her doctors and nurses when they ask her medical history."

Corwin started plucking adjacent strings at the same time. The instrument sounded true, but then the D slipped, so he adjusted it again. "With that information, and Dad incapacitated, it's a perfect storm if you pretend to be that missing Castleton. I refuse to be a party to their deception. I'll send my DNA kit, and if it turns out I'm in the system twice, they'll tell me I have an identical twin."

The D kept going out of tune. "It's not the peg," Lindsey observed. "That string is dying."

"Not a surprise if it's been in someone's basement for a hundred months. Once I tightened it all the way, it lost the plot." Corwin tucked the instrument under his chin and laid the bow on it. "Linz, I need some rosin."

"You need a better bow. That thing looks like it's been through a war." Lindsey took it from his hands. "This must have been a student-grade instrument, but right now I wouldn't even give it to Jason."

Ashlyn laughed.

Corwin said, "To celebrate my capitulation, Lindsey had me make nachos. Go ahead."

Ashlyn settled herself in the empty seat as Lindsey got a rosin cake from the music stand in the living room. Corwin had buried the nachos with anything he'd found in their house: seasoned ground beef, cheese, olives, salsa, sour cream. They didn't have an avocado or else there would have been guacamole. Ashlyn loaded a plate and armed herself with napkins.

Lindsey returned. "Remember that night the vendor meal was nachos, and Jason refused to eat because he didn't want to get his fingers greasy?"

Corwin rolled his eyes. "Suddenly I remember why I switched to guitar."

"Fretted violins never made a big splash." Lindsey sat at the table rosining the bow. "I know why he refused, but at the time I was like, dude, that's why we have wet naps and soap and water. No, he'd rather starve than risk oil residue on the fingerboard."

Ashlyn rubbed her chin. "Linz, remind me: how many shreds of remorse did we experience as we devoured his share?"

"None. Not even one. Life is far tastier that way. Plus, he uses chopsticks on cheese puffs. I get protecting the wood finish, but for me that's a bridge too far." Lindsey took the violin from Corwin. "Is the D still off?"

Corwin snorted. "It's in freefall. Play way up the G string if you want any of those notes."

Lindsey played a three-octave G scale, starting with the open string and working all the way to the top of the E string, her wrist cocked back over the body of the violin as she reached the highest of the high notes.

Ashlyn applauded. "You did that even after nachos."

"I'm going to go ahead and believe this poor sweetheart has seen a lot worse than taco grease." Lindsey went back down the scale, using the D string this time. "Oh, foul. You're right, that string is dead."

Ashlyn looked at Corwin. "You'll send your DNA kit tomorrow? How long do the results take to come back?"

Lindsey said, "A week or two. Corwin's nominally going through a different service, so their timing may be different." Lindsey played a series of notes on the higher strings. "The tone isn't too bad. I may offer to buy it on behalf of the school, especially since Jason borrowed the star violin."

Corwin squinted. "Am I forgetting something, or does Jason not have a violin worth more than this house?"

"It's worth less than this house, but he was adamant that humidity not taint his precious darling." Lindsey turned to Ashlyn. "What did he name it?"

Ashlyn shrugged. "I'm not aware that he gave it a name."

"I can't imagine he didn't give that violin a name." Lindsey kept playing. "Did you play the stage crew a private concert? I don't suppose the theater-owner rushed down the aisle with tears in her eyes, begging for the quartet to come serenade the town?"

Corwin said, "Which theater?"

Ashlyn took more chips. "Haverstock Community Playhouse. We were building props for a performance next week, so no owner was around. At least the director applauded."

"Bummer. Because can you imagine a whole concert night dedicated to just us? No wedding marches, just Mozart and Beethoven and Haydn." Lindsey switched up the melody. "This bow is the pits. I'm not sure it's even worth rehairing. It's stiff, and it's too heavy."

Ashlyn raised her eyebrows. "Any chance it's a viola bow?"

Lindsey's eyes flared, and she held it away from her. "Criminy, you're right. The frog is rounded."

"Might explain why it's too stiff for you, then." Ashlyn chuckled. "And why I didn't notice a difference."

"How'd they even get a viola bow paired with...you know, forget it. I've seen dumber things."

Corwin's brows contracted. "Back up a minute. You went to Haverstock to build props for a community theater production. You were with Michael?"

Lindsey clamped the violin back under her chin. "Corwin, can you check the time? Because I think it's *Hey Look Ashlyn Is A Grown Adult* o'clock."

"I get that, but you don't know anything about him other than he's hot."

Ashlyn swallowed her bite of nachos. "That's all it takes

for me. A hot scammer bats his eyes, and I drive two hours to assemble theater sets."

Corwin growled, "And steal their violins."

Ashlyn wiped her fingers on the napkin. "The violin called for help from their basement. I needed to move four sofas, a sleigh, and the prow of a sailing ship before I could extract it."

"Traitor." Corwin could have been joking, but his eyes were narrow. "You're betraying Dad by messing around with this guy without even establishing who he is." He stood. "I came here to talk things out, and fine. But that's treachery. How do I know *you* didn't find out about this mystery baby and steal my DNA?"

Ashlyn's stomach clenched, but it was Lindsey who exclaimed, "Corwin! That's beyond paranoid—it's bonkers!"

"Bonkers is coming on to a guy who's claiming to be the long-lost kid in a family you're already a member of. That makes him your step-brother."

Lindsey huffed. "It makes him no such thing, even if we'd adopted her, which we didn't. She and Michael didn't grow up together, and they share exactly zero DNA except the stuff that keeps us from being chimpanzees." She laid the violin back in the case. "Paranoid is assuming Ashlyn uncovered a secret baby and then stole your toothbrush to obtain DNA."

Corwin's eyes glimmered. "Or one of the people who knew about the secret baby paid her off to steal my toothbrush."

Ashlyn's eyes filled with tears. "I would never."

Lindsey pointed to the door. "Out. Get out of my apartment. You're not insulting Ashlyn at her own table."

Corwin glowered at Ashlyn. "You always wanted to be a member of the family."

She had. From the minute she'd met Bob and Susan, she'd wished she were a Castleton.

He snarled, "Conning our mother is not how you do it."

Lindsey yanked open the door. "Out. I'll shovel chips

into a bag for you, but go."

Ashlyn could barely see Corwin standing over her, arms crossed. "You know I'm right."

Lindsey said, "Submit your DNA, and when you turn up as Michael's identical twin, we can start accusing one another of fraud. Until then, you're just being a toad."

Ashlyn pressed her face into her napkins, and her shoulders jerked.

Corwin sneered. "Crocodile tears?"

The door slammed behind him, and then Lindsey was kneeling beside Ashlyn's chair, arms around her. "I'm so sorry. I shouldn't have brought up where you were."

Ashlyn wouldn't hurt Mom and Dad. She would never hurt them. She owed them her life. She owed them for the home they'd given her when she'd have been shunted back into the foster care system. She owed them for the endless music lessons and the encouragement to look further than surviving the next day. She owed them for her first instrument and then for a place to live with that instrument. With her mother, she'd never have been able to do that. She'd never have been able to go to college. She'd have come home one day to find Rachel had sold the viola for a hundred bucks to get her next fix, and Ashlyn would have been screamed at to go back to whatever minimum wage job she'd landed just to keep food on the table. Rachel spent months at a time living in a car, lately not even her own car.

Ashlyn would never hurt Mom and Dad.

If Michael was scamming them, then Michael was a threat, but she'd never willingly participate in that. Except... Except the more she entangled herself with him, the harder it would be to recognize if he wasn't who he said he was.

She shuddered. Lindsey held her tighter.

Ashlyn choked out, "I wouldn't do that."

"No one thinks you would. Even Corwin doesn't. Think about what he's suggesting. How would you even get his DNA?"

"Apparently I stole his toothbrush."

"A toothbrush wouldn't do it. They'd tell Michael he was related to the Procter and Gamble corporation and shares forty-seven percent of his DNA with a tube of Colgate. Corwin's such an idiot."

Ashlyn pushed away her plate and crossed her arms on the table. She laid her head on her forearms and went limp.

Lindsey said, "What did you play for Michael?"

"The 'Ave Maria'." She struggled to breathe. "They had a penny whistle too. I played 'Nearer My God to Thee'."

"Sweet. Is it in your backpack?" Lindsey went looking. "We could clean this up. How's the sound?"

A long clear note reverberated through the apartment.

"Oh, that's darling." Lindsey went back to her seat.

After a few minutes, Ashlyn murmured, "I shouldn't get close to Michael. Not until we know for sure."

"Mom verified every bit of his story, and he supplied the name that would have been blocked out on his amended birth certificate. Even if Mom told medical staff she was pregnant four times, she wouldn't have told them the baby's name." Lindsey waited a moment, and then added, "Think about the baby pictures he showed us."

Michael had come last Wednesday armed with a dozen baby pictures. There were the first photos of him at two days old, but then in addition were a few from the next months, and one from his first birthday. There were some from when he was older, as well. Mom had gone through them all, but most especially she'd focused on the earliest photos.

She'd recognized her own baby. In that photo of Michael's first day with the Knolwoods, she'd seen the baby she'd last laid eyes on two days before.

Lindsey said, "If this team of phantom scammers went through the trouble to obtain the real Dalton's newborn photos, then they have the real Dalton."

Ashlyn closed her eyes.

"Not only that, but you saw his high school graduation

photo. He looked exactly like Mom in her graduation picture." Lindsey huffed. "If Michael is working that hard to defraud us, I'm kind of rooting for him to succeed," and that startled a laugh from Ashlyn.

"Corwin disagrees."

"Corwin is being a jackapple because Michael just dethroned him as son and heir to the resplendent Castleton empire." Lindsey raised her eyebrows as Ashlyn picked up her head. "There isn't a judge in the world who would entertain the case he made against you, so try to laugh at him for being an idiot. Or pity him for grasping at straws. But don't under any circumstances give what he said a second thought. I certainly won't."

Ashlyn sighed. "Michael, though. Should I back off until everything settles?"

"That's up to you." Lindsey frowned. "I'm a little worried that he might be attaching to you as a way of getting closer to the rest of us. Not in a scammy way. Just that he's so excited to be here that he wants to make sure he stays."

Ashlyn bit her lip. "He told me horror stories about adoptees who find their birth families only to get disowned or rejected."

"Whereas if he married you, we'd have to invite him to Thanksgiving. Unless we go all-in and disown you too." Lindsey flinched. "Oh, crud. Thanksgiving. The holidays this year. I can't even imagine."

Ashlyn put her face in her hands. "Then don't."

"Yeah." Lindsey picked up the violin and started unwinding the dead string. "I'd rather imagine good things right now. I'd rather imagine that Michael is really my brother, and someday, if you marry him, you'll really be my sister."

CHAPTER NINETEEN

Ashlyn became mysteriously unavailable all week just at a time when Michael wanted her more than anything.

Instead he spent the evenings at the theater in a race to ready all the props for the premiere performance on Friday. He'd scheduled the day off work because invariably they'd have far too much to do and not enough time to do it, plus the company was holding dress rehearsals every night.

"It's so much easier when a traveling group comes through," Emma muttered.

Michael suggested, "You could have Ashlyn's quartet perform one night, just to get bodies in the seats."

The community theater aimed never to have an empty weekend, primarily to keep people in the habit of checking back to see what was going on. Still, Emma didn't think there'd be interest in a string concert.

Ashlyn was terse over texts. Had he overwhelmed her by

calling her beautiful? Was she upset because they'd been kissing in the stairwell?

"Will you come to one of the performances?" he asked.

She replied, "Not sure. We picked up another client for Saturday evening."

She could get there for the Sunday matinee. He knew she could. Or the week after. "If you can, I'll hold free tickets at the box office."

To which Ashlyn only replied, "Okay."

Okay.

Not okay. Not okay that she wasn't sending him pictures from the ice cream stand or random thoughts throughout the day, nor even responding to his own texts with more than one-word answers.

He did get a message from Susan, though. "I wanted to see you next week if you're free one night. Maybe Monday?"

He replied, "I hate to be *that guy*, but we're having five performances this weekend. On Monday, I planned to sleep."

She sent back, "That's funny. Church musicians usually feel the same on Easter Monday. Will you be caught up on sleep by Wednesday?"

When he agreed, she texted, "Is six too early? What do you want for dinner?"

Your mother should know what you like to eat. This weird mix of intimacy and strangeness kept Michael off-balance. The only one he felt comfortable with was Ashlyn because he had no expectation that she'd be alike to him, so he texted Ashlyn. "Susan invited me to dinner on Wednesday. You'll be there?"

Half an hour later, Ashlyn replied, "She didn't invite me, so no."

He replied, "Are you that formal over there?"

Her answer: "Yes."

He studied that answer far longer than it should have taken to parse one single word. The reason? The Castletons weren't in any way that formal. From everything he'd seen, the family members moved in and out of each others' lives with a casual ease. If an extra person showed up for dinner, everyone shifted the chairs closer together. It might be different for Ashlyn because she wasn't theirs by blood, but he'd seen nothing to indicate she was ever unwelcome.

Instead he finally addressed the actual question, and he did it by calling from the back of the theater in the few minutes before dress rehearsal.

She answered, which he'd figured wasn't going to happen. He'd have downgraded to texting if she'd sent him to voicemail. "Hi."

"Hi." He braced himself. "Why are you upset with me?"

In his head he had a list of evidence in case she tried to deny it, but when she finally spoke, she said, "It's hard to explain. I'm not upset really. Not with you."

Okay...? Michael said, "So...unsettled? And who with?"

He heard a door shut. Had she gone somewhere for privacy?

"I don't want to move too quickly. There's a lot going on."

He said, "You're being vague. Did I hurt your feelings?"

"No!" There were background noises. Wherever she was, she was puttering around. "Um, I talked to Corwin. He's going to submit his DNA kit, so in a couple of weeks you'll get a notice that you have a brother. I thought I ought to warn you."

Michael paced through the back of the auditorium. "Corwin was boycotting his DNA."

"Yeah."

She sounded miserable. Corwin had to be the key. "Corwin was also boycotting me. You're using Corwin's DNA as a cross-check to make sure I'm who I say I am."

Anger bubbled up, but Michael tried to keep it contained with movement. Right. Because after their mother confirmed everything, of course Michael still wasn't trustworthy. Of course he was still orchestrating some major scheme to...to do what? To infiltrate the Castletons and steal their worldly possessions? Which were nothing? If everyone in the quartet was working a day job in addition to playing three gigs every weekend, then guess what? A scammer wouldn't be going after them. He'd be going after a high-class family full of professionals who wore suits to work.

Ashlyn said, "Corwin doesn't believe you, but weirdly enough, he also doesn't believe Mom. He accused me of all sorts of things. I don't want to hurt your feelings."

"You're failing at that," Michael muttered.

"I'm sorry." Her voice broke. "This got too complicated too fast. If there's any chance Susan or Bob would get hurt, I can't participate."

"Susan invited me for dinner at her house on Wednesday."

"I know! But Corwin wants proof, and I don't know how to give him that." All background noise had ceased.

"I've given you everything I can. If you want to re-submit my DNA yourself—as in, actually do a cheek swab and seal it up and mail it off yourself—then I'm game with that. If you want to have a doctor test all of us, that's fine too."

Ashlyn went silent.

"But you're treating me like a criminal because Corwin's indulging in a snit, and that's not fair."

She breathed, "You're right. It's not."

"You're acting like I'm asking you to change loyalties. Of course you're loyal to them. They're your family." He made his voice stern. "You're saying you don't want to move too quickly, but what you're doing is stalling until everyone else approves. It doesn't work that way. I didn't beg permission from my parents before I asked you out."

His mother wouldn't have given it, that's for sure. If Corwin thought Michael a scammer, Michael's parents would by the same scorecard consider Ashlyn a social climber and a leech.

Ashlyn softened her voice. "You're the only one here in possession of all the information."

Michael said, "On the contrary, you're the one with all

the information because you're the one who grew up there."

"That's not what I mean, and I wish you'd stop asking me about everything. I can't give you my childhood, and you wouldn't want it." Ashlyn struggled to get a grip. "The information I mean is, you're the only one who knows your goal."

He huffed. "I thought I was being clear. What else do you think my goal is?"

"I have no idea. Do you want to replace your family? I don't think so. Do you want to mine us—by which I mean me—for details so you can flounce back to your upper-class life with all your questions answered? Do you want to cozy up to us so you have a second family? I can't tell."

Michael stopped in place.

Ashlyn said, "Tell me, then. What's your endgame?"

He found himself staring at the designs on the theater wall. "I... That I never figured out."

A pause. "Really?"

"Really. Whatever happened next was going to depend on what I found. This moved a lot faster than I expected."

Her chuckle sounded nervous. "Didn't you think you'd find someone?"

"Not this. I figured eventually I'd get the name of a man who might have been my father, and he'd be just as surprised as I was. We'd track down my mother someday, and she'd maybe want something to do with me or maybe not. There might be half siblings, and I'd have to locate them one by one."

Ashlyn said, "Not so very different."

"It's completely different. I found an intact family. That's like hitting the lottery. Instead of piecing together everything like a puzzle, there's the same combination of traits in all of them." Michael was breathing faster. "I don't have to imagine what my biological parents would have been like together because they were together. I've got a complete story behind all the mysteries."

Ashlyn sounded stunned. "Yeah. I can see that."

Michael said, "As of now, I have a medical history. I have a genealogy. I have ancestors. I have names and places. If someone asks me where my people came from, I know. When I find myself favoring one thing over another, I can look backward." He stopped. "That's it. I can look backward. Before, I could only look forward. The Castletons have given me a rearview mirror."

Ashlyn was awed. "If you have something quirky, like you've always been able to put your palms flat on the floor with your knees locked, you have three other people who might be able to do it too."

"Exactly! I never grew up seeing anyone quite like myself. Except now I can. Susan says there's evidence in things like how I stand, how I move." Emma was on the stage waving him over, but he shook his head and kept talking. "I never planned on that. I thought every answer would lead to another question."

Ashlyn said, "You're off-script too?"

"Very much off-script." The tone of her voice had changed. Michael decided to take a chance. "Do you trust me?"

"I..."

Wow, that note in her voice. She was torn.

That meant she did trust him, but other people were pouring their fear into her. "You, Ashlyn. Not everyone else. If it's just you and me, do you trust me?"

Ashlyn lowered her voice. "I think you're telling the truth."

That wasn't trust, but close enough. "Then don't let Corwin get to you. I will offer to Susan that we can re-do my testing howsoever she wants so there's no doubt. But now answer another question: even if Corwin hires his own private physician to perform DNA tests on every one of us, in his presence, and the results come back the same, would Corwin back down?"

Ashlyn said, "Corwin isn't like you. Corwin responds with a lot more energy."

Michael said, "I'm also older than he is."

"What does that have to do with anything?"

"I used to be stubborn too."

Ashlyn laughed. "You're plenty stubborn. This whole conversation is you being stubborn. I'm the one who's balancing everyone's concerns. You want what you want."

Michael raised his eyebrows. "Well."

"Look, if Mom asks us to see you on Wednesday, I'll be there. I still don't want to rush. I'm emotionally tapped out, and it's even affecting my playing. I don't have the energy for a whirlwind romance."

Michael laughed. "Whirlwind?"

"You're doing the Castleton thing to sweep me off my feet, right?"

Was that what Bob had done to Susan? Swept her off her feet, out-stubborned her, impressed her, convinced her, and then what? Waited another five years for her?

Michael frowned. "I wasn't aware whirlwinds were a requirement."

Ashlyn hadn't tried to sweep him off his feet, but she'd been doing it. Instead of grandiose gestures, she was doing it with peekaboo glimpses into her soul. She revealed the most tantalizing bits of herself through her music, through her touches, and through her concern for Susan. Then she'd cover them back up and slip away again.

After the pain of her childhood, she'd want to be cautious. He wasn't her mother, though. He wasn't going to feed his own needs at her expense.

Ashlyn said, "Maybe it's like playing multiple instruments. Maybe sweeping people off their feet is a learned behavior rather than innate."

Michael said, "Can I meet you again and give it another shot? Now that I know you require a whirlwind, I'll work on my technique," and Ashlyn laughed.

He added, "Can you come to one of the performances?"

"Maybe Sunday evening," she said, and with that, he'd beaten Corwin.

CHAPTER TWENTY

Wednesday evening, Ashlyn got home from Rockway's long enough to take a five-minute shower before driving with Lindsey to Mom and Dad's.

Mom's. Mom's house, drat it.

They arrived to a house smelling of roasted chicken, onions, and potatoes. Lindsey set the table while Ashlyn made herself useful assembling a salad. Although cheerful, Mom seemed nervous.

Not as nervous as Ashlyn. Blast it.

Michael could rush over her defenses like seawater. It made no sense. He was forceful, sure, but Lindsey and Corwin were also forceful, and they didn't railroad her. Not that Michael was railroading her. It wasn't manipulation either. Somehow, she'd walk into a conversation knowing what she wanted and come out the other side wanting something else. Was that a Knolwood thing? Maybe he should have been a lawyer.

Alternatively, maybe he'd inherited Susan's knack of looking right at you and reading your heart. Susan could ask just the right questions to turn you around. She kept it subtle, though, never completing the turn in the same conversation. Instead she'd leave you sitting with your discomfort so you kept tending it, and the next time you spoke, you'd find your mind changed about something you'd always known to be true.

When Michael arrived, Ashlyn hugged him, and he didn't make things awkward by kissing her. During dinner, he played the role of polite guest. "Everything is wonderful." "Please pass the rolls?" Mom had questions for him, but mostly surface-level. Michael again dived deep: did you guys always do dinner together? Did you usually have friends dropping in? What kind of activities did the kids do after school?

He didn't talk to Ashlyn through all this. What would happen if she rose from the table, walked out the door, and just didn't come back? Would he notice before dessert? But then he smiled at her, and she warmed back up. It was all the different people competing for his attention. There would be time for him and her later.

Mom said, "You have no idea how much noise this house has endured."

Lindsey snickered. "If you use a stethoscope, you can still hear vibrations in the two-by-fours."

Ashlyn said, "Corwin would be in the basement with the band of the week. Sierra was usually in the living room with either the piano or the harp. Lindsey and I had the violin and the viola, but sometimes we'd go on a jag with some other instrument."

Lindsey said, "Every so often, Dad would pay one of us to sit on the front porch waiting for a delivery, and you knew another instrument was coming. We'd make the delivery guy wait while we uncrated the thing to make sure it arrived okay, and inside, there could be anything."

Michael raised his eyebrows. "Anything?"

"Bagpipes," Ashlyn teased, and Michael's eyes flew wide.

He'd probably never considered bagpipes an instrument, but then again, bagpipes had as many jokes about them as did the viola.

Lindsey said, "My favorite was the tubax," and Mom sighed.

Ashlyn said to Michael, "The tubax is taller than Corwin."

Susan said, "No, you're thinking of the contrabass sarrusophone."

Ashlyn giggled. "Oh, right."

Michael bit his lip. "I didn't know those were instruments that existed."

"Oh, and the soprillo." Lindsey reached across the table and patted Michael's hand. "No one knows these instruments exist. My father had a slight problem with collecting instruments that served exactly zero purpose. I don't think you can move a contrabass sarrusophone unless you have a truck, so what are you going to do with the thing? The tubax is a mere three feet tall and weighs only twenty pounds, but even that only got invented in 1999, so it's not like you're going to wander into the music store and impulse-buy sheet music to play Disney tunes on it."

Ashlyn said, "Dad transposed everything in his head. So he *did* do a medley of Disney tunes on it. Or a dozen Beatles songs."

"Yeah, but realistically speaking? He got those instruments because he wanted them."

All of them. Dad had room in his heart for all the kids and all the instruments. He'd have loved Michael. He'd have loved him so much, and there was no way now to be sure he'd understand.

Mom shook her head. "Your father always believed 'tax deductible' meant it was free. We had some tight years where I'd tell Bob the income tax return was earmarked to pay for an oil delivery, and he'd say, 'But I wanted a contratuba."

Ashlyn rested her chin on her hands and looked at

Michael. "Mom and Dad loaded us into the car one day, and we drove five hours to Boston, where someone slipped us into the backstage of the Boston Pops. We were supposedly there for a performance, but we arrived two hours early."

Mom said, "Remember that our students ended up all over the world, which is why no one was surprised when Jason landed in the Los Angeles Philharmonic. One of our former students was performing that night at Symphony Hall, and Bob asked him to sneak us into the backstage area because they had an octobass, and that was the only way he'd ever get to play one."

The look on Michael's face made Ashlyn laugh. "No, really, he went right for this bass fiddle that was like twelve feet tall and had only three strings. Then he started figuring it out because obviously you can't play that with your hands. It had pedals and levers and clamps, and the player had to stand on a platform. None of us should have been anywhere near that thing because there are only seven in existence. Dad bowed this super-low note, and the floor boards shook."

Lindsey said, "That note is still rolling its way through the earth's core, and in nine years, someone in Australia is going to wake up hearing a C."

Michael exclaimed, "How do you even tune that? Do you get on a ladder?"

Ashlyn said, "Remember how much trouble I had with that broken violin's pegs? Multiply that by fifty."

Lindsey huffed. "Mom complains about *our* noise, but she conveniently ignores Dad's noise."

Michael grinned, and he looked amazing. "Maybe that's the point of living, to make as much noise as you can."

"Beautiful noise," Mom corrected. "Some people's noise is just cacophony."

While they cleaned up after dinner, Mom stood, looking nervous. "I have a few things to show you."

She brought out a cardboard box, something for shipping a few paperback novels. The flaps were marled with age, the top labeled "Instruction manuals and warrantees." Ashlyn had never seen this before.

As Mom started removing the contents one at a time, each in a plastic bag, her voice was thin. "These are your things. Everyone wanted me to forget you, so I was able to keep only what I could hide. I couldn't have a real memory box, and I labeled this with the most boring thing I could think of."

Ashlyn blinked back tears.

Mom was wistful. "A lot of this won't mean anything to you. This is a receipt from the day before I confirmed I was pregnant, the last 'normal' day. This is an appointment card from my doctor's office when I was seven months. After you were born, I saved whatever scraps I could find of your existence because everyone had thrown away anything that might remind me of you."

Michael sat looking pale. "Why would they do that?"

"They thought I could be happy." She set aside a letter, the envelope taped together. "This was from Bob, laying out a scheme so we could get married and raise you. My parents ripped it up. I climbed out the window at two o'clock in the morning to get it from the trash so I could tape the pieces back together. After that, Bob had to send letters to my friend Amanda's house." Then she paused as a pink and blue stretchy cap came out, still in its plastic bag. "This was your baby hat, the one they put on you right after you were born. I didn't like the hats on you, so I kept taking them off, and the nurses kept getting another to put on. This one ended up in my bag, and I sealed it in plastic because it still smelled like you. I wanted to keep the smell as long as I could."

At the bottom of the box were a few photos. "These are the only photos I had. Amanda took them, so my parents didn't know they existed." She spread them out so Michael could see. A picture of his face as a newborn, wearing the pink and blue stretchy cap and with his clenched hands up by his face. Pictures of a very young Susan holding her baby. She looked exactly like a younger Sierra, but baby

Dalton was wrapped up and hard to see. And finally, a picture of Dalton's hand resting on hers.

Lindsey said, "He looked a lot like Sierra."

Mom nodded. "I thought that too. It was hard when I had her."

Ashlyn said, "And Dad never saw him?"

She shook her head. "Dad was in England by then. I wasn't pushy enough and didn't insist on enough. I trusted them. I should have stood up for myself." She looked down. "I regret a lot about the way things worked out. I parented you three very differently because of what happened with Dalton."

You three. Ashlyn looked at her lap.

Michael looked again through the pictures. "I can ask my mother if she can copy her photos for you."

Mom tensed. "Please don't involve your parents."

Michael shrugged. "It's not a problem. My mother has said she'd love to meet you."

"I don't want to meet them. I'm sorry, but that's not something I can handle." Mom took everything back into the box. "I can't have your babyhood back. I accept that. But there's no way I can deal with your parents."

Michael cringed back into his own skin, and Ashlyn reached for his hand under the table. He started, as if he'd forgotten Ashlyn was even there. She let go, stung.

Mom blinked hard. "We don't have the past, and Bob's illness is forcing me to accept that we don't have the future, either. All we have is the present, so that will have to suffice."

Before the end of the evening, Lindsey had a mandolin on her lap and was picking through "Boléro". Based on Michael's expression, in his world that wasn't exactly normal.

What was normal? Ashlyn's mother hadn't had a household littered with instruments, but there hadn't been food either. Once Ashlyn had arrived here, food was just there in the fridge, and instruments were just available. If you picked up an apple out of the bin, you could eat it. If you picked up a trumpet, someone would offer a couple of pointers before turning you loose.

Mom said, "Do you want to see the instrument room?"

Lindsey looked up abruptly, and Ashlyn thought of Jason snapping at her not to give any violins to Michael. Thought of Corwin accusing Michael of scamming them to get their valuables.

Michael laughed. "Can I see that tubax thing?"

Corwin's boyhood bedroom had become the instrument repository. The lights flared on, and Michael gasped.

"Yeah, it's a bunch." Lindsey walked through stands of instruments and hefted a case out of the back. "I think this one's the tubax."

Michael kept scanning the room, wide-eyed. Instruments were rack-mounted to the walls. Chairs and music stands and instrument stands clustered at the center, and between the windows towered a floor-to-ceiling bookshelf packed with sheet music.

Lindsey shifted the tubax out of the velvet form inside the case, then stood it on the floor. "It's coiled differently so you can sit while playing it, but see, it has feet." She laughed. "Kind of like the cello has that peg. This weighs a ton, though."

Ashlyn said, "Some of the big ones, in order to play, you need to do deadlifts on a regular basis."

Michael gestured around the room. "You guys play all of these?"

"Maybe not often," Mom said. "Bob got the tubax for fun. The lowest notes vibrate the floor boards." She positioned herself in front of the tubax while Ashlyn took Dad's viola off the wall and started tuning.

Michael said, "You told me if an instrument doesn't play,

it loses its voice."

Mom blew into the tubax. It called out, resonant. She did half a scale, then ended with a deep, "pop goes the weasel," which made Michael laugh.

She said, "Not a risk in this household. I let the students play these, and we've loaned out violins to professional musicians who don't have the resources to buy a professional grade instrument. Jason borrowed one for a few years."

Lindsey looked over her shoulder. "I didn't know that."

Mom played the tubax again, the theme from "Ride of the Valkyries." Michael was goggle-eyed, and it was hilarious. What was that he always said about "just" being a musician? When you could "just" pick up any instrument and "just" play it? As if.

Ashlyn drew the bow across the viola's strings, then adjusted the tuning on the A. The moment after, Lindsey had a violin off the wall. Not Dad's best (a German violin he'd named Frederika), but still a sweet instrument. When Mom stopped playing, Lindsey asked, "Which one did Jason borrow?"

"I don't honestly remember."

"Ah well. I'm not curious enough to ask him. Ash, give me an A," and then Lindsey tuned to Ashlyn.

Michael folded his arms and leaned against the door. He was so tall, his legs so long, his smile easy but at the same time a little smug. "Do I get a private concert?"

Ashlyn beamed at him. "Either that or a private lesson. Pick an instrument and I'll show you how to make some noise of your own."

Michael's brow furrowed. "Why would I want to do that?"

Ashlyn froze, but Lindsey rolled her eyes. "Dude, it's in the genes. You make the noise, and then you turn that noise into joy. *That's* why you should want to do that. There is no *just* about being a musician."

Lindsey started playing. Ashlyn identified the song, then jumped in. She faced Lindsey to get better cues, so a moment after it was a surprise to hear Mom filling in on the keyboard.

Beaming, Lindsey nodded to Ashlyn, who stepped up into the melody line, and then Lindsey took off, ornamenting the melody and fooling around with the high notes and the low notes. The violin line punched in and out of the main line, turning it inside out and then rejoining to keep pace with the viola. Mom stayed in the background, supporting the melody while Lindsey went insane with the descant.

Ashlyn swayed with the music, and Lindsey joined in, watching Ashlyn for movement cues while Ashlyn watched Lindsey for musical ones. Together they filled the room with sound and motion and melody. Ashlyn worked hard not to get distracted by Lindsey's musical acrobatics. It must have been even harder for Mom, who was predicting Ashlyn's melody line ahead of her in order to lay down the right notes to harmonize.

Lindsey changed tactics, repeating Ashlyn's line in staccato a moment after she finished it, and then Ashlyn threw the melody line to the wind. She took the main riff and powered it out at Lindsey, who repeated it right back at her. They sent that back and forth until Ashlyn moved onto the next repeating motif. Lindsey changed that up by playing it at the same time Ashlyn did, and now they were in unison but one fifth apart. Ashlyn shifted up to Lindsey's key, and they finished the last three lines of the song. Mom gave a number of closing chords, and they stopped.

"Wow!" Michael applauded. "You were just—you were making that up?"

Lindsey bowed, so Ashlyn tucked her viola under her arm and bowed too. Michael kept clapping, and then Mom stood to take her bow.

Michael said, "That was a one-off? You just let it fly!"

Ashlyn said, "We did that all the time. Most visitors would be like, 'Wow, I can't wait to hear that again on the recording!' and we'd be like, 'Recording? You recorded that?'"

Michael said, "But you can't recreate it if it's just off the top of your head."

Mom said, "That's what a jam is. Enjoy it and let it go."

Ashlyn said, "Once you've identified the key, you know which notes are most likely to come up. Find the highest note and the lowest note, and there's your range. Mom insisted on one improv session per month for every student so we'd get comfortable with it, but we were doing it a lot more often." She gestured to the wall. "That's the real reason for all these. We had some insane parties."

Lindsey said, "You should see Corwin when his friends start jamming. They'll go on for an hour."

Wide-eyed, Michael only shook his head. "You don't understand how magical this is."

Lindsey stroked the violin in her arms. "It's not magic. It's wood and strings and vibrations. It's a lot of practice, a lot of knowledge, and a lot of opportunity."

"It's time," Mom said. "It's all those plus time."

"It's even more than that," Ashlyn said. "It's everything they said, plus love."

CHAPTER TWENTY-ONE

After the final curtain call of the final performance at the community theater, Michael didn't even have the luxury of collapsing onto a prop couch. Emma Hall was in his headset peppering orders, and the costume room resembled the aftermath of a hurricane.

Also, Ashlyn was here.

Still wearing his headset, Michael pushed his way into the auditorium and found her approaching the stage. Right into his arms, she fit so perfectly and so well. He hugged her, eyes closed, savoring for one moment the reprieve of having her near.

She breathed in his ear, "Is that thing transmitting?"

He shook his head, so she kissed him.

Unfortunately, the headset was receiving. "Michael?"

"Hang on," he said, then switched on the mic. "Yeah, Emma? What do you need?"

"Meet me by the makeup station."

He escorted Ashlyn into the backstage area where actors were in a tumult, some half-undressed, others gulping down bottled water. Every flat surface was covered with clothing and props, nothing in its right place, and the entire stage area needed to be cleaned.

Agape, Ashlyn stared. "I'll help."

"I don't even know where to start."

At the makeup station, Michael negotiated a truce between two actors arguing over an eye pencil. Ashlyn started setting clothing on hangers, then hanging them on the rolling racks. "I need to sort them," Michael told her.

"They'll be easier to sort if they're not in piles."

They were still hard at work when performers and their relatives started bringing in food for the cast party. Michael tried to stuff down his frustration that the same people who'd made the mess were eating rather than cleaning. He instructed the stage crew to break for now. "Eat while the food is hot—and before these people devour it all."

He and Ashlyn camped on the floor, surrounded by the rest of the stage crew. It was hardly romantic, but there was laughter and cringing as the cast rehashed everything that had gone wrong, or might have gone wrong.

Ashlyn leaned up against Michael. He rested his arm around her as he slackened back into the wall. Well, maybe it was just a bit romantic.

He loved these performances. He'd gladly do three plays every summer until the day he died. Still, by the time any one of the productions ended, he was spent like a one dollar bill.

One of the lighting guys turned to Ashlyn. "Did you ever fix that busted violin?"

"Our quartet's first violinist fixed it." She walked her fingers up Michael's arm. "It's in the trunk of my car, so you should take it before I go home."

Michael shivered at her touch. "I thought you were keeping it for the music school."

She traced a line back down to his wrist, again shooting

thrills through him. "It's the theater's violin, so it belongs with you."

The lighting guy said, "You could play for us again."

Michael bristled, but Ashlyn only replied, "Tonight's for you guys, not for music."

He imagined she got hit up for free music on a regular basis. Or hit on. He tightened his arm around her waist. "You've already done quite a bit for us."

After the food, there was more cleanup. Michael had no expectation of escaping the theater before midnight, which meant Ashlyn would be driving until almost two. "Are you working in the morning?"

"I traded shifts for tomorrow." Ashlyn helped him carry the prop couch to the elevator. "Lindsey's quiet in the mornings, so I'll sleep in."

Next they moved the grandfather clock to the elevator. Michael said, "We'll have to send the mantlepiece downstairs on its own," and lowered the elevator into the sub-stage area. He and Ashlyn followed it down by the stairs.

"You had a nice cast party." Ashlyn helped him shift a box to make room for the sofa. "What are the odds we'll have to clean that up as well?"

"That's a problem with parties." Michael considered. "What did the Castletons do for birthdays?"

Ashlyn frowned. "Nothing huge. Cake. Friends over."

Michael said, "Did you guys go on vacations?"

"Not so much. Any time we weren't in school was busy time for Bob and Susan. They were both playing independent gigs, plus the quartet, plus teaching. They ran something like a music summer camp for a number of years."

Interesting. They'd met at a summer camp.

Michael tried to remember the other questions he'd written down. He kept a tickler file on his phone with all the things he wanted to know. Everything from how long they'd lived in that house to which of his extended relations might still live around here to whether anyone other than Lindsey had allergies. Had Susan kept baby books for the kids like the one his mom had kept for him?

Also, when could he meet Bob again? Were they going to tell Bob who he was? Or would Bob not be able to handle the emotions of meeting his son for the first time while in a state of mental and physical freefall? Susan had been vague about that, and once they'd detected Susan's reluctance, Lindsey and Ashlyn had become equally vague.

Ashlyn helped Michael lift the grandfather clock. The trail they'd cleared last time remained in place, and they hefted the thing back into the corner. The sofa was harder to maneuver. Then Michael looked around feeling defeated. "Where do we put the fireplace? That thing is huge, and it's new."

Ashlyn scanned the area. "If we move those book shelves in front of one another, we can set it there, against the wall."

Michael said, "And all the stuff on the shelves?"

Ashlyn opened her hands. "If you have a better place...?"

He didn't. They started moving things around. Michael said, "There were two fireplaces in the Castleton house. Did you guys burn wood?"

"When the power was out. For real efficiency, you'd need a woodstove."

Michael said, "And you could have sleepovers in front of the fireplace when the power was out? Keep everyone in the same room for warmth?"

Ashlyn said, "Could we not talk about this right now?"

Michael stopped in place.

She wouldn't look at him as she kept moving things from shelf to shelf. "You're mining me for information. I'm getting to know you, and you're getting to know someone else."

Of course he was getting to know her. For a lot of the things he was asking about, she'd been right there. Like sleepovers during power outages. There had been a storm just this past winter that knocked out power for five days on the coast. She could have told him about surviving that, right?

Nevertheless, he said, "I'm sorry," because she expected him to. They went back upstairs to reload the elevator, and this time there wasn't any kissing in the stairwell. He was exhausted. She must be, too.

The stage world was returning to a blank canvas. Michael walked through the rooms backstage, ensuring the costumes hung in the right places and all the props sat where they belonged. By eleven-thirty, he and Ashlyn were on the street, the theater door locked behind them.

He should ask her back to his apartment. That made the most sense, even if he slept on his couch. She wanted to take things slow, but by the same token, she shouldn't fall asleep at the wheel.

She yawned. "This was fun. And I'll get to see you next Friday night, too. I'll meet you at seven?"

"How about six? That gives us time to get dinner before the movie." Michael took her hand. "Are you too tired to drive all the way back?"

She shrugged. "I'd better not be."

He squeezed. "You could stay here."

She shook her head. "I'll be fine. But if you'll walk me back to my car, I have a violin for you."

He'd much rather cuddle her than a violin. Regardless, he followed her to the parking lot where hers was the only car left. Ashlyn's car, alone. Ashlyn, also always alone. Alone until she'd found a family the same way he had.

As she unlocked the trunk, he said, "Did you guys all get lessons at the same time?"

Ashlyn stopped in place, her hand on the handle of the violin. "I can't do this."

Her voice was brittle.

She turned to him, the violin up and down between them like a pillar of misunderstanding. "It's not me you're interested in. You've pretended to be interested in me from the start, but you just want access to them."

Michael frowned. "This again?"

"Because you're doing it again. You say you care about

me, but you don't. It's never about me. You want information about them, and you're using me to get it."

He stared at her. "How can you say that?"

"The constant never-ending questions about Bob and Susan and Lindsey and Corwin and Sierra." Ashlyn blinked hard. "You're a great guy, but you think you're better than me. You're higher class; you're better educated; you're in a better profession; you come from better people. You'll permit yourself to slum with me on the bottom floor, though. Because even though I'm just a musician, I've got something you want."

Michael's throat tightened. "Haven't we been over this before?"

"Yes. And you keep coming back to it afterward." Ashlyn wouldn't meet his eyes. "Do you not even see what you're doing? I get it, that this is huge for you. You said you'd be able to start something with me anyway. The thing is, you're not. You're starting something with *them,* and you're using me."

Michael folded his arms. "I'm not using you."

"Then it's all the worse because you haven't even noticed me. It's all about them, about what I did with them, my experiences with them, what I did with Susan, what I did with Bob. Have you asked me about anything else?"

Michael opened his hands. "The ice cream stand."

"My day job that you look down on. Tell me, what do I want to do in the future? Do I want to stay in Maine? Do I want to have kids? Did I go to college? Where? What was my degree in?"

Ears ringing, Michael found he had no answers.

She slammed the trunk and walked to the side of the car. "That's what I mean. You can tell me where I went to school and what I did every Christmas morning after I was twelve. But you don't know much about the time before, and you can't tell me a thing that happened between when I was eighteen and twenty-four. Why? Because that doesn't matter to you."

"It does matter." It was weak. It was lame. He was tired. He couldn't find any of that information in him to spit it back at her.

She said, "Prove it. Remember when Corwin yelled at me? What did he accuse me of?" Her hands clenched. "What did he say to me, Michael?"

He didn't know. He hadn't asked.

"Remember your epiphany, *know your own value.* I'm worth more than that." Her eyes glistened, but in the low light he couldn't tell if she were crying. "If you ever were to say you love me, how will I know you really do? You don't know me. You'd only love what I was giving you."

He squared his shoulders. "You're repeating what Lindsey said about Susan, that she wouldn't know Bob loved her if he'd come back because of me."

She clicked the unlock button. "I don't exist. I can't even talk without you drawing a parallel to the Castleton family."

The hair stood up on the back of his neck. "You're being paranoid."

She opened the driver's side door. "And you're being jealous. Yes, I have something you didn't have. I'm not a sibling, but I was raised there. You are but weren't. I can't give you what you deserved to have. I can't give you back all those years."

Cars passed on the street. No one else was in the parking lot to witness her fury, his shock.

"I'm just a musician." It wasn't just the light. Her eyes really were tearful. "I'm not a professional advertising executive and I'm not an insurance agent. But as it turns out, I'm a person. Not your stand-in. Not the person who took the thing that should have been yours. You're not a scammer, and I'm not a thief."

Numb, Michael heard himself say, "I never said you were a thief."

"I'm the gutter brat who pick-pocketed the childhood that should have been yours. Now you want it back." She shoved the violin case at him. "You win. I need to go

185

home."

She shut the door, and a second later she had the engine on.

He tapped on her window, but she only shook her head and put the car in gear. His fingers tightened on the violin case, and he tapped harder.

She wouldn't look at him as she pulled out of the space. He could have pounded on the hood, but instead he let her go.

CHAPTER TWENTY-TWO

Hollow.

Ashlyn felt hollow all day Monday and Tuesday. Being hollow kept her from hurting worse.

She scooped the ice cream and wiped down the tables and mopped the floors. She managed the inventory and argued with an employee who'd no-called/no-showed for the fourth time. She stood in front of a customer who was having a full-on meltdown because she'd asked for a mocha chip frappe and gotten a mocha chip frappe rather than a mocha frappe with chocolate chips. After the customer finally finished screaming, Ashlyn apologized for the confusion and offered to remake the frappe. The customer refused. She stormed off with her defective dessert, and Ashlyn returned to doing inventory, hollow.

She'd begun to believe she was something special, but apparently not.

Back when Bob and Susan first took Ashlyn in, they'd sat

her down in her room and shut the door. Ah yes, one of *those* meetings, that special time when the foster parents laid out the ground rules. Ashlyn tucked herself up on the bed near her pillow, bracing her heart for the list of conditions to maintain her good standing. The bedtime, the chores, the restrictions on the phone and the TV, and then the threats if they even once caught her stealing or breaking things. She'd learned to ask the foster parents to write these down, that way she had it on record to defend herself against jack-in-the-box rules. The bio kids would have one set of expectations, and she'd have a second set. She'd be told what she could eat and when she could eat it, and she wasn't to ask for new clothes or shoes unless and until the first check came from the state.

Bob was sitting on the desk chair. "We need to set up some ground rules for the time you're here. You've been through a lot, and we want to make this a safe place for you."

Susan had sat on the foot of the bed. "As long as you're in this household, you're one of us. Consider yourself one of the kids. When I call them down, you should come too. When I ask what everyone wants for dinner, you should tell me what you want too."

Bob said, "One of the things we tell our kids over and over is to know their own value. If something's bothering you, tell us. If you need something changed, let us know so we can change it."

Ashlyn looked from one to the next. "Okay?"

Susan went on, "We don't want you to think of yourself as our guest. For as long as the state lets you stay here, this is your home."

Bob said, "How could you be comfortable if you thought you needed permission for everything?"

Susan added, "Like if you need help with your homework, we'll help you. But you'll be expected to keep up with your schoolwork the same as the others, and you'll need to contribute to the household chores the same way they do. I'll show you how to operate the laundry, and if there's anything special you want, like strawberry shampoo or your favorite breakfast cereal, you can write it on the shopping list. I may not get it," she added, "but you'll notice Corwin doesn't get half the things he puts on that list either."

Ashlyn laughed. Yesterday, Corwin had printed "Elephant Ears" on the shopping list. Beneath that he'd put, "Chocolate cereal." Susan had returned from the grocery store bearing neither.

Susan said, "If you want to play the instruments in the house, go ahead."

Bob said, "We'll keep you posted as the system chews on your placement. These cases are never fast, but I'm hopeful you can stay a long time."

Susan said, "Now, what do you need?"

Ashlyn swallowed hard. "Can you..." She looked at the carpet. "Can you write down my chore list? That way I won't get in trouble by forgetting." Or if they randomly added surprise chores.

Dead silence from both of them. Then, finally, Susan said, "Yes. I will write it all down for you."

It would have horrified Susan back then to know that well over a decade later, this list would still be saved in Ashlyn's desk drawer. It listed items like, "If something runs out, please add it to the grocery list" and "When your room gets messy, either clean the room or close the door."

Unsure what they expected, Ashlyn had shifted her pillow in front of herself. "I'm sorry I got you in trouble."

Susan had looked sad. "I'm only sorry you were in that position. From now on, if there's a problem, we want you to come to us sooner."

That had been it. Those had been their expectations. Ashlyn got into trouble every so often for breaking the rules, but whenever she panicked that they were going to eject her back into the system, that never materialized. Instead they kept insisting on only those first rules: Consider yourself one of us. Value yourself. Speak up about things you don't like.

She'd spoken up against Michael, and he hadn't responded. He hadn't even tried to understand.

She'd thought he valued her, only instead he viewed her as a package to smuggle himself into the Castleton family of yesteryear. You can't crawl inside something that's already got stuff in it, so he'd needed her hollow. Her identity was just a hindrance.

Kind of the opposite of valuing her.

It stung. It stung because for a little while, she'd believed he cared. He'd called her beautiful, and he'd acted enthralled by her music. Instead, she was his means to an end.

"Think about my daughter," Rachel used to beg her landlords. "You can't throw my daughter onto the street." Once she'd pleaded with a judge, "Have pity on my daughter. My family won't take her in."

Even Ashlyn's grandmother had used her. "Don't you care about your daughter? You're going to lose her if you don't get your act together."

I don't exist only to make everyone's life more convenient. She thought it out to the universe, out to Michael, out to Rachel wherever she happened to be. Right now, Rachel was probably wringing sympathy from some halfway house worker. "I have a daughter who never writes back."

Michael might be wringing sympathy from his adoption support groups. "I found a near-sibling, and she got mad when I asked questions about my own parents."

I am not a crowbar to pry open the barriers in your life. You are not allowed to use me again.

Of all the people Ashlyn had ever known, only the Castletons had asked nothing in return. She'd made herself useful to them, but they'd never placed a priority on that. Her inclusion hadn't depended on the support funds from the state or on having her cook dinner three nights a week or her potential to baby-sit Corwin.

The peppermint chip tub was nearly empty, so Ashlyn decided to pack a quart with the last of it. Packing quarts was honest work. She could send away her brain and cram thirty-two ounces of peppermint chip into a paper carton, one wrist-twist at a time. She slapped a label onto it with the flavor, the date, and her initials, then pulled out the empty tub and carried the quart to the freezer. When she dropped the tub to the ground, it made a hollow thunk.

Then she thought, *Hollow isn't bad.*

A viola is hollow. The interior of a viola is empty space, with only a soundpost beneath the C string that conducts the vibrations and supports the hollow space. Otherwise it's beautiful and spare like a midnight cathedral. There's a little rosin powder and a little atomized wood, and when you fit your chin into the rib of a viola and inhale, that hollow space smells like time.

That's a good hollow, and a necessary hollow. The hollow is what allows the viola to vibrate, allows it to sing. Without that hollow space, there would be no resonance. The strings would twang and be done.

A mute viola is a block of solid wood.

"Value yourself," Bob had said. "Speak up."

Ashlyn grabbed a full tub and hauled it back to the freezer cases, then used a pry tool to claw up the lid. How dare Michael treat her like a tool? She was more than an empty space for him to step in and fill. She was an instrument playing a song, and if her heart went hollow right now, that would make her sing louder.

At practice, Ashlyn tuned while Lindsey sorted her music. Jason came in a couple minutes late, per usual, but in the same hand as his violin case he was holding a black plastic bag. "I come bearing brilliance! Behold!"

He dumped out the bag onto his chair, and Ashlyn reached for one of the boxes that clattered down.

Lindsey exclaimed, "Literal brilliance!"

Jason said, "Lights that clip to our music stands. USB-chargeable, too, so we can charge them en route the next time some rich yacht-owner decides he wants his musicians playing blind."

Lindsey picked up another. "Excellent timing, pretty boy! Do you know why? Because that selfsame rich yacht-owner called this afternoon wondering if we'd like to set sail on Friday night."

Hannah's head jerked up. "Amazing!"

"You don't sail a yacht. You pilot it." Jason unstrapped his violin from the case, then turned to her. "Wait, you're serious?"

Lindsey opened her hands.

He sat with the violin on his lap, wide-eyed. "I had no idea boats were the upcoming place to play."

"You still have the star violin, right? Keep it singing for us. How much does the quartet owe you for the lights?"

"It's on me because I don't feel like not playing our best work for our richest clients." Jason shot her an evil smile. "Call me crazy, but it's worth forty bucks to impress people."

"Thanks. I'll drop forty bucks in your account next time I do the books." Lindsey shook her head. "Is this weekend insane, or what?

Hannah said, "I'm going with the 'what' because money's coming in."

"Totally not arguing with more money," Ashlyn said. "Friday evening boat party, Saturday morning library reception, Saturday evening wedding, Sunday morning concert at the Ellsworth town green and farmer's market."

Jason said, "Sunday afternoon nap?"

"I'm in negotiations about a Sunday afternoon performance too. I love summer." Lindsey shrugged. "If we get that gig, by the way, it won't be anything unusual. We could repurpose the entirety of the yacht party playlist because there won't be any crossover."

Jason said, "Please tell me there will be recording executives with contracts and enormous checkbooks."

Lindsey studied him. "How much do you like being lied to?"

Ashlyn said, "I'm good with the enormous checkbooks."

"Newspaper reporters?" Jason prompted. "Photographers?"

"No promises. It'll have to be your rabid fans sustaining us."

Jason sighed. "You know my fans. Rabid, indeed." He ran through a three-octave G-scale, then finished off with a series of perfect fifths.

Ashlyn's phone buzzed, and since they hadn't started playing yet, she checked it.

Rachel again, from a different number. "Honey, it's Mom. You need to answer me or I'm going to call the cops."

Ashlyn silenced notifications so she wouldn't get the next five prompts until the drive home. She didn't even need to read them, though. "Tell me you're all right. That's all I want. A mother has a right to know these things. Did you send me money? I wish I had a daughter who loved me like I love her."

Go ahead. Call the cops. They're probably laughing at you at headquarters anyhow. Does that make you feel as embarrassed as it makes me?

Of course not. Her mother had no shame.

When Jason's violin's tuning answered Jason's exact demands, he turned to Lindsey. "We need to go over the new Beethoven piece again. Last time, we were pretty rough on the third movement."

Lindsey didn't hide her annoyance. This tension wasn't sustainable. Jason couldn't keep insisting on whatever he wanted. The whole point of a quartet was harmonizing, splitting apart, and then rejoining in harmony. At some point, they were going to split apart and never rejoin.

They ran through the first two movements without a hitch, but the third was, in fact, all over the place. Hannah's line was difficult, and she instinctively sped up during those parts. Meanwhile Jason's supposedly supporting line drowned out the first violin. Ashlyn felt like she should just stop playing entirely, for all the good she was doing.

Lindsey gave a thin, "Let's take it from measure fifty," and Jason turned his music back to the correct page.

A knock on the door, and Mom stepped in. "I hope you don't mind. My seven o'clock student cancelled, and I wanted to listen."

Jason said, "You're always welcome, Mrs. Castleton," as though he had any right to welcome Susan into her own school.

Mom tucked up on the floor in the corner. Lindsey said, "Okay, then. From measure fifty."

Again the dynamics were awful. Hannah worked harder to stay on tempo, but that made her playing much more mechanical. Ashlyn played a fraction louder so Hannah would hear her better, but Jason and Lindsey once again became the dueling violinists. He was playing louder, bowing with more flair. Visually as well as audibly, he was overpowering the primary line.

Lindsey ended the run-through, then turned to her mother with a tense smile. "We're still working on this."

"I didn't expect a concert." Mom shrugged. "Remember, I used to stand in sometimes for second violin."

Jason tilted his head. "I didn't know that."

"When he first started the quartet, he didn't have a roster of substitutes who could just come forward when someone got sick. I learned enough to keep the quartet sounding good."

Hannah said, "Didn't Mozart say when he was five that you don't need lessons to play second violin?"

Jason's eyes darkened. Mom said, "Well, none of us is Mozart."

Lindsey wasn't in a hurry to start playing again, and Ashlyn wondered if they would just chat until Mom left. Lindsey had no control over the quartet. Her mother had been the one to recruit Jason back to the quartet, and Lindsey didn't want her mother to see Jason in open rebellion. Lindsey also didn't want her mother to see Hannah foundering on a difficult piece, and herself unable to settle her down.

Lindsey didn't want her mother to see failure.

Dad would have toned down Jason enough to get him comfortable in the supporting role. He'd have relaxed Hannah so she freed her heart into the music. He'd have noticed Ashlyn dissolving into the background.

Lindsey wasn't Dad. Dad wasn't coming back, and without his bracing, the quartet was warping apart at the seams like a violin left too long in the heat and humidity.

Mom waved them on. "Don't stop playing because of me."

Lindsey braced herself. "From measure fifty."

They went through it again, no better than before. Ashlyn was playing so softly now that when she did mess up, no one noticed. Jason was staring at Hannah rather than Lindsey. Lindsey was just frustrated, and she ended the run-through at measure eighty.

Ashlyn ventured, "Maybe we don't have to play this on the weekend?"

Jason said, "I really think we should. This dinner party should have a different lineup than the first time."

Lindsey said, "We filled it with forty minutes of solos the first time, so we've got plenty of slack. If this piece isn't ready to go, I'm not playing it."

Jason said, "You alone don't get to decide."

Ashlyn said, "As first violinist, Lindsey does get to decide."

Jason smoldered.

Mom said, "You're very close to getting it right, you realize. It's just the dynamics."

Lindsey's brows contracted. "It's always the dynamics."

Hannah offered, "I'll work on the third movement on my own. I'm having a hard time in the group because the other lines are out of rhythm with mine, but I'll practice with a recording."

Jason said, "If you don't mind, Mrs. Castleton, may I ask

you a question? Lindsey told us about Michael. Are you sure he's legit?"

Heat rose inside Ashlyn, but Mom only smiled at him. "Yes, I'm completely sure."

Jason said, "This is a vulnerable time. I don't want to see you taken advantage of."

Ashlyn's hand tightened on the viola, and Lindsey glared at him. Mom said, "I appreciate that."

Jason said, "Let me know if he asks for any of Bob's violins."

Lindsey muttered, "For crying out loud, Jason."

Mom met Lindsey's eyes and gave a cue so subtle that only a world class musician would have been able to give it —or to decode it. Lindsey went silent.

Ashlyn said, "If it makes you feel better, I repaired a junk violin from the theater prop room, and he didn't even want that."

Mom shook her head. "Michael's not interested in the instruments. He doesn't play, and because there are so many in the house, it's never occurred to him that they might have monetary value."

Jason leaned forward. "That's not my point."

"I understand your point." Mom waved a hand. "Don't let me derail you. I like to listen."

Looking at Jason, Lindsey seemed equal parts annoyed and defeated. "Let's take the whole movement, and we'll run through to the end." She turned to Hannah. "I want you not to worry about the dynamics. Play one volume straight through and let us work around you."

Jason said, "But—"

"No." Hand raised, she turned to him. "We have too many balls in the air. I want Hannah to act like the long pole of the tent. She's going to play the notes and the rhythm, and nothing else. You are going to back off your volume as much as you possibly can without sticking a mute on your bridge, that way she can hear herself better. You're a good enough musician to work that way for one play-through, and if you can't, then I'll have you stick an actual mute on your bridge. We're backtracking to basics. If we can't get this working by the end of tonight, I'm scrapping it from Friday's playlist."

Jason said, "And play what instead? We need to do this one."

"Then quit being bullheaded and work with me." Lindsey raised her violin. "From measure one. One, two, three—"

She wanted them to work as a team, so when it was a question of overruling someone, she seldom did. For the music to flow, she always said, everyone needed to work together. That meant not silencing one another, except that gave Jason endless openings to silence the rest of them. But for once, Lindsey had shut him down.

Ashlyn set her mind free into the piece. Like a dreamer, Lindsey envisioned how it ought to be: each instrument voicing its own line while contributing to the whole. Each musician, micro-adjusting to accommodate. Acknowledging. Listening.

Listening.

Michael hadn't listened. Tears stung her eyes, but Ashlyn blinked hard so they'd stay put. She wasn't the kind of player whose own music brought her to tears, so she'd never be able to pass it off as that—nor was this an emotional enough piece that it would sound believable if she tried. Admitting she was crying over Michael would be dumb.

She wasn't crying over Michael, though. She was crying over her own invisibility. Even in this exchange, with Lindsey's attention divided between her mother and Hannah and Jason, none of them had noticed her. The one time Ashlyn spoke, she'd been ignored.

Michael had ignored her. As long as he was getting what he wanted, why pay attention to the misbehaving bonus kid? As long as the quartet had the viola's sound, why pay attention to the violist? Ashlyn's own mother ignored her until she needed something.

They hit the dreaded measure fifty and kept going. Hannah ignored the dynamics as if she were a second-year student. No emoting, no change in volume. She was, however, able to stay on track, and once Hannah managed that, Ashlyn found she didn't care anymore if Jason cranked his volume and drowned out Lindsey, or if Lindsey overemphasized her part in order to combat Jason. The music trudged on, but at least it moved. Ashlyn flubbed her line, but she corrected, and no one noticed. As if they would. The viola always has the softest part in the performance.

They passed the point where Lindsey usually stopped them. Lindsey said, "No repeat," so at least they didn't have to circle back through it again. Now they were in relatively unpracticed territory, and Ashlyn fought the urge to get even softer. She knew this part. She'd practiced it for three weeks, sometimes solo and sometimes with Lindsey.

It didn't matter. It didn't matter if they ignored you. You still existed. Invisibility actually freed you. People didn't criticize what they didn't see. Not being noticed was a skill Ashlyn had worked hard to develop as a child. Be quiet and Grandma won't threaten to send you to an orphanage. Be quiet and Mom won't yell at you. Hide in one room so Mr. and Mrs. Castleton won't detect you living in their home. Play viola and let everyone notice the first violin and the cello.

They reached the end of the piece, and Ashlyn sat with her viola on her lap, her eyes lowered.

Mom clapped. "You got through it!"

Jason muttered, "We sound like a hot mess."

"You got through it." Mom stood, then put her hand on Ashlyn's shoulder. "Are you okay, honey?"

Ashlyn looked up, brows raised.

Mom said, "You're really tense."

"I'm just tired," she said because that response always got the least attention.

"You're more than tired." Mom brushed her hair back from her forehead. "You did great. Maybe a little quiet, but I was listening for you. The viola adds a lot of dynamism to that movement. Through most of it, you're anticipating the first violin line by about three measures, so you're cuing the listener as to where the piece is headed."

Fighting the hollow feeling, Ashlyn only nodded.

Mom said, "Don't stifle your voice. They need you."

Lindsey huffed. "All our dynamics are off."

"It's a difficult time." Mom turned to her. "You're all still adjusting to the changes. It would have taken a while under the best of circumstances, but it was springtime when you started working together, and a month later when you started your first performances. You had to hit the ground running."

Ashlyn stroked the scroll of her viola.

Mom added, "I know you each want different things, but you've all pulled together for me and for Bob, and that means a lot."

Lindsey said, "Sometimes if feels like all these different things are incompatible."

Mom put her hand on the door. "You need to listen to each other. You've all got good hearts. If you listen, really listen and then really respond, it's going to be okay."

CHAPTER TWENTY-THREE

Friday afternoon. Restless, Michael kept thinking of Hartwell.

He hadn't talked with any of them since last Sunday. He'd texted Ashlyn, but either she'd blocked him, or else she was doing an excellent impression thereof. He'd sent an apology. He'd called. He'd tried to video chat.

Now it was Friday. She'd said her weekend schedule was two gigs on Saturday and one on Sunday, but nothing Friday night. They'd planned on dinner and a movie, so she should be free.

He texted her with, "Are you around? Can we talk?"

By the time he was ready to leave work, Ashlyn still hadn't replied. The message only said "delivered" but not "read." That looked like blocking to him, but he couldn't be sure.

Unacceptable. He called Susan. "Michael!" she exclaimed. "How nice to hear from you! What's going on?"

He said, "I'm about to head out of work, but before I went home, I was wondering if you have anything going on this weekend."

Ashlyn would go nuclear. First, she'd say, he used her to get information on Susan. Now he was using Susan to get information about Ashlyn.

"Nothing much. I'm taking care of paperwork at the school tonight, and tomorrow I've got two performances, then Sunday morning at the church." She laughed. "What about you? You're probably still recovering after last weekend's show."

Michael got off the phone with just enough information to know Susan hadn't planned anything with Ashlyn and Lindsey. That made it more than likely they were home.

Once again, this was the reason Michael had a car. Even if she'd blocked him, Ashlyn wouldn't leave the door shut if he turned up at her apartment. They'd have to deal with one another sooner or later, like family gatherings they were both at, so they needed to get the awkwardness out of the way.

In Hartwell, he headed right for her apartment, and there he met the first snag: neither her car nor Lindsey's were in the lot.

Okay, where might they be?

He cruised past Susan's house to find no cars in her driveway and all the lights off. Again, not very useful. Michael went back to the main strip and drove the length of the town. At a chain restaurant, he pulled into their parking lot and searched the quartet up on Google. Nothing turned up as a public performance tonight, but he already knew that because he and Ashlyn had been planning to meet at about this time. Ashlyn still hadn't replied to his text.

This was inconvenient. He drove back to the Mexican restaurant they'd eaten at the first time. Her car wasn't there, but he went in anyhow since he needed dinner and wouldn't think very well while hungry and annoyed.

He'd accepted the risk that she might not be available

when he decided to drive. There just hadn't been anything else at home for him to do, and the only way she'd talk was in person.

During dinner he read a book and played with his phone. It was noisy tonight, unlike the last time when it was just the five Castletons. The waitress was the same, but fortunately she didn't recognize him, even though Michael would have remembered one customer throwing her arms around another and gushing that this was her long-lost brother.

Now that was a thought. Michael texted Sierra. "Who's around tonight?"

Before the check arrived, he got a response. "Maybe Mom. I think everyone else has a gig. I'm doing a dinner party in Brighthead."

He texted, "Thanks."

Michael had come all this way, so he paid up and went for another drive because despite what Sierra thought, he knew Ashlyn wasn't supposed to be performing tonight. Again, no cars at Ashlyn's apartment; none in front of their mother's house. He searched up the music school and drove to Granite Cross Road where the only car in the lot was Susan's, and there was only one light on at the top floor. He kept going.

He wanted to see Ashlyn, and there was no way to do it. Annoying as everything.

Wait: with everyone working tonight, Ashlyn might have gone to see Bob. She did say she usually went with Lindsey, and Lindsey was missing too.

At the rehab hospital, the parking lot was mostly empty, but not enough for him to be sure Ashlyn's car wasn't there.

Whether Ashlyn was here wouldn't matter if security blocked him at the entrance, so he grabbed the violin from the back seat.

A glance at the violin was all it took. "Oh, you must be here for Bob Castleton!" The guard buzzed Michael right through. Mission accomplished.

Michael remembered enough of Ashlyn's route to get himself to the elevator, but then he had a momentary confusion trying to recall which floor. He guessed three. It looked familiar, so he continued down the corridor until he found the nurses' station. "Excuse me?" he asked, wishing he remembered the names Ashlyn had so casually used with the nurses.

The nurse saw the violin. "Oh, thank you for coming! Bob was asking if anyone had come to see him. He's so disappointed when I show him the guest book and he sees he's already had all his regular visitors."

The other nurse said, "I was about to head down and ask if he'd teach me the Happy Birthday song on the keyboard, but it's better this way."

At the end of the hallway, at a doorway decorated with music symbols, at last Michael found someone.

Bob was sitting up in bed, the wheeled table at full stretch and covered with adult coloring books and colored pencils. He wasn't using them. Instead he had an audiobook playing on a tablet computer. "Come in!" He looked Michael up and down without recognition. "Come in, always welcome. Come in."

Michael drew up a chair, and Bob said, "You brought my violin?"

Now that the violin had gotten Michael into the building, he had no use for it. "No, sir, it's not a nice violin like you have." Based on Ashlyn's comments, that had to be true.

"What did I tell you?" Bob shook his head. "It's not about the violin. It's about the player." He reached for the tablet computer, but he had trouble turning off the playback. Michael helped him wake the unit and pause the story. He also hit the "back 15 seconds" button twice.

Fine motor, Ashlyn had said. Bob had gone to the doctor when his fine motor coordination deteriorated until he couldn't play, and shortly afterward his memory started to slip. Here was another terrible thought: could Bob remember from time to time what audiobook he was even listening to? Or was he cycling through the same audiobooks, unable to remember he'd already visited this town, these characters, this resolution?

Bob told Michael to open the case, so Michael withdrew the violin for him. Bob took the violin, gazing at it like a man regarding his former lover.

Michael's heart gave a pang. Ashlyn. Would Michael look at a picture of her that way someday? They'd had almost no time together. Most likely he'd just move on. She'd settle in her mind that he'd treated her badly—by whatever definition of bad she was using. Then she'd move on too.

Bob plucked a string, but his hands tremored. "Here. You do it."

He held it out, and Michael took it. "Do what?"

"Play that song for me. The one you worked on."

Michael laughed nervously. "I've never played."

"You don't like to play." Bob looked sad. "But I know you can play."

Michael said, "I promise you, I've never played this."

"Don't do that to me." Bob frowned. "My memory's going, but I gave all three of you violin lessons."

Michael's throat seized.

I'm not Corwin.

Instead he said, "Dad?"

Their eyes met, and Bob said, "Yes. Now play."

Michael plucked the third string on the violin, and it twanged. Wishing like crazy for Ashlyn's ability with any musical instrument, Michael tucked the violin under his chin and shoved it into place with his left hand. He gripped the bow in his right, and he dragged the bow across the first string. It squeaked, but a note came out.

Bob shook his head. "You're pushing too hard. It wants to make a note, but not if you grind it. Give the instrument its freedom. Let the bow rest on the string."

Michael lowered the instrument. "Do you remember Dalton?"

Bob's face crumbled, and his eyes flickered to his lap.

Michael leaned forward. "Tell me about Dalton."

Bob slumped back onto the bed. "Just play."

Michael tried again with the second string, only to end up hitting two strings at once. Ashlyn had made this instrument sound like heaven, and he made it sound like hell.

Bob didn't seem to notice. "She told you? So sad."

Michael paused. "Dalton was sad?"

"Dalton made her sad." Bob plucked at his blankets, hands trembling harder now. "I made her sad. She cried so much. They wanted me in Paris, but I had to come back."

Michael said, "You came back for Susan?"

"Dalton." Bob whispered. "My boy. My little boy. It was so hard on her when we had you. Finally had a son, they said, but we already had a son."

I am Dalton.

I'm your son, but I'm not Corwin.

I am Michael.

Bob murmured, "My little boy. My little boy."

Michael put down the violin, but then Bob pointed at him. "Try again."

The empty case beckoned as though the violin wanted nothing more than to escape back into it. Bob reverted to murmuring, "My little boy," and Michael tried to make another note.

It sounded terrible. "I'm not very good at playing."

Bob stopped his under-the-breath chanting and said, "Because you're forcing it. Violins are love. You can't force love. Draw out the sound. A light touch works wonders. You'll make a lot of mistakes." Abruptly his face looked haunted. "So many mistakes. *My little boy. My little boy.*"

Michael tried again, this time on the lowest string. He had to keep his bowing arm at a weird angle in order to reach it, but at least this way he wasn't hitting two strings at once. "Dalton wasn't a mistake."

"I should have stayed." Bob pulled his blankets tighter around his legs. "I made her so sad."

Michael shuddered. "I'm sorry."

Bob said, "You? You need to keep playing."

Michael lay the violin and bow across his lap. "I'm no

good at this."

Bob plucked at the skin of one hand with the other. "Stick with it. You'll learn."

Michael shivered. "I wish you could teach me now, the way you're teaching the nurse to play piano."

Bob turned to look at the window, but it was black outside and only reflected them back at themselves.

What was Bob seeing? Was he seeing a copy of a photograph with a baby tucked up in a blanket? Did he remember the face of a girl he'd left behind so he could study in England? Was he remembering the young woman who'd waited four years in the hopes that they could restart their family and track down their missing son?

A smile transformed Bob's face. "I met Dalton once."

Michael's head jerked up. "You did?"

Bob relaxed into his pillow as if staring a hundred miles away. He sighed. "Don't tell her. He had such a smile. He was so smart."

The room had no air. "When?"

Bob kept looking into the past. "I saw he was fine. I didn't tell him either. How could I?"

"But when?" Michael wracked his brain for any time he might have met Bob Castleton. "What did you say to him?"

"What good would it have done?" Bob looked at Michael again. "You're my son?"

No, no, no, don't clear the cache and reset the conversation. "I am. You were telling me about meeting Dalton."

Bob's face fell. "I should have stayed. My little boy."

Michael reached for Bob's hand. "But Dalton is fine. You said you met him."

Bob didn't reply.

Michael ran his fingers along the violin's strings, then rested his fingertips in the curvy holes. Ashlyn had told him to inhale through those holes to smell the scent of centuries, but instead he kept tracing the tailpiece to the button at the bottom, then back up again. "You said Dalton is fine."

Bob murmured, "Susan isn't fine." He pointed to the violin. "It's empty inside. I'm worried. About your mother. About what will happen to her."

What was it like, knowing death was not only inevitable but also soon? Michael never thought about his own death. There seemed no point. For Bob, though, it must be the sensation of standing on a cliff face, watching the sand slide out from beneath the rocks, waves crashing into the base, long portions tumbling into the sea, and every crash accompanied by a tremble beneath the fragile spot on which you stood. The edge, always closer. The support, always less.

Michael looked down. "She's got the kids. They'll look after her."

Bob said, "I should have done better."

He retreated into himself then, as if the conversation had exhausted his own structures. Tears in his eyes, he sat back into his pillows, his gaze focused on a blank part of the ceiling. The conversation was over.

Michael shut the violin back into its case.

Dalton was fine. Michael was fine.

Susan would grieve, but she'd be fine.

They sat in silence, Michael with the coffin case across his lap. He'd used the violin to get into the building because anyone bearing an instrument had only one reason to be there. Music had been such a part of Bob's life that no one questioned it, and they wouldn't think to mention it afterward. Michael would escape this meeting, and he'd be fine.

Ashlyn? Would Ashlyn be fine?

Months ago, Michael had been struggling with a relationship when a voice broke in on him: *Know your own value.* He'd forgotten how to value himself because Kristen had only valued what he brought to her. Now here he stood, a mini-Kristen, having valued Ashlyn only for what she could give. And that was wrong.

He'd used Ashlyn the same way he'd used the repaired violin, only Ashlyn's voice was real. Her heart was real, and she'd seen through what he'd done.

Michael had no intention of playing the violin, but he'd had every intention of getting closer to Ashlyn. Why hadn't he actually done it? Instead he'd gotten bedazzled with the allure of everything she could offer: the information and the inside track. As if she were a violin carried under his arm, her presence could slip him right into the heart of the Castleton stronghold and give him the experience of growing up there without having lived through it.

His parents had provided an upper middle-class lifestyle, with computers and video games and vacations and trendy clothing. They'd paid his sports fees and driven him to travel soccer, and for his fifteenth birthday he'd taken three friends on a ski trip. He'd never shared a bedroom, never had a combination Christmas-birthday gift, never had to wear someone else's outgrown boots.

Because of that supposed superiority, he'd styled himself as judge and jury. Ashlyn was just a musician. She was just a ward of the state. Michael was a professional. He was educated. While he'd known his mother would consider Ashlyn beneath him in every way, he'd never stopped to consider how he himself considered her, as if dating him would be a boost up in the world. She would give him love, and he'd give her status and class—whereas by accepting him as he was, she'd outclassed him. She'd valued him for who he was, and he'd valued her because of what she could give.

Michael had overlooked Ashlyn's love in favor of access. She'd accused him of trying to co-opt her experiences, her life, and her memories. She wasn't wrong.

Meanwhile, every day Bob was losing his memories. Ashlyn had tried to coordinate Michael's introduction to the family while Bob lost his coordination. Ashlyn was making music while Michael was rewriting the lyrics.

Bob looked confused again, seeing Michael but groping for Corwin. He was a shade under six feet, but in the hospital bed he looked small. "I'm sorry. You're my son?"

"Yes." Michael reached for his hand. "You're my father,

and you've shown me so much."

Chapter Twenty-Four

Jason's mini lights were an awesome addition to their performance, and every so often Jason reminded them of his (ahem) brilliance in having procured them. "If you'd check your bank account," Lindsey murmured between pieces, "you'd notice I reimbursed your savage brilliance."

Jason sighed. "I'm disappointed that the going rate for my savage brilliance included parts but not labor and expertise."

She looked him up and down. "Two minutes of labor, and I'm pretty sure you got reimbursed for expertise."

Hannah whistled, and Jason's eyes widened.

Ashlyn said, "I recall Susan Castleton saying something about us working together...?"

Jason gave a mock pout. It was, of course, beautiful. "You singed my poor violin with that burn."

"Yours? That little darling you're borrowing is mine, and after so many students, it's survived worse." Lindsey arched her eyebrows. "The last piece for the night is your beloved Beethoven, so shall we get started...?"

Ashlyn said, "Are you watching the time? We may not get all the way through the third movement."

"Last party ran over by half an hour. I'm betting we'll take all the repeats and still have to backfill with something else. Our overtime rates will make it all worthwhile." Lindsey raised her bow, then counted them to start.

Michael had texted Ashlyn tonight. Again. She'd been leaving his messages unread like digital compost in her message app, but she'd seen the notifications as they came through. She ought to have been at dinner with him, or maybe cuddled against his shoulder in a movie theater.

The first movement of the Beethoven was an enthusiastic call to action, so she tried to imagine herself and Michael watching one of the superhero movies dotting the cinematic landscape. The next movement, slow and thoughtful, would work better with a literary film, something with subtitles. The third movement finally (finally) would sound epic. They'd nailed it at practice on Thursday evening—just after the point where Ashlyn felt ready to hang up her viola and sit on the roof contemplating a career change. Ditch-digging sounded okay. So did stuffing her worldly belongings into a backpack and hitch-hiking around the country.

Drifting worked for Rachel, at least. Her mother had texted again from a different number. For the time being, Ashlyn had turned all her ringtones to silent except for Lindsey, Mom, Sierra, and the town's reverse-911 system.

Today's message said Rachel was hiring a private detective to track Ashlyn, and Ashlyn had better have a good answer for her silence. Also, Rachel hoped Ashlyn was still alive.

The private detective thing made Ashlyn snort. Her mother couldn't pay for her own phone service, and private detectives generally preferred cash to palm reading or whatever her mother did nowadays to buy food.

Beethoven soothed a lot of ills. Ashlyn tackled her line with a gusto that made her wish Beethoven had wanted a viola to scream.

Much as she hated this, Ashlyn would just have to trust that Beethoven knew what he was doing. Susan said the viola line laid down the path for the first violin, but that irritated her too. When did Ashlyn stop laying down paths for other people? When did she get to be herself and make her own choices? When did other people take responsibility for their own lives?

Rachel would never wake up from the guilt trip she was using to hitch-hike her way through life. Whether because of addiction or mental illness, or mental illness medicated with addiction, her mother would never be able to do that. She'd always want Ashlyn to provide for her, mother her, be strong for her. Like that time her mother had texted, "Why would you destroy our relationship over fifteen dollars?" Ashlyn had stared at that, wondering exactly the same thing: why would her mother destroy their relationship for fifteen dollars? Again and again and again, why would you destroy your relationships over a tiny thing that isn't tiny at all?

They started the second movement. Ashlyn's mother had shown up once at the Castleton household. Bob had gone out to talk to her, followed minutes later by Susan. Ashlyn had fled into Corwin's bedroom over the porch and, crouching beneath the sill, slid up the window half an inch. Her mother kept whining, "But I want to see her," while Susan kept giving variations on a theme: *There's a court order in place, Rachel. You can't take her with you, and you're only allowed to see her with the social worker present.*

It was like a duet of futility. Rachel had mewled and threatened and finally picked up her phone because she was going to call the police to accuse the Castletons of kidnapping. Ashlyn had nearly flown down the stairs to stop her, except Susan had said, "That's a wonderful idea. I'll call them myself."

Abruptly Rachel had backed off. No, it wasn't like that; they didn't need the cops. She wanted to see Ashlyn because a mother cares about her daughter, but did they have twenty bucks so she could get food?

Susan had gone into the house, and Ashlyn crept down the back stairs into the kitchen.

Ashlyn made no noise, but Susan heard her. "I'm not going to stop you, but there's a court order in place for a reason." Susan pulled money out of her wallet, then got bread and lunch meat from the fridge. Ashlyn helped Susan make three sandwiches, with just a little mayo and salt the way her mother liked it, plus some apples and granola bars. Last of all, Ashlyn tucked a bottle of water into the bag. Susan gave the bundle to Rachel, and afterward, Susan sat on the couch cuddling Ashlyn while Ashlyn sobbed.

Michael had in effect come to Ashlyn's door to beg not for money, but for information. She must have a sign on herself: "Ring bell for service."

The second movement ended, and Ashlyn shivered in the lake breeze. Lindsey raised her violin and began the third.

At last night's practice, Hannah had successfully reintroduced the cello's dynamics. Lindsey had made them play the troublesome measures four times as slow as they ought to, and Jason eventually calmed down about his part. It was either that or not play it at all, so faced with Lindsey's ultimatum, he'd dialed it back. That left Lindsey free to play her part with more range of feeling, and then she'd turned her attention to Ashlyn.

"Forget what Beethoven noted. You've got an awesome line. Sing it."

Ashlyn only said, "What?"

Lindsey nodded. "Every quartet puts their own stamp on a piece, and after Mom pointed out what the viola is doing, I saw so much potential. Go right ahead and voice the living daylights out of this one. Jason and I will back off," (she'd said that with a fiery glare at Jason,) "but you're going to lead. Hannah's line is subtle enough that you're going to weave in and out of hers. Do whatever you want."

Tonight, Ashlyn felt through the wood and the strings, through the hollow at the center. With the wood vibrating and the strings sounding, she let the music emerge from between her heart and her left ear. The sound traveled through her chin and her spine and her sternum, and it went up both arms. With her eyes on the notes more for guidance than direction, she let her line swell and call and keen, and then build.

As Beethoven did so often, this final movement ended in triumph. The instruments trilled with victory and unity, the dangling threads from the previous movements weaving together into one precious whole, and it was in Ashlyn's line that they braided together.

The yacht was approaching the shoreline, and Ashlyn closed her eyes as they worked through the repeat. Music was everything. Michael was nothing.

He'd treated her like she was hollow, but that hollow could make a whole lot of noise.

She had a place in this world. Without her mother... without Michael...she'd be fine.

Ashlyn pulled up at home a minute behind Lindsey. Friday evening gigs were rough in that she had to bring her concert blacks to Rockway's Ice Cream Stand, change in the restroom, and then drive directly. She much preferred splitting the drive, especially when the evening ended this late.

Lindsey held out her arms and spun in the lot, her violin case tracing an arc in the air. "Oh, that worked so well! The water echoed our music out for miles. I hope everyone asks who that was, and then we'll get a dozen other clients with boats."

Ashlyn laughed. "Or a dozen other boats hire their own quartets, and then it sounds like a riot because Haydn's finally duking it out with Beethoven."

"Hush. I'm going to enjoy our victory while we have it." Lindsey bounded up the porch steps. "Dad never told me how much fun it was to play on a lake. I'd have been reaching out to the yacht-owning community ages ago."

They quieted down in the stairwell so they wouldn't disturb the other dark apartments. At the top of the stairs, though, Lindsey stopped. "Um, Ashlyn?"

On the landing stood a vase of yellow roses, carnations, and gerbera daisies. The neck of the vase was wrapped in a yellow ribbon, and on a plastic fork was an envelope with her name.

Lindsey unlocked the door and reached back to take the viola case. Ashlyn carried the flowers inside and set them on the kitchen table. "Should I even bother?"

"Yes, you should. Either he's groveling or he's being smugly superior, or else it's not actually Michael and you're in the early stages of a reverse harem. For that matter, it could be an overdue apology from Corwin." Lindsey shrugged. "At the very least, I'm dying of curiosity, so that's why you need to do it."

"I'm voting for Michael and smugly superior. *Dear Ashlyn, I'm sorry if you still feel hurt, but I only did it because you were being unreasonable.*"

Lindsey snorted. "It won't be anywhere near that direct. Imagine how Jason would write a flower card. *Dear Ashlyn, You must be pretty hurt to ignore me for a whole week. Let's talk so I can explain again.* You know, just in case you were too stupid to understand how right he was the first time." Lindsey nudged her. "Open the card before I die."

With a sigh, Ashlyn took the card.

Ashlyn,

> *I was wrong. I'm very sorry. There's no excuse.*
> *Michael*

She handed the card to Lindsey, whose eyebrows went all the way up.

"No weaseling," Ashlyn said.

"Agreed. Not even one weasel." Lindsey bit her lip. "Well, there goes all my suggestions on how to respond. I was going to bring the bouquet to the nurses over at Dad's hospital."

"I may bring it there anyhow."

Lindsey snickered. "I wonder if he called in a Jason-esque non-apology and the floral shop changed it."

"That's Michael's handwriting. Did he drive all the way just to deliver these?" Ashlyn shuddered. "I was supposed to see him tonight, before we ended up with a gig. And before he acted like a giant snot. He must have thought I'd be home."

Lindsey shook her head. "Don't try to mind-read him now. That's an apology. If you accept it or don't accept it, do it tomorrow. You've got time."

Ashlyn leaned in to inhale the scent of the largest yellow rose. It smelled of beauty and longing.

Lindsey put a hand on Ashlyn's shoulder. "If he's sorry, he'll understand if you don't forgive him right away. He of all people would know relationships don't end just because of silence, and he'll know they can't start again without consent."

CHAPTER TWENTY-FIVE

On Tuesday afternoon, Michael got an email from DN-Amazing. "Congratulations, we've updated your close relatives!" followed by a series of graphics. Corwin, obviously, although he'd used the name Clare Enigma. They shared forty-nine percent of their DNA.

So much for Corwin's assertion of stolen DNA. At this point, all four of them were in the database, and Michael was an exact match to none but nearly a fifty-fifty match to all.

An hour later, a text arrived from Corwin. "Well, bro."

Impressive he got that much acknowledgment, but at least it wasn't about rusty shovels and unmarked graves.

Later, he got a text from Lindsey. "Corwin says you're legit, although I think that made him even angrier."

Michael replied, "What? Why?"

Lindsey texted, "You just one-upped him. You know, by being yourself."

Michael replied, "Shameful."

Lindsey sent, "Tsk tsk" but that was the end of the conversation.

Tuesday evening, the quartet would be practicing together, so Michael expected silence. Instead Michael got a call from Susan. "Do you want to come for dinner tomorrow?"

Michael said, "Everyone, or just you and me? I'm given to understand there's still some anger."

Anger from Corwin. Anger from Ashlyn.

Susan chuckled. "That's Corwin. You'll get used to it. I'm making pecan pie for dessert, and guaranteed he'll stay for pie, even if he plugs his guitar into the living room amp and makes thundering sounds every time you speak."

Bemused, Michael said, "That will make things interesting."

"It's actually kind of standard."

Ashlyn mustn't have mentioned anything to Susan. That didn't seem standard.

Wednesday evening, armed with the DNA encoded in every cell of his body, Michael arrived at Susan's house. He'd accounted for tourist traffic, but the roads had been unexpectedly (and blessedly) clear, so he arrived first. He parked next to Susan's car, then rang the bell even though he could see her through the screen door.

"Oh, for heaven's sake," she called from the kitchen, "walk right in. Everyone else does."

He entered through the dooryard and then the foyer with the grandfather clock and the creaky stairway. The house smelled of roast beef and onions, rolls and pie. "Do you do this all the time?"

"Not when it's over ninety degrees. We're still getting used to each other, and when you're cooking for six, you're really cooking for eight anyhow." Susan dried her hands on a towel looped to the oven handle with a button. "We have a grill, but that's Corwin's thing. Usually he wants to grill burgers and hot dogs and corn, so I let him."

Michael said, "Can I set the table?" so she put him to

work.

He couldn't remember his mother cooking for six people. Sometimes Michael had a friend over, or Kristen had come for dinner, but six people would have had his mother reaching for the phone to make reservations.

As he set out the napkins, Michael ventured, "Did Bob ever meet me?"

Susan shook her head as she got the butter from the fridge. "He was in England when you were born, and they took you two hours after your birth."

Michael kept his gaze away from her. "Something he said... He seemed to think he met me."

Susan brought the butter to the table. "It's hard. He has trouble with faces, so a lot of the time he'll talk as if he recognizes you. He's buying time while he figures out who the person really is. He probably thought he should recognize you because you were with Ashlyn."

Michael wanted to protest. Bob had been very clear that he'd met Dalton. Dalton had a great smile. Dalton was smart.

Still, Susan looked so sad that Michael had to let that mystery stay a mystery.

So much was a mystery. Like, for example, how he and Ashlyn would deal with one another.

Sierra breezed through the front door, arms loaded with flowers and a shoulder bag weighted with books. "I just got recruited to play harp at the public school one afternoon a month." She set the bouquet on the counter. "The preschoolers are supposed to be exposed to culture during their afterschool program because that's what it says on the fliers, except no one bothered figuring out what that meant. Now the parents are asking, and it turns out that although yogurt snacks contain active cultures, they are an insufficient amount of culture. To supplement, they've hired a musician."

Susan huffed. "Mozart would turn over in his grave if we knew where it was."

"We can find it now if we look for the disturbed earth."

Sierra hugged Michael. "I'm so glad you didn't just disappear out of our lives. We need to teach you an instrument, though, even if it's just the harmonica."

The front door banged. "Sierra, if you just suggested that man play a harmonica, I'm leaving the state." Corwin strode into the kitchen and extended his hand to Michael. "No offense, but you'd be one of those annoying harmonica players who makes people's teeth fall out of their heads."

Michael shook Corwin's hand. "I wouldn't take that bet in a thousand years."

Corwin stepped back and studied him. "Are you tone deaf?"

"It's better that way. I'm told perfect pitch is a curse."

Corwin folded his arms, and then picked up his head. "Okay, maybe you're tolerable."

Good to know.

Lindsey entered, and Michael looked behind her for Ashlyn. Lindsey said, "Hooray, I didn't miss the fireworks! Shall I lock up the steak knives so you can do the manly thing and battle to the death with tablespoons?"

Corwin looked Michael up and down. "I could take you, but I don't see a reason right now."

Ashlyn wasn't at Lindsey's heels. The front door didn't bang open again.

Sierra was doing the same thing Michael was. "Where's Ashlyn?"

Lindsey glanced away as if she'd accidentally meet Michael's eyes. "She's home. She said it should be just us tonight."

Corwin's head shot up. "Is she still mad at me?"

Lindsey snorted. "*I'm* still mad at you, if that counts."

"No." Michael stepped forward. "It's me she's avoiding, and that's not fair."

Corwin brightened. "I'm off the hook?"

"You still owe her an apology in lights, you reprobate." Lindsey folded her arms. "But Ashlyn said tonight should be for Michael to get his questions answered."

"Not doing that. This is her family." Michael gestured around. "I'm not stepping in here if it forces her out."

Susan turned. "Why would Ashlyn think she's not welcome? I'll give her a call."

Lindsey folded her arms and made her voice flat. "She knows she's invited."

Corwin strode up to Michael. "Did you hurt her? Because I might have a reason to take you down after all."

Lindsey said, "Yeah, dude. If someone hurts her feelings, it ought to be you?"

Corwin growled, "I said I'd apologize."

"You've had two weeks to apologize. Are all the apologies on back order?"

Corwin rolled his eyes.

Michael said to Susan, "How long until dinner's ready? Do I have time to drive over there and talk to her?"

Lindsey recoiled. "I really don't think that's a good idea."

Susan walked away from the stove. "What happened? Did you two actually have a thing going on? Because I didn't mean to make her break up with you."

Corwin glowered. "I certainly did."

Lindsey muttered, "Quit being a toad."

Michael said, "I'm the one who messed things up. I'm the one who needs to apologize."

Sierra's lip quivered. "I'll call her. She'll answer."

Susan shook her head. "She's not stupid. She'll know a call from any one of us is a request for her to come over. This sounds bigger than a phone call." She turned to Michael. "Go apologize. I'll hold dinner for twenty minutes." She looked to Lindsey. "Give him your keys. I'm not having him drive over there only to have her not open the door because she's practicing. Plus, you parked him in."

Corwin said, "And don't bother coming back without her or we *will* have to battle to the death."

Susan sighed. "Not on my kitchen floor. I just mopped."

Michael was about to get into Lindsey's car when he glanced in the back seat of his own. He was still carting around that violin.

Well. It got him into the hospital, so he might as well carry it now. At the very least, Ashlyn could yank it back from his unworthy hands.

He drove to Ashlyn's still agog over that whole conversation. Corwin wouldn't kill him (probably) but Susan was by turns worried about Ashlyn and then joking as if a dead body in her kitchen were only a problem if it got blood on the newly-mopped linoleum. If Corwin had offed him before mopping, would it have been fine?

The dynamics were so different. The expectations. The unspoken understandings. No one had bothered explaining that to Michael: by stepping into a ready-made family, Michael had done more than hang his swing on a branch of a family tree. He was becoming bilingual in a new set of relationship parameters. Don't bother ringing the bell. Pick up any instrument in arm's reach. Joke about things that shouldn't be joked about. Include people who've never been included. Hand over your car and house keys. Accept people's outrageous behavior not as an act of tolerance, but because you love them and that's part of who they are.

At Ashlyn and Lindsey's apartment, he didn't knock. Music filled the stairwell.

The viola had a gorgeous range. Ashlyn was right that he couldn't hear it well when it was buried in the other musical lines. Since last week, he'd downloaded a few string quartets by Mozart so he could learn what they were all about. The first violin was pretty obvious, as was the cello. Michael could usually pick out what was the second violin. The viola blurred into the background, even with only four voices.

Now, though, it was just Ashlyn, playing something he almost could recognize but not quite.

Then it came to him as if from twenty years ago, the second part of a song where he'd only ever heard the first part: "I Vow to Thee, My Country." He must have heard it in grammar school. Slow and sad and sweet, and brimming with love.

He let himself inside, then closed the door lightly, that way he wouldn't interrupt her. The yellow flowers were standing on the kitchen table, but the card was missing.

He stepped forward to where she could see him.

Ashlyn started. "What are you doing here?"

He held up Lindsey's keys. "I'm here because if you're not going to the Castletons' for dinner, then I'm not going either."

Ashlyn shot him an annoyed look. "You belong there."

"*You* belong there. I'm the interloper. Look, I apologized because I meant it." Michael stepped forward. "I treated you badly. I will tell them exactly that if you want: I was selfish. Don't retreat into the shadows just because I pushed you out of the light."

"You're only barely getting to know them." Ashlyn righted her viola on her lap, the scroll leaning against her shoulder. It looked almost like a shield. "If I'm not there, you'll get your information directly from them. That's the way it should be."

Michael said, "And what if my focus was all wrong? It shouldn't be about the information. If I want information, my DN-Amazing profile has a lot of information about specific genes and what they do. Family should be about the people, and if meeting those people means I'm cutting off one of them, then it's my duty to step back out again."

Ashlyn quivered. "You'd break Susan's heart, and you know it."

"Losing you would break her heart too." Michael took the seat across from her, in front of Lindsey's empty music stand. "If you don't want anything to do with me, I deserve that. I won't ask you out again. I won't tell you you're beautiful. I won't hold your hand if you don't want it, and I won't kiss you. You have every right to set those terms, but stepping back out of that family so I can step in isn't the right thing to do."

Ashlyn opened her hands. "And if I refuse?"

"Then I drive home to Haverstock. Susan's got a roast

beef in the oven, but I will drive to my apartment instead and pick up a fast-food burger because I will not be the reason you leave the only family you've ever had." Michael leaned forward. "You've told me five different ways that your existence is a mistake and that your mother traded sex for drugs, as if somehow that makes you less than me, or your mother less than Susan. I'm not letting that stand. You are valuable. Your mother made mistakes. Susan made mistakes. But I'm the only one here who actually did something *wrong*. I'm the one who devalued you, and I'm sorry."

Ashlyn tucked her viola under her chin and drew the bow across the strings, then played a phrase of music he couldn't recognize.

Michael had no idea how to interpret that, so he pivoted. "Can you teach me to play?"

Ashlyn said, "I'm not much of a teacher. I train the new employees to scoop ice cream, but they have to weigh the cones for the first couple of weeks, otherwise some of our clients get these tiny marbles instead of the baseball-sized heart attack bombs we're world famous for."

Michael pulled the violin from the case. "World famous?"

"We got into the northern Maine tourist association booklet three summers ago, and someone must have carried a copy back to Berlin, so yeah." Ashlyn studied him. "You're serious?"

Michael picked up the bow. "Sure, why not?"

"Because you didn't even tighten the bow, and that thing can't be in tune." She extended a hand, and he passed her the bow, which she adjusted with a screw at the end. She rosined it, then traded the bow for the violin. "Dear heaven," she muttered, fixing one of the pegs. "Okay, not so bad."

Michael jammed it back under his chin and she huffed. "See, even holding the violin is its own lesson. You're shoving it into your throat with your arm." She tucked the viola under her chin and let go of the scroll. The instrument didn't budge. "Your chin and shoulder are supposed to do the work. Your hand needs to be free to go up and down the neck. You're holding the bow like a baseball bat. Hang on."

She moved behind him and put her arm over his, her bow out a bit further. "Use a lighter grip than you think you'll need. Let the bow rest on the strings." She showed him how the bow would swivel if she raised her arm. "You're keeping a stranglehold on the thing."

She was so close that all his hair stood on end. "Some things never change."

"But they *can* change." Ashlyn set her bow on his music stand and rested her hand on top of his. "Relax your fingers. Sure, it's valuable, but you're not going to drop it if you give it a little freedom." She had the handle part in her grip, so he did as she said. Then, with the violin tucked under his chin, she drew the bow across the strings.

For the first time, Michael felt an instrument vibrate right through him. Responsive to her touch, the violin sang one long note that conducted down his collar bone, expanded through his sternum, then poured out of his heart.

She angled the bow differently and pushed it upward, and again the instrument let loose a summons. She reached around him and pressed the string at the top of the neck, and the sound went higher, then higher again as she changed her fingering.

"The violin wants to make the sound." Her voice was in his left ear, her breath on his neck. Heat flushed through his core with her surrounding him. "It's longing to sing. Give it freedom, and it expresses its own song."

Michael choked out, "Do that again."

She released him but stayed behind with her hands on his shoulders. "You do it."

Tense, he tried to drag the bow back down across the strings, but it squeaked. She adjusted his arm. "Relax your hand. Let the bow move." Then the violin sounded stronger. Not strong like her tone, but louder and steadier.

He reversed the bow to go back up, and he wrapped his finger over the neck to push the string. That wasn't a real note, but it did change the tone. He shook his finger a little on the string the way he'd seen Ashlyn do, and she giggled. "Ooh, a vibrato."

He said, "What?"

"Well, a lame and terrible attempt at vibrato. That's a fourth-year student thing, but you've watched us enough to try doing it." She returned to her seat. "That's your first lesson. Go home and practice until you're relaxed when you hold it. Maybe ask Lindsey to give you lesson number two."

Michael looked her in the eyes. "Come back with me."

Ashlyn's shoulders dropped.

Michael didn't look away. "Please. Come back to the house with me. You let me hear you playing. I want to hear more from you. Not as a Castleton, but as Ashlyn Merritt."

When Ashlyn trailed Michael into the house, Susan rushed past to engulf her in a hug. "You're always welcome here. You know that."

Lindsey called, "Corwin, put down the reciprocating saw. Ashlyn's home."

"Now what are we going to do for entertainment?" Corwin leaned in the doorway with folded arms. "It's always so much more exciting when the cops show up."

Ashlyn stepped back from Susan. "If you don't mind, I'd prefer no cops."

"Cops, no cops, it just depends on your definition of a good time." Corwin rolled his eyes. "Can we eat now? Before everyone starves to death?"

Susan raised her eyebrows. "So soon? Don't you have something to say?"

Corwin cringed. "I'm sorry I called you a traitor to the family."

Susan's eyes flared. "You called her what?"

Corwin muttered, "I was mad."

"That's not an excuse!"

"Well, that's why I said I'm sorry!"

Ashlyn snickered, and apparently that meant, "Apology accepted."

Sierra called from the kitchen, "Food's ready! Come on!"

Michael at least remembered to wait until Susan said grace for everyone, and then he relaxed into the chaos as the serving dishes crisscrossed the table. What would it have been like—

No. Stop. This wasn't about the past. Tonight was about the present.

This time, Michael kept his focus on here and now. Sierra told Ashlyn about her assignment with the afterschool program, and Lindsey sat upright with dollar signs in her eyes, asking who she could contact for a similar arrangement. Corwin interrupted to talk about a brawl at a concert he'd played this weekend. ("We were the warm-up act, fortunately, so we were way off stage by the time the tourists started throwing beer bottles.")

Susan had nothing nearly as exciting. "Bob seemed better this week." She looked sad. "It's still hard, though. During the good weeks, he hates being at the facility. The bad weeks come again, though, and the bad days become worse."

Through the meal, Ashlyn laughed when everyone else laughed, and she looked sad for Susan, but she volunteered nothing. Aching, Michael wondered if that was because of him or if she normally kept herself to herself. He should have paid more attention. Did she consider herself an outsider all the time? How could he get to know her if she didn't want to be known?

It took ten minutes for everyone to get the kitchen put away. (Except Susan, whom Corwin told to sit her butt down for once since she'd cooked everything. It was rude.

Susan didn't seem to mind.) Ashlyn put away the leftovers. Corwin washed dishes and sprayed Lindsey with a stream from the sink's retractable hose. Lindsey threatened him with death and a bad online review. Sierra handed Lindsey a towel.

Michael's DNA had to come from somewhere. He was grateful it was from these wingnuts.

Susan gestured to the living room. "I could get our old photo albums if you want to see some pictures from years ago."

Michael avoided Ashlyn's glance.

"Not tonight." He approached the table. "You've told me a lot about the past already. You've been talking about the present and the future tonight, and I'd like to hear more about that."

CHAPTER TWENTY-SIX

"It's with great pleasure that I welcome the Castleton String Quartet. Lindsey Castleton, Jason Woodward, Ashlyn Merritt, and Hannah Staples."

The four of them walked onto the stage, bowed, and took their places. Lindsey met all their eyes and raised her bow. They began.

Their lineup for tonight's music festival featured a good mix of the instruments' voices. The first piece was violin-centric, but halfway through it yielded the main line to Hannah, after which the cello carried the song while the violins and viola served as backdrop. The second piece, to make up for that, featured Ashlyn doing a very nearly solo rendition of "Let It Be" while the violins evoked the human voices and the cello laid down drone notes.

Their thirty-minute slot at this festival was special for a number of reasons. First, tonight was a weeknight, so despite their half-hour performance they could still carry a full roster of weddings and special events over the weekend. Secondly, they had a table in the fairgrounds where they could sell performance CDs and hand out their flyers and business cards. Thirdly—and best—that table was being manned by Michael.

Ashlyn couldn't see him at the back of the crowd, but they'd spent time together before the performance, and they would again after. He'd driven there early to set up, then stayed put at the table while they went inside to tune and await their slot. Performing in the bandshell after nine o'clock at night, their quartet had quite a crowd of listeners spread out on blankets and lawn chairs. Lindsey hoped that would translate into future clients.

Ashlyn hoped Michael would translate into a musician. He'd asked Ashlyn for violin lessons, and she'd taught him bits and pieces on that battered violin with its mismatched bow and a neck that would eventually need a full reset.

He promised that learning violin would help him get to know her.

After the quartet's first two pieces warmed up the audience, they began the Beethoven they'd worked so hard to polish. For tonight's performance, they'd cut all the repeats so it fit better. To Jason's horror, Lindsey had also cut quite a few sections so it ran a distressingly short fifteen minutes. The fight about cutting segments of the piece had lasted longer than the piece itself would last, but in the end, Beethoven would just have to rise from his grave and haunt them. That way, they could finish strong with their own arrangement of "Sweet Caroline".

"Get the audience on their feet," Lindsey kept urging the quartet. "Get their blood pumping. Leave them knowing something phenomenal visited their town."

Once again, Ashlyn let the viola's song dominate the third movement while Lindsey backed off to a supportive role. It worked so well this way. Beethoven would have hated it, but everything about music was interpretation. Notes on the page didn't sing. Notes from hollow spaces certainly did.

At the end of the Beethoven, Lindsey swiped her bow across the strings to start Sweet Caroline, and then she and Jason were on their feet. Ashlyn joined them, but she stayed in place because Hannah couldn't dance with the cello. The violinists were out front and center, getting people to clap. Lindsey let Jason solo for a bit while she waved the crowd on, and then she slipped back into the song before they finished in unison.

Lindsey raised her violin in the air, and Jason stood beside her to bow. They both turned and gestured to Ashlyn and Hannah.

Those were the best moments: the applause. You didn't get applause at a wedding where you were required to fade into the background. But here, here on stage? When people were listening only to you? This was the best.

The announcer gushed thanks to the Castleton String Quartet, and they cleared the stage.

Jason muttered to Lindsey, "You need to learn to dance."

"You need to learn when people don't want your opinions." Lindsey turned to Ashlyn. "You did great! We'll make a performer out of you yet." Then she turned to Hannah and high-fived. "Amazing work on the opener. You get the most heartbreaking sounds out of that cello."

Hannah smiled. "Thanks. I want to get back out front soonish. You saw who's following us."

Ashlyn teased, "Some pianist?"

"Yes, some pianist—and *our* vocalist."

Jason said, "Oh, that's interesting. I want to hear Enrique when he's singing for someone else. I never get to really listen."

Hannah gave a shy smile. "I'd like to hear him too."

They hustled to get the instruments in their cases. Once in the night air, the piano music washed over and through them as they headed for their table at the back.

Lindsey said, "It was odd knowing Michael was watching."

Jason said, "And you're sure—"

"Oh, for pity's sake." Lindsey huffed. "If you want to

analyze the DNA results, get a subpoena."

Jason snickered. "I love it when you talk like a bottom-feeder lawyer."

They quieted down as they passed through the audience. The pianist was Declan Hatcher, a fellow Castleton Music School alum who payed jazz. As someone who could only plunk out a tune, Ashlyn savored the way Declan had eighty different degrees of pressure for the keys and the way he could coax different tones from the instrument.

Michael met them at their sales table, looking delighted. "You were awesome! By the end, you had the audience on their feet."

"Corwin kept sniping at us about playing for old people." Ashlyn snickered. "We needed to prove we could make them young again."

"It worked." He wrapped Ashlyn in his arms. "Help me out here. Is a piano a string instrument, or a percussion instrument?"

Jason said, "Strings," and Lindsey said, "Percussion."

Hannah waved them down. "Quiet, guys. Enrique's on."

Enrique stepped out under the lights, leaning on the side of the baby grand. When he opened his mouth, out came the most amazing melody. Jason was right: when they were playing, they were too busy analyzing and adjusting and watching one another to truly listen. Now, with their focus on him, Ashlyn could enjoy the richness of his voice.

Hannah sighed. "Isn't he amazing?"

They stood there, the four members of the quartet plus Michael. Michael remained behind Ashlyn with his arms around her shoulders. They were to the back of the others. A breeze came in off the ocean, and she shivered now that they weren't under the lights.

Michael breathed in her ear, "I never knew a human voice could do that. Or instruments. It was all just sound in my headphones."

She relaxed into him. "You'll be able to do this yourself

someday."

"I doubt it. You'll always have to be the music-maker."

She pulled his arms tighter around her waist, so he nuzzled her hair. Her cheeks flushed, and warmth shot from her stomach to her throat.

Michael ran his hands over her arms. Enrique was singing a love song, and Ashlyn craned back her head to rest on Michael's shoulders. He breathed against her ear.

Michael murmured, "Am I doing better by you?"

Ashlyn closed her eyes. "You are. It's good working with you and the violin. Talking, spending time. I like that a lot."

"If I mess up...tell me." Michael squeezed her. "You're important to me. I want you to feel valued. More than that. I want you to feel treasured."

Ashlyn wove her fingers through his. Treasured. Not useful, just wanted.

She had no idea how that would feel, but she'd like it very much.

Michael said, "There's so much I never understood. The world is far bigger than the walls I had around me. The music, the art—my universe expanded all at once, and it's dizzying." Michael pressed her closer against him, her back to his chest. "I want to see it all. I want to see it with you."

Ashlyn half-turned to snuggle into his arms. "And listen to it?"

"Especially listen to it." He brought a hand to her chin, then lowered his face toward hers. "I love you."

Warmth flooded her, and she stretched up to kiss him. Michael held her, his lips soft against hers, his arms strong and warm. When he pulled back, he breathed again, "I love you."

Ashlyn tucked against him, the wind teasing her hair from her face. She rested her head against his chest and listened to his heartbeat, the backdrop of the music of his life. "I love you too."

Once more he kissed her, surrounded by the darkness

and the stars, the breeze, the voice of the piano, and the voice of the singer. Her memories, his future, their future, their family.

Epilogue

The gymnasium echoed with a thousand voices at the statewide grammar school art competition, and in the aisle for the sixth graders, Michael Knolwood wove his fingers together and kept shifting his weight. The judges were working down the aisle, table by table, asking the presenters a dozen questions and then ticking off boxes on little grading sheets. This was it: nine weeks of work came down to numbers in boxes.

Mom and Dad weren't allowed on the floor during the judging, so Michael waited, teeth locked, watching the judges bear down on his station with the inevitability of a nor'easter. It was better not to have his parents here. Mom would have had a blizzard of questions: "Are you nervous?" "Are you sure you aren't nervous?" "Do you remember all your answers?"

And then, if he blew it? If the judges hated him? His parents would see it and remember it forever. No, thank you.

Michael swallowed hard as the judges reached the next table. The girl there had done a mosaic, and he strained to hear the questions they asked her. Except he'd practiced all the most likely questions. He'd gone over it with Dad dozens of times, even in the car driving over. If they came up with a showstopper question, what was he going to do? Make up the perfect answer right now?

Get it over with. Just get it over with.

Michael glanced at his display: a computer, and behind that a poster board with bullet points about computer animation, stained glass, and human history. It was so inadequate. He wanted to run, to hide, to scream. Dad had worked hard on it with him. If Michael messed up now, it was all for nothing, and Dad would be so disappointed.

Looking over all the other projects, though, it was

obvious he'd never had a chance. Fifth and sixth graders from around the state had carted in what amounted to a museum. Sculptures, pottery, paintings, collages, jewelry, lace—things Michael hadn't even known were art were all represented at the competition, and that wasn't even considering the live performances of music and dance. The judges weren't just district teachers, either. They were professionals, used to judging other professionals. Michael and his glorified cartoon had no chance of making it to nationals. None. Which stank because the principal and the art teacher had all been on top of Michael once he'd made it past the regional: he was the first kid in twenty years to make it to the state level, so they were counting on him to represent the school really well.

Michael's breath shuddered through him as the judges handed the mosaic girl the copies of her score sheets, and then they approached his display.

"Entry number seventy-eight," said the first judge, a humorless woman. "'Origin Story,' a work of digital animation."

It wasn't just Michael's project getting sifted down to numbers. The judges didn't know his name or his school because the competition touted its "blind judging," as if some judge would hear it and suddenly remember he owed Michael's father a half million dollars. Michael had told his father that was dumb, but now it was a relief. If he botched the whole thing, they wouldn't know who he was afterward.

The judges introduced themselves as teachers from area schools, including one guy from a music school who looked at Michael and started—as if he did owe Dad half a million dollars.

The first judge said, "Please tell us about your project."

All Michael's words fled his brain. He looked at the poster board and the computer, and everything was a blank. "I— Um— My project—"

He turned away, afraid he was going to start crying, and the fear of breaking down was only making him more terrified.

"Hey." It was a commanding word, and Michael pivoted. The music teacher was looking right at him. He was tall and dark-haired, but with kind eyes. "Deep breath. We know you worked hard, and your work is good because you got all the way here."

Michael still couldn't speak, but neither could he look away from the man's eyes.

"What you're feeling is stage fright, and my students get it all the time." The music teacher's voice was gentle but firm. "I'll tell you what I tell them: get out of your own way. You've practiced this in private, so you can perform it in public."

Michael closed his eyes and struggled to breathe.

The man said, "We're judging your *work*. Not you."

With his hands clenched, Michael couldn't look up. "My school is counting on me."

The musician judge said, "Your value as a person doesn't depend on giving other people what they want."

Michael glanced up, expecting a stern expression, but the man looked worried. Maybe he thought Michael was about to have a nervous breakdown.

"Take it from the top, just like you practiced." The music teacher's voice was low, assured. "Face the board so you can't see us. Pretend we aren't here and your parents are on the couch. Then, tell your parents your Origin Story."

Michael turned to the poster board. He'd done this a dozen times. Mom and Dad would have been in the dining room. The project would have been on the table. He'd have been in jeans rather than a suit. Dinner might have been on the stove. "For my art project, I created an animated short that showcases a hundred thousand years of human history." He was talking far too fast. Dad always urged him to slow down, and he tried to do that now. "I plotted it out to give six seconds each to the thirty most important advancements. I chose to use the animation style of a stained-glass window because when people weren't literate in the middle ages, they used picture windows to teach themselves their history."

Just in time Michael remembered to show the judges a stained-glass transparency he'd bought at a museum gift shop. His hands had stopped shaking. The musician nodded that Michael should keep going, but the pre-rehearsed words were gone, so Michael gave up. "Can I show you the video?"

Michael hit the button for playback, and then he stepped aside so they could see the screen. It began with an early human running down a gazelle for food. Next, a figure stood awed before a domesticated fire. A figure planted food. A figure learned to spin fiber. More modern scenes were a figure inventing the computer and a figure standing awed before the A-bomb. The final scene mimicked the first, with a rocket launching into space.

Michael had seen his video often enough that he watched the music teacher instead. The man wasn't a long-haired rock star. Instead he wore a suit and carried himself with poise. Still, unless he designed music videos, how was he possibly going to judge an animated film? It made sense to have a musician judging the orchestras or the dances, which Michael had just sat through two hours of, but why was a music teacher judging art?

The video ended, and the judges applauded. Then the first judge asked, "What made you try digital animation?"

Michael had practiced an answer to her question. He stumbled over the words and forgot one sentence, but he added that in at the end. Another of the judges asked about the storyboarding process. Michael also had an answer for that.

The music teacher looked amused. "You didn't include any musical innovations."

None of those had seemed important, so Michael said, "No, sir. I could only pick thirty events due to the format."

One of the other judges laughed. "But you chose the domestication of the dog?"

The music teacher perked up. "Oh? Do you have a dog?"

That was throwing Michael a softball. "No, sir. My father's allergic."

The musician gestured toward the screen. "The human figure in your pictures is always alone. Do you have brothers and sisters? Friends?"

The first judge said, "Oh! Good catch."

Afraid of looking pathetic, Michael said, "I don't have brothers and sisters, but I have plenty of friends. It was too hard to animate more than one person per scene."

The music teacher nodded. "Now that was an interesting choice for background music. How did you pick it?"

Michael cringed. "Well..."

It sounded cool. That was the answer.

Of course a musician would notice that, but the music was the last thing Michael had done. Dad had said, "You know what's missing? You need something for sound," and he'd turned Michael loose on a website that provided royalty-free songs. You could search things like "dramatic" or "sad", "vocals" or "no vocals", "synthesized" or "orchestral".

Michael said, "I wanted something that sounded triumphant. With no vocals. And this one, its first three minutes fit right into the three minutes of the video."

Please don't ask what it is, please don't ask what it is...

The music teacher nodded. "Yes, after the three-minute mark, Holst's 'Jupiter' transitions to 'Thaxted,' which is sometimes played as a hymn called 'I Vow to Thee, My Country.' Well, Holst was composing not only about the planet, but also about the god, so in effect you're combining the religious imagery of the stained glass with the religious story of the ancient Romans, and simultaneously weaving in the outer space theme of the ending image."

Michael gave a nervous laugh. "Yes, sir."

Meeting Michael's eyes, the music teacher stifled a smile. Blast. The music guy recognized exactly how hard Michael had biffed that one.

Another judge asked Michael how he'd programmed the animation, but the whole time they talked tech, Michael felt awful. The only judge who'd seemed to care wasn't on his side anymore. Dad would want to know why Michael scored so low, and Michael would have to admit: because he hadn't known what the judges would look for. He'd tried to tell a story about the past, but what he'd needed to do was predict the future.

The music hadn't seemed important. Sometimes the transitions even lined up well, but it was obvious to the music teacher that Michael had devalued the only thing the guy could do, first by not including any musical inventions and secondly by not carefully picking the song. He'd let everyone down, and it was his own fault.

The judges filled out their score sheets while Michael felt faint, and then they handed over their grades, each paper folded in half. Michael couldn't meet their eyes.

The musician passed Michael his paper last, then shook his hand. "You did fine, don't worry. But I have two more questions for you. First, were you born in May?"

Michael gave a startled laugh. "Yes, sir! How did you tell?"

The musician winked. "Lucky guess. And secondly, what instrument do you play?"

Michael shrugged. "None. My school offered either orchestra or French, and my dad said it was better if I took French."

For the first time, the musician looked disappointed. "Well, young man, I think you would be great at violin." He handed Michael a business card. "If you ever want to learn, have your parents give me a call. The first three lessons are free."

Michael took the card. "I got stage fright. I could never play music in front of people."

The musician lowered his voice, and Michael found himself paying total attention. "Listen to me, and always remember this: know your own value. People may judge your work, but no one has the right to judge *you*."

Michael quavered. "You're a judge."

The music teacher's smile made Michael relax. "Then trust me. Your value is much more than what you give to other people."

The judges went to the next display where a girl had an oil painting. As they left, the first judge said to the music teacher, "You were great at calming him down, but now you look rattled."

The music teacher demurred, "Something about that project hit a bit close to home."

That sounded ominous. Michael steeled himself to check his score.

Whoa! Mostly fours and fives! And the music teacher— even though Michael had totally messed up the background music, the music teacher had given him all fives!

Michael looked back at him, astonished. The music guy glanced at him with an embarrassed smile, then turned again toward the student with the oil painting.

The guy thought he'd be good on violin, but Michael had never considered orchestra after he'd opted for French. He hadn't been any good with the recorder when he'd learned it, and Mom and Dad said you couldn't make a decent living with art unless you went into design or advertising. That's why they'd made him do this project on the computer, and why he'd be attending animation summer camp.

Michael kept going over his score sheets, thrilled with relief. Yes, the music guy had said your value was more than you gave to other people, but at least Michael could give his teachers and his school and his parents this much: he'd scored well enough that he'd place, even if his project didn't go to nationals.

His parents returned, and Michael showed off his score sheets. Mom hugged him, and Dad clapped a hand on his shoulder. "I knew you'd do great! You certainly impressed the judges."

Michael felt eyes on him, and he glanced up the aisle.

The musician had gotten distracted at another display and was looking back at him. Michael met the musician's eyes, then turned to his father and hugged him. "I guess they think it's really important that we know both the past and the future."

THANK YOU!

Thank you so much for reading Ashlyn and Michael's story! I loved these two so much.

I'd like to thank the people who helped: Mallory Crowe from Crowe Covers, my editor Michayla DeToma, and all my early readers for feedback and typo-blasting.

Want to hear more? Sign up for my newsletter ("Mondays with Maddie") at http://eepurl.com/dEJjI1 Once a week, I'll send you something cute as well as news about my stories or recommendations of other books you might like.

The Castletons play on in *Soul of the Cellist*! Always a rock for her mom, Hannah has just discovered her phone is loaded with spyware and a tracker—and her creepy stepdad is the one tracking her. Hannah's longtime crush Enrique never really noticed her until now, but seeing her distress, he'll do anything to protect her. As bombshell after bombshell detonates in Hannah's life, she starts to redefine her family, and maybe that makes room for Enrique to become a permanent part of it.

The Castleton
String Quartet
Book Two

SOUL OF
THE
Cellist

maddie evans

Printed in Great Britain
by Amazon